THE
SURVIVOR

by JAMES FORMAN

THE
SURVIVOR

JAMES FORMAN

Farrar, Straus and Giroux New York

Library of Congress Cataloging in Publication Data
Forman, James D.
   The survivor.
   1. Jews in the Netherlands—Juvenile fiction.
[1. Jews in the Netherlands—Fiction.   2. World War,
1939–1945—Jews—Fiction.   3. Concentration camps—
Germany—Fiction.   4. The Netherlands—History—German
occupation, 1940–1945—Fiction]   I. Title.
PZ7.F76Su   [Fic]   76-2478
ISBN 0-374-37312-4

For four good friends: Mike and Gigi O'Melia, Barbara Gelber, and Phoebe Wells. May their roads go ever on and their beards never grow thin.

CONTENTS

THE
SURVIVOR

ONE
LATE AUGUST, 1939

An old man and a boy stood on the high dunes overlooking the sea, which was dark as indigo and feathered white where the wind kissed it. No boat was out. Below, the beach lay golden yellow in the late-afternoon light. A horseman trotting his mount splashed through the shallows. The hoofmarks were brief silver coins.

There were other figures on the beach making the most of summer's end, and the old man smiled to see them there, his family. The boy beside him was his favorite grandchild. Moses Ullman was seventy years old. Curious, he looked at his watch: just seventy. He had found much pleasure in growing old. The years had been good and full of adventure. They had turned him from a rather ugly, gangly youth with a diving nose, so fiercely hooked that it might have chopped wood, into a patriarch with a splendid snowstorm of silver-white hair. Lines of ugliness had come to rest in lines of strength and repose. He still had his strength: strong bony wrists, hands gnarled and knotted, the nails yellow and thick as sea shells. His digestion was perfect. He could eat anything.

"Do you know, David," he said to his grandson, "I never stare off at the horizon without seeing it beckon to me." He stood for a moment, hand on hip, shading his eyes like an old sea captain beached at last. Still no sail, no smudge of smoke to mar the perfect curve of water.

"It's a marvelous view," David agreed. He wanted to communicate, but he preferred to feel himself part of the whole summer scene rather than just a spectator upon the dune.

The old man overlooked the reluctance of tone. He was borne away. "Yes, you can see what I mean. It's the permanence of the ocean. A view like this—you can look at it forever. Feel it. Smell it. The cradle of life. Life began there in the sea." At the edge of the tide his family played: son and daughter-in-law, three of their children. He smiled again but added, "It makes me sad somehow."

"Why sad, Grandfather?"

"Oh, because summer's over now," and there was more he did not say; all the years so quickly gone, squandered as a boy will spend coppers for candy. Yet how else could it be? "Maybe I'm getting those growing pains of old age at last," he tried to joke. "Something you know nothing about, David, but you will know one day, unless medical science makes more progress than I anticipate. Maybe I miss not setting out to sea on another adventure." There had been many when Moses was young. "I suppose, too, the autumn makes everyone a bit sad. The leaves falling. Of course, summer comes again and we'll be back." He put his weathered hand on his grandson's neck and gave a special pressure of affection. The boy felt the shiny calluses that only years at sea can leave on a hand. David's own hands were large for a boy of fourteen, but unmarked except by the chafing handlebars of a bicycle. He was long in the leg, nearing six feet, with reddish hair that curled without his instigation and lightly freckled skin. His grandfather's face was nearly the color of dried beef from the summer sun, but David only burned and peeled and burned again. Suddenly he yearned to break away and catch the last combination of sea and sand and sun, to run jumping, half-falling, down the long dune to the beach where he could hear, faint as the cry of gulls, the shouts of the last bathers tumbling in the sea. The tide was running out and a crescent bank of sand lay warm and dry. Amid the bars and yellow banks lightly clad figures were gamboling. David brushed his ear, which held a few grains of sand. He felt the salt air on his lips and tasted it with his tongue, but he did not pull away. He had grown too fond of the sailor turned doctor and now, in his old age, nostalgic sailor again. Perhaps it was the shadow of a younger Moses that he loved, a Moses who had lately taken to filling his pockets with little bundles of things: lists and calendars, rubber bands and old pens that would not write. David dropped a pink shell into the leathery hand.

"Do you miss going to sea?" he asked, and Moses replied without hesitation, "Every night I dream of those times in the South Pacific."

"I envy you all that."

"And I envy you. You have what matters, David. You have time, and all your discoveries lie ahead."

"Grandfather, how many times have you sailed around the world?"

"About as often as the sun and moon. Not quite, perhaps, but sometimes I feel as if I'd rowed the whole way. I've told you how, when I was your age, I would take out a map and look over the blank places that had no names and then I'd stick in a pin and say, 'When I'm a man . . .' But those were different times, or seem so now. Maybe it's because I'm getting old, but the world seemed carefree and really young at heart then. There was nothing drab, nothing boring. I think the world was sane in those days, even if I was a little mad. Now it looks as though the world's gone daft, and young people like yourself will have to try very hard to keep your heads. Be a doctor, boy, but not a ship's doctor in the East India trade. Follow your father's example."

There had been doctors in the Ullman family since time out of mind; doctors since the family had come from Portugal in the fifteenth century, if one could trust traditions that old; doctors in Spain before the Inquisition at a time when Christianity forbade surgery and only Jewish physicians had access to the great writings of Hippocrates and Galen. But Amsterdam had been the Ullmans' home for as long as there were written records and family heirlooms. Apart from a great-uncle in the diamond trade, men of the family had practiced medicine in that city, except of course for Moses, who had carried his profession to sea and been more of a vagabond than a healer during those early years.

"Old, old stories. Why fish them up again? You've heard them all before," Moses admitted.

"But they're good stories," David insisted, and so they were, though worn and smooth as the colored pebbles a boy carries in his pocket all summer until the pocket frays and the treasure slips away. So the old man once more recalled aloud the natives fishing by torchlight in dark-green lagoons and the long, white beach near Mindanao where the dhows rested on their sides waiting for the winds to turn again toward Africa. He pictured village streets paved with grass where spotted dogs, looking as though they'd been crossbred with pigs and lizards, zigzagged like silent lightning and fled from his approach. He told how the wind lulled in the silvery palms at night, and how he'd delivered a brown baby with the only light from oil burning in a human skull.

"I've told you how I met your grandmother," he said, pausing.

"Not all the details," David lied. This part was always strange, his grandmother pictured as a white queen of the jungle, like some real-life heroine out of *Green Mansions*. Vera had long ago entered the sedate tea-and-cake time of life, and for David she had always been an imperious, thick-bodied authoritarian, both loved and feared, and very often made fun of from a safe distance when they called her "Big Banana" in accordance with a joke the origins of which were forgotten.

"It was in Java," the old man said, smiling more to himself than to his grandson. "The ship was laid up with a bent shaft and we were out for a good time. Except for the native women, and most of them tattooed, there was just this sort of mission band. Lady musicians. Oh, the noise, boy, and the sweating in that heat." The old man's body had settled a bit into a timeless repose. A faint wrinkle strained between his eyes as he experienced again the uproar in that bamboo ballroom. The instruments roared, whirred, thumped, twanged. He had wanted to flee, but curiosity held him despite his offended senses, for there was said to be a main attraction come all the way from just east of Suez. He had half-expected a belly dancer, but it had been Vera the vocalist, clad like any Victorian, more girl than woman, seemingly defenseless and lost with her long, red hair, slender waist, and slightly nasal voice. She sang songs popular five years before in England and Holland, sang them haltingly and yet too fast so that the effect was that of a quarrel between irate squirrels.

Moses had laughed out loud. Vera had cried. It was love at first sight and they had been married before Moses' ship had been repaired. His shoes had creaked as they had gone before the captain. There was no rabbi on the island and neither one had really cared. They were not devout, though a formal service had later been performed in Amsterdam, at which point Moses' roving youth had come to an end. His spice islands had shrunk to a pink conch shell on the mantel and an occasional dinner of Indonesian rice table prepared by Vera in honor of those days and because it was her husband's favorite meal.

She would be preparing it now, for the evening had been set aside for Moses' seventieth birthday party.

"I wish she would do something simpler," he mused. "Your grandmother puts too much energy into things. She isn't that well. David, will you help with the serving?"

David agreed to this. It was no secret that his grandmother had suffered a stroke the year before.

The crowd on the beach had thinned. Apart from the returning horseman, only the Ullmans were left, aflame with light. A small group in the distance, without proportion, they might have been sea birds printing their delicate graffiti. David lost them in the dazzle of sunshine, saw them again, caught the heliographic flash of Saul's eyeglasses. Saul was his twin brother, no carbon copy, but thinner, with a face like a bird, thoughtful eyes, and a beak of a nose like his grandfather's. More imaginative than David, Saul was the innovator in their games, though he suffered from the initial contact with strangers. While David had gone to school full of curiosity, it had been a nightmare for Saul. Now it was Saul who turned in the better grades and viewed the coming semester without regret. When their mother became pregnant with Rachel, Saul had nearly died of asthma. Now he and Rachel were building a sand castle. They would call it a temple, however, or perhaps a monastery in playful honor of Father Lebbink, who often walked on the beach reading *The Little Flowers of St. Francis.*

Rachel, the youngest of the Ullman children, was going on seven: the result of a seven-year itch, her father had said in fun. Rachel took after her mother, being pretty in a dark and secret way, with deep, polite eyes and a mouth that moved when she was worried. This wasn't often, for Rachel remained the baby in the Ullman household. She believed that all men and animals—they had only a cat and a canary—were guardian spirits, and that the world had not fundamentally changed since the Garden of Eden.

More flamboyant in manner and appearance was Ruth, aged nineteen and already launched as a dancer in Amsterdam despite her mother's objections. She emerged now with an explosion of spray from the cruelly cold sea and raced toward the family group. Wrapped in a large beach towel, she looked to David like a yellow narcissus.

Arms arched over her head, hands limp as the wings of a newborn butterfly, then up on her toes for an instant, Ruth waltzed round the family group, ended with an arabesque, and finally flopped down, graceless as a toad, before the nearly finished sand castle. She was a puzzle and a wonder to David. How had she become a member of the dark and bookish Ullman family? Ruth was no hesitant comma in the family genealogy. She was sometimes an exclamation point, but most often was a question mark. Taken feature by feature, Ruth was not beautiful, but all together, with her hair blond enough to suit a Norwegian and her laughing eyes, she was made to turn men's gaze to admiration. Even if she had not been so pretty, men would have fancied her for her easy good nature and her half-boyish grin that spoke deceptively of invitation. Not that Ruth was dishonest; she was simply an enigma to herself as much as to David and her parents. No horsy Brünnhilde, though her appetite was appalling, she remained petite and slim through dancing, tennis, and horse-back riding. Her list of beaux was endless, yet she kept them all, particularly the most ardent, at a friendly but frustrated distance. Why? Did she distrust men? David wondered. Amid all her laughter and tireless good cheer, was she secretly unhappy? He had heard her cry once, alone in her room, but she had denied it even when he had pointed out a tear. That was Ruth, who was posing now, a sort of winged victory, for her father's camera. The summer was to be recorded on film in its waning moments.

Abraham Ullman, intent now on the camera, was an Amsterdam doctor who had never roamed the world. He had always been a family man, dignified, headmasterly, with strong, heavy features and fine hair, black as a rook's wing. Most of his time and energy was devoted to his patients. For him, this was a rare visit to their summer place, made in part because of the need to close the cottage down for the winter. David did not really know his father, neither unreservedly loving nor actively disliking him. In family crises, Abraham was often absent or unreflectingly tolerant. Sporadic periods of concern for his children's development, usually stormy because of their unexpectedness, had alternated with long periods during which he almost seemed unaware of their existence.

The real pillar that held the family up, the maypole around which all danced when matters were serious, was his wife, Rebecca. Rebecca was a small woman, thick-waisted, full-bosomed, but never fat, for she was always bursting with vitality as if it were actually surging against her littleness. A motor might be expected to sputter and die at the pace she set, but Rebecca showed few signs of an aging organism about to break down: no rapid pulse, no shortness of breath, though she was a heavy smoker. Only occasionally she complained that her legs were cold, even sometimes in summer when they were scorched pink. Her voice had always been throaty with a hint of a warble, as though it barely confined some profound emotion.

Now it carried as far as David and Moses on the dune. "Time to go home, everyone. Time to wash up for Grandfather's party."

Seventy years had to be celebrated. So many candles would melt the icing, and it seemed to Moses that finally his life was rounded off. He had done what he had wanted to do as a youth, and more. He had even built up a good practice in Amsterdam. He had reached a time in life to relax and drowse in the sun, dreaming of ships with tattered sails.

Too late now for David to run to the shore. He saw the camera glint in his father's hands, then disappear into its leather case, saw them all gathering their possessions as the gulls languorously flew down to claim dominion of the beach with shrill, sad cries. Summer was over, but David thought not of that or of the lowering sun or even of the party to come. He was concentrating on the camera that hung from his father's side. It was a coveted mechanism that Uncle Daniel had brought from Germany, one of the few possessions he had been allowed to carry away from that strange country of marching bands and broken windows.

Uncle Daniel had stayed with them most of the summer, a worrisome skeleton broken out of the closet. He spent much of his time combating the crackling static of the summer cottage's one radio. Frequently he would sum up the political situation in his own fashion. "In Germany and Italy everyone's wearing uniforms and talking peace. The English and French put on their frock coats and talk war." Uncle Daniel

was a bitter man. His shoulders drooped, but his body was
well kept, hard and flat, with no paunchy collapse into middle age. His jaw was set, his cold eyes bleak as family death.
Under the left eye was a jagged scar, part of the same street
encounter that had given his nose a leftward drift. He had
stories to tell of those memorabilia, but David no longer
asked. The eyes stopped him. They made him afraid.

Until the passage of the Nuremberg laws that curtailed
Jewish rights in Germany, Uncle Daniel had practiced law in
Berlin. As he explained it, Hitler had seemed but a crazy joke
at first, his *Mein Kampf* a mad fairy tale, ugly as Hansel and
Gretel's witch. When Hitler had become Chancellor of Germany in 1933 and made his "Give me four years" speech,
Daniel had decided to emigrate. There had been a running
correspondence on this subject between him and Abraham
that lasted more than those four years. Not until 1938 were
Daniel and his wife actually packed, but at the last she could
not leave the dog and the four-poster bed behind. Then had
come Crystal Night, the first really violent persecution of the
Jews.

"Was it terrible?" David had asked.

"Very terrible. Fearful things happened," his uncle had admitted.

"Many Jews were beaten up?"

"Many. Many were killed. Synagogues were burned."

"And shops broken into?"

"All that. All over the city. And the fires—my God, the
fires."

If no longer an influential attorney, Daniel had still been an
outspoken man and his home had been a particular target. In
the flames his wife had suffered fatal burns, as had the dog
and the four-poster bed. Everything that had bound Daniel to

Berlin, except hatred, had gone up in smoke that night in 1938, and he had departed Germany, which he now referred to as the Lion's Den. He had meant to leave behind that part of the world permanently, and in May had set sail on the ship *St. Louis* with other Jewish refugees, bound for asylum in Cuba. The trip, as he told of it, had begun like a vacation cruise. They had sunned, played shuffleboard, and observed the tiny flag on the purser's map that marked their progress into warmer Gulf waters. One morning the *St. Louis* had weighed anchor off Havana. Relatives and friends had come out by launch, but disembarkation was always "mañana." Food on board ran short. Rumors spread of the ship's return to Germany. A young passenger hurled himself overboard to his death, and presently they were sailing north. To Miami? To New York? In the end it was back across the Atlantic to Antwerp, from which Belgian port the refugees were parceled out among the more friendly countries of Europe. Before he had time to contact his relatives, Daniel found himself at the Lloyd Hotel in Amsterdam. Later a central camp for refugees would be set up at Westerbork, but these earliest arrivals were swiftly placed. Abraham found his brother a secretarial job, though most of Daniel's time was given over to the SRJ, the Society for the Defense of Cultural and Social Rights of Jews. Even David knew this was no beer-and-pretzels debating society, but a group of hardened fighters who trained with guns.

Abraham was against all this preoccupation with foreign affairs. After all, Holland had not known war since Napoleon. When he visited their summer cottage he was on vacation, and that especially meant seeing no newspaper, hearing no radio, being absolutely indifferent to the world's fate. In his mind, this was the best medicine a doctor could prescribe.

Sometimes, when Hitler's voice barked over the radio loud enough to make the teacups dance on their saucers, he would reach out and turn the volume down. Just as often Daniel would switch it up again, saying, "Consider me as your wasp in Eden."

"You should forget all that," Abraham would admonish.

"Some things you don't forget."

The brothers were in stalemate. Only blood loyalty kept them under the same roof, for they saw different worlds out of different eyes. For Daniel, man's presence on this planet was no more than an unforeseen accident, a hollow mockery, and it was clearly bad luck for those gentler creatures whose instinct was to survive while man's one talent was destruction.

Abraham, the radio shut down again, would argue against this. Hadn't civilized people learned anything from the last war? If all decent men demanded peace, how could there be war? Enslavement? As he had tirelessly explained to his children, the globe was not automatically parceled up like a map into patches of alien color. The world was too small now for that sort of thing. Much of this, David knew, came second-hand from his mother, whose soul had a pure and sky-blue tint. She could think ill of neither God nor his creations, but Daniel dismissed her point of view out of hand as deadly idealism. He rejected as well Abraham's more medical arguments on the subject of race. Scientifically, Abraham maintained, there were no purebred Aryans, no Hottentots, Jews, or Irishmen.

"Tell Adolf that," Daniel would reply. "Hitler's a sleepwalker. He says so himself. He hears no voices but his own, and just now he's sleepwalking Germany and the rest of those little colored patches on your map right to the brink."

So throughout that summer of '39, Daniel Ullman had been a wasp in Eden, but Eden seemed just then a big place and David scarcely heard the buzzing. He listened instead to the singing of larks, which seemed to lift the sky into the clear and blinding blue of outer space. There was so much to do that he felt always on the run, always looking forward to the next thing—swimming, fishing, exploring. Even when it rained there was the huge jigsaw puzzle. It was a picture by Rembrandt, which they never completed because Rachel kept hiding the pieces for fear the others would finish their parts first.

The best days were spent exploring, by land or water. Their bicycles, called *rijweils*, or riding wheels, pounded down the cobbled dike roads under the trees. Saul usually set the pace, his glasses flashing, his legs pumping, though David would have liked to go faster. They were not identical twins, but enough alike to cause comment and occasional jokes. Such embarrassing pleasantries and the intangible fact of having come from a single birth had bound them together and encouraged them to invent a secret language that they employed only when they were alone. Often Rachel rode with them, past the small houses with their big square windows open and polished as Dutch faces, along the enclosed polders, that land reclaimed from the sea. Here and there wind-driven windmills still turned their left-handed blades to keep the water level down. Along the coast, farmers still wore baggy trousers and blue smocks, but the once-common wooden shoes were more and more being limited to garage mechanics and fishmongers. On one particularly clear Friday they had pedaled as far as Alkmaar, where the big round cheeses like cannon balls were being auctioned off from sledges in the market square. Midday excursions to the pretty old town of

Leyden involved the whole family and the family car, with
Moses presiding over a stupefying meal at the Golden Turk.
Here the waiter had but one objective, to make food available. He lacked the grace of French waiters, according to
Daniel, but he refrained from the German approach of dump-
ing food like hay from a pitchfork. On hot days, his white
waiter's jacket was soaked through and purple under the
arms.

"Does he drink a lot of red wine?" David had whispered.

"Maybe he's a true blue blood," from Saul, and finally a
"Hush" from Ruth, who always had to have the last word.
"Probably he wears purple undershirts."

In Leyden there were women in full skirts and golden ear-
rings, ignoring the times, or perhaps wisely preserving the
past for the weekend tourists who came to see the famous
town that had been saved from the sea by the gallant boy
who had put his finger in the dike. Of course, there had been
no such boy and no monument had been cast for him. It was
rumored, however, that the town council had in mind melting down the monument to the Waterloo dead as a reminder
that Leyden would never again muster so many men for war.
The metal could be reshaped into a statue of the fictitious boy
who represented the proud idea that even as God had made
the earth, Holland had made and still preserved itself.

Weekdays often found Saul and David on the canal that
passed near the cottage. The boat belonged to Moses and was
his for fishing whenever he made the demand. Most often,
though, it fell to David and Saul, and in Viking tradition
they had mounted a wooden horse head on the bow and
christened it *Raven of the Wind*. Numerous sailboats tacked
back and forth on the waterways just on a level with the graz-
ing cows. The *Raven*, as they called her for short, had mast

and sail available, but usually they made better time with the oars. They passed shaggy-haired gypsy children with their dark ribs showing through green and yellow rags, barge gypsies in craft that seemed barely able to float, and road gypsies who filled their copper pots with water while swans flowed rapidly by in dignified tandem without seeming to move a feather.

It was one of these boating expeditions which led to a discovery that marked not only that summer but their future lives beyond any imaginings. They had passed the broken-down old mill many times before. Few wind-driven mills survived in service. There was one large paint mill in the village that was said still to make a profit, but the everyday business of draining Holland's sub-sea-level fields had been given over to motor-powered pumping stations. Of the old wooden-frame and canvas-sail pumpers, not one functioned within a day's rowing, but often Saul and David passed this mill with its naked blades still intact and its door swinging invitingly. Clearly it was abandoned, and just as clearly their obligation to explore it increased as the days passed, even though Ruth said they would be trespassing. Finally, on a day of low fog that had driven all but the business-bent barges from the canal, David and Saul knew the time had come. No words were necessary. They went at it like well-rehearsed burglars, their skiff hidden in the tall, thick reeds.

All mills at one time had names. This one curiously still bore a flaking legend, *The Hero Joshua.*

"Anyone home?" This was Saul's shy inquiry of the gloomy interior. "What if it's haunted?" He had seen a ghost once, or so he insisted, though David guessed it had been a dream. No phantom answered this time. There was not even the alarmed scamper of mice. The mill had long been stripped and plundered beyond service, yet structurally it remained sound. Their visit might have been final and disappointing had not Saul, in rolling aside a millstone, made a discovery. Behind the stone was a passage, dark, smelling of bats.

"Yay-hay-hay!" David shouted with pure piratical delight. He was plunging in when Saul held his arm. "I don't trust it," he said. "It might be a trap."

"It might be," David echoed, no more deterred than iron approaching a lodestone. He led the way down a low passage. Saul kept close behind him, but he'd begun to wheeze. They emerged into a room or vault of some size, lit only by a hole in the wall. "Good place for killing butterflies," said Saul as David lit a match and observed, "I like it. You could hide out forever in a place like this."

"If you were a brigand or a highwayman," agreed Saul, his imagination at last won over.

The passing of a car overhead told them that they were directly under the dike itself.

"I wonder if this wasn't one of those storerooms that were built for gunpowder. You know, so the fields could be flooded and the town saved from invaders." That was Saul's romantic notion, and he was beginning to share David's joy in their slightly criminal discovery. He felt the place needed a purpose. Then the afternoon would be truly crowned.

All this transpired toward the end of July. Before another month had passed, the hole had been cleaned, and given shelves and furniture of a sort. Then, because they needed a homey touch, and it was truly too big a secret to keep entirely to themselves, they had brought Rachel along under pain of torture should she make any revelation.

"But it hasn't any windows," she complained, "except that little crack."

"That's the whole point," Saul admonished her. In the end they did force a small rusting pipe out through the inner bank. "There. Now are you satisfied?" and Rachel had said at least she could breathe, though the narrow view enclosed only a portion of the high ground near Father Lebbink's Catholic church where the villagers were buried. The graves were placed well above the high-water mark, as though the dead could drown.

The mill with its secret vault was a good three miles from the Ullmans' summer cottage and the high dune where David and his grandfather now watched the sun lowering over the North Sea. The rest of the family, hand in hand, progressed toward them over the soft sand, laboriously as insects. These were natural sand dunes, through which the hammering North Sea surf had never broken. To the north, the barrier was artificial and paved with heavy stone blocks, a man-made fortress against the water's ceaseless attacks.

The clear sea breeze laughed behind them, blowing Ruth's hair around her face, lifting Rachel's skirts. It wafted their voices up to David and his grandfather as it must somewhere have swelled unseen sails. The evening, the sun and wind, gave a restful well-being to Moses' heart. It was good to see them all together having such a happy time. He could hear Abraham's protests, "Oh, you're too big," as he hoisted Rachel to his shoulders, swinging her around his back to let her dangle upside down. "And now what do you see?" he demanded with mock ferociousness. "Jerusalem!" came the reply that set her free.

Rebecca linked her arm with her husband's, half pulling

him along. They were devoted to each other, and wanted
only that their children should become respectable citizens of
the Netherlands, leaving the world, if possible, a better place
than they had found it. In method alone did they differ.
Abraham relied on a laissez-faire policy of good example,
while Rebecca saw to it that things were done her way. When
her children were infants she had relentlessly trained them in
cleanliness. With her, washing was a compulsion, more of a
family joke now than something to be taken seriously. "What
a sandy mess we all are," she was saying. "We must all take
baths for your grandfather. Do you hear me, Saul?"

Another one of Rebecca's obsessions was editing magazines
brought into the house. All scenes of violence, mayhem,
death, came under her scissors before her young ones could
look. Now only Rachel remained subject to this surveillance.

Rachel, Abraham, and Rebecca led the way. Saul straggled
behind and with him was Ruth, reluctant to give up the
golden beach. They pointed out to each other, as though the
other were blind, the great rocky head rising from the running tide. Then they, too, surrendered and bounded after to
catch up. They were all together when they reached David
and Moses, and together they came in sight of the summer
cottage with the sun shining from its windows as though a
fire burned inside. Indeed, as if to announce ruin, Vera
emerged on the porch with the dinner bell. Thick and heavy,
she gave the effect neither of flab nor of real vigor, but rather,
of solid purposefulness. She wore a feathered hat against the
sun's last glare that had set only a freckled stain upon her
hands for all its summer's burning. The hat's primary feather
was fractured and drooping, and David knew that when he
got near enough his grandmother would smell of camphor.
Imperiously she rang the bell to tell them what they already

knew, that it was high time to honor her cooking and her husband, now in his seventy-first year. Then she turned back inside without waiting for their arrival. As automatically as the second figure in some mechanical clock tower, Uncle Daniel emerged to take her place. He strode toward them down the last few yards of path. The beach was no longer visible, but the sea glittered to the horizon.

Daniel walked like an athlete. There was an air of stubborn youth about him, though David had noticed that lately he often arose in the morning with bloodshot eyes. His expression, as he drew closer, was that of a messenger carrying diplomatic papers against a deadline.

"It's war," he announced, his speech sharply accented from the many years lived in Germany.

"What war?" Abraham retorted. War in China? War in Ethiopia? They had all forgotten the radio with its inventions and alarms.

"Germany and Poland. There's sure to be war now."

So it was not for them after all, but only Uncle Daniel reviving his old predictions.

"You really believe it this time," Abraham allowed grudgingly.

"Believe? I'm damned sure. Hitler and that Stalin mean to slice the Poles up like capons."

"Yes, I'm afraid you're not the only one who expects that. But after all, Poland and Germany—surely the Dutch have too much sense to get involved in what isn't our business. We kept out of it last time."

"Times change, brother," Daniel persisted. "The Dutch are dreamers from the chin up, while the rest of their anatomies are strapped in the guillotine."

"Honestly, Daniel, you talk as though you weren't Dutch

yourself." This was Rebecca taking charge. "Must we dwell on such speculations, especially in front of the young people? It's been a happy day. Think of all the beauty that's left in the world, and try to be content."

Daniel at this point held his tongue. It seemed to require a big effort. "Oh, Daniel," she went on, bent now on appeasement, "you missed such a lovely time on the beach. Just look at the sky."

A fan of golden light had spread across the horizon. The evening was shot through with colors saturating the canal with prismatic hues. A boy from town, riding home fast before the dark, sounded his bell on the dike road.

"Yes, it is lovely," Moses agreed, lost in the miracle of its flowing through him. Then the first blue-winged bat flickered by, a tenant perhaps of the ruined mill, and gulls, jet-black against the sky, rose above the dunes, then flung themselves down like reckless dive bombers upon the small fish trapped in the low tidal pools.

There was much hasty bathing and scrubbing before Vera, her face dusted into a pale-pink mask by a large powder puff, could unveil her culinary triumph and receive the necessary compliments. As her hearing became fuzzier, she more and more frequently accused people of whispering. "What's that he said?" She was looking at Uncle Daniel.

"Why, he said it's simply splendid," Moses told her, putting his arm around his wife as far as it would go. "You have really outdone yourself this time, Vera."

David's stomach rumbled with anticipation. He had always enjoyed this Indonesian feast in which there was no sad testament to animal slaughter—the bones, the anatomical shapes of legs and wings—for all of it was carefully minced, sliced, and sauced. Nevertheless his mother, Rebecca, would la-

boriously remove the nearly unrecognizable meat with her
fork, passing the bits on surreptitiously to her boys, for she
was an adamant vegetarian. "We're only beaks and fangs for
tearing at murdered flesh," she'd once asserted, though this
opinion she had not tried to inculcate in the rest of her family.

As they were sitting down, Daniel announced, "Father
Lebbink's here," with the air of someone handing over a par-
cel. There had been a place set for the priest and, on entering
with a bouquet of flowers, he said, "God save all here."

Except for his clerical garments, Father Lebbink looked
more like a genial blacksmith substituting for the regular
priest, for he was big of waist, arm, and shoulder. On a short
pillar of neck sat a monolithic head, gothic rather than clas-
sical sculpture. There was only one thing out of tune with
this majestic picture. His fingernails were bitten painfully
down to the quick.

Father Lebbink had been Moses' summer friend for years,
never tiring of the old sailor-surgeon's tales from the missionary islands that he had visited only in books. The priest
was not a deep or profoundly thoughtful man, but sincere
and well intentioned. Except in jest, he no longer tried to
convert his tribe of lapsed Jews. He called them his pagans.
As a younger man he might not have accepted defeat so easily. Upon assignment to the church above the canal, he had
dutifully abandoned his hope of service beyond the sea. God
had assigned him a place. "Like a bridegroom," he had once
remarked to Abraham, "I came here bearing gifts of pure
faith." He had been and still was very popular. His sermons,
dredged up from vast lungs, were pleasantly resonant and
generally unintelligible. With the years, Father Lebbink had
hinted only to this "pagan" family of his that he had become

inwardly harassed by questions. Why did the ladies of his parish sell cakes to one another so that the church might have a new bell? It had a fine bell already, but people in Armenia were starving. Why did they put on their best hats and dresses to hear him mumble on about the Virgin Mary and the Holy Ghost while Ethiopians were being slaughtered by Italian machine guns? And there were even more painful questions. Had Christ, for instance, really saved the world by martyrdom? Yes! Yes! No other answer, but still the questions rose like chronic indigestion. Was his sacrifice really necessary? Was civilized man born so evil that he really required saving? Or conversely, in moments of gloom, was he wicked beyond any hope of reformation? Was God really employing His priest to the utmost here in this little old water town in Holland? These were speculations that rose in gloomy times. Normally he fought them off, becoming more zealous in expiation for having ever entertained such thoughts at all.

"To be honest, Father," Moses had said once during such a discussion, "I think you're a missionary by temperament. You'd be happier winning over Dyaks or being boiled alive by cannibals than puzzling about theology."

There was no time for philosophizing now. Rebecca had found a vase for the flowers. Abraham said the blessing, and Vera dished up.

"Ouch! That tastes good," Rachel exclaimed, her fork still in her mouth.

It was a feast enjoyed by all and most especially by Moses, who washed it down with five glasses of French wine before spilling gravy on his shirt front.

Outside, darkness was falling. The late-summer evening was full of subtle colors, while from the kitchen emerged the sugary buttery smells associated with birthday cake. In baking Vera excelled, and she was as stubbornly proud of her products as she was nearsighted. David shivered, remembering certain sugar cookies that he had once declined, saying, "Grandmother, I think ants have gotten into them."

"Nonsense. There's not a bug in my kitchen." And she had eaten the cookies herself, ants and all.

No ants tonight, but seventy candles blazing. How Vera had gotten them all burning at once was a wonder. The heat would have turned ants to ashes. Moses threatened to use a fire extinguisher to save his eyebrows from singeing, but the candles were finally quenched and the cake portioned out. David filled his mouth, coughed, caught Saul glancing at him, his face a full-mouthed image of his own. Both were about to explode with laughter but both, eyes widening with effort, managed to swallow first.

They were well into the traditional birthday ritual by now, and all, including Father Lebbink, joined hands around the table to sing. David and Saul barely murmured, but Rachel's voice rose fragile and pure as a crystal thread. It was a sweet voice for little songs but ill designed for operatic renditions, the sort of voice that had carried her grandmother to the South Pacific but no farther. Ruth's tone was low as a boy's, while the priest's song soared earnestly. He might have been trying to lift a hymn to the church rafters. Next they toasted each other in the rosy glow of the scarlet candles, which stood unwinking in the still air, and Rachel remarked that when she had last had a birthday there had been a movie with Rin-Tin-Tin. Moses patted his knee and his granddaughter went to him, observing with genuine admiration, "Grandfather, you have such nice, long, yellow teeth." At this they all laughed, Rebecca with her face shut down so that her eyes completely vanished, and the priest tilted back in his chair, his head rocking to and fro. David's stomach went up and down until his sides hurt and his eyes filled with tears. He saw them all briefly as through a glittering kaleidoscope. They looked so happy, his family, and it seemed just then that they must be together like this forever. Why then was he suddenly touched with sadness? The candles were so bright, the faces so glowing, and yet through all the brightness he felt the winds of change. Surely it was only the first tiny stirring of a sea breeze, nothing more.

Rachel hinted again about Rin-Tin-Tin, but Moses said that this was an old man's party, and it was more fitting that he do the barking. "I'm a man of a few words," he began.

"But all of them long," interrupted Abraham.

"Have a cigar first," offered Uncle Daniel.

Moses, who did not smoke cigars as such, crumpled his up into his pipe, a sure sign that he was preparing to enjoy himself. Old memories were stirring, many beautiful and pleasing, others ragged as scar tissue, but all worth preserving. He held up his glass. "To times gone by." The old man knew he was about to speak of those times, but the details, as they came from his mouth, often surprised him. Like most long-distance storytellers, he relied on inspiration, and sometimes what came forth was as novel to him as to anyone in the room.

"When I was a man you could call a man," he began, playing for sympathy, "my first patient was a murderer. He'd been almost killed himself when he was captured." Moses remembered the muscles on the man, sliding blue on the nut-brown skin. "They'd be hanging him for murder all the same. By rights he should have died there in the street. Nearly cut in half he was—blood, entrails spilling out. I had to stuff them back with both hands."

"Really, Grandfather," Rebecca protested. "The children . . ."

"No, no," the old man insisted, "there's a point to all this. It has to do with the will to live. I remember once . . . Have I told you about the typhus epidemic among the Malayans?"

"I believe you did," Abraham interrupted. "Wasn't it just before your ship was laid up in Fiji?"

Moses turned quickly to his son. "That's right. I guess you've all heard that one." But the children were not to be put off.

"I like that story," said Saul, who meant to be a doctor. There was more of the sailor in David.

"It's one of my favorites," from Rachel.

"Go on, Moses, do tell us." Father Lebbink settled the matter.

"Well, those Malayans were dying like flies, you see. No medication, no immunity, and about all we could do was shovel the poor fellows under the ground as soon as they went stiff. But the point I'm trying to make is that the warm soil revived some of them and they crawled out, just like Father Lebbink's Lazarus. They came back to life." Moses was groping now for the one string to tie all his remarks together. It had to do with the tenacity of human nature. "What I'm trying to say, looking back now from seventy years, is that life is a baffling gift. We're not always sure what we should do with it, but it's the only thing we have and it's to be cherished. Even a wounded murderer, or a beggar who by all rights ought to be dead of typhus, knows that in his blood even if he can't put it into words. So, with apologies to our

beloved Father Lebbink, whose concern is with the hereafter
. . ." Moses raised his glass, paused like a comedian timing a
joke until all glasses were raised. *"L'Chaim!* To life!" They all
echoed him, Lebbink too, smiling and looking down at his
plate. "Life is nothing but the happiness you take out of it.
So—long life, my children. It is all we have."

To this the Ullman family drank solemnly again, all save
Vera, who, after straining and boiling rice, cleaning meat and
fish, chopping, mincing, grating, cooking, arranging the food
on the table, and supervising its transmission into the appre-
ciative stomachs of the only people on earth who mattered to
her, had fallen asleep. She had once been a rosy-cheeked
bride. Now, all wrapped up like a molting pigeon, her face
was more wrinkled than a last year's apple. Moses put his
dry, warm hand on the dowager's hump of her neck in memory. "She's not such an old girl," he said.

In fact, Vera's age was a secret known only to herself and
possibly to Moses, who, if he did know, was not saying.
"She's got a song or two left in her yet." But there was no
music for him now like that sweating, booming mission band,
no time like those times. His eyes filled up with tears so that
he could not find what he was looking for, and Rebecca had
to hand him the corkscrew. "Oh, the past, Vera, the past,"
he whispered.

David could scarcely imagine his grandmother other than
she was now, though it was said she had stirred great pas-
sions in her day and still kept a porcelain box in her vanity
table full of love letters in six languages mailed from five conti-
nents. He saw her only as a grandmother, her hands covered
with big cabbagy veins, all gray except for the brown spots the
sun had left her. Was she gray all over? He imagined undress-

ing her, but his imagination grew timid. How gray her legs must be.

Outside, crickets screamed, frogs debated, and a breeze lolloped up from the sea and blew open the front door.

"Who's there?" whispered Saul.

"Ghosts," David told him.

"I'm cold," Ruth said, and clasped her arms about her chest. Rebecca, who always sensed the cold first, pulled on a sweater, and David felt gooseflesh rise on his arms. Abraham went to close the doors and windows, but Moses stepped outside with David to taste the wind from the sea.

"Did you ever see such a black night? No moon. Not one star. There! A wink of lightning."

"Where?" David had missed it.

"Out to sea. There's a storm about. I can feel it in my bones. It's a nuisance, becoming a barometer. The way I ache tonight, it can't be anything less than a hurricane. Just as well." He clapped a hand on David's shoulder. "Summer's finished. But that's not so bad. It only means the next one's that much nearer. Tomorrow and tomorrow and tomorrow. Snap your fingers and summer's back again." His words drifted off but David would long remember the moment, the darkness of the night, the golden radiance of the candle-lit cottage, the air filled with laughter, and the tinkle of china and silverware being cleaned for the trip back to Amsterdam. August was ending for the Ullman family. September, 1939, lay ahead.

TWO
MAY, 1940

David wakened with a jolt as though his *opklap* bed, the sort that folds back into the wall to look like a bookcase during the day, had overturned. "Whew!" He squinted into the spring sunshine. "Why's it so bright?" He was only partly conscious of Saul and Rachel. "Why'd you wake me up?" He was still too laden with sleep to be argumentative, but clearly he was aware of some irregularity in the day's events. The calendar said Friday, May 10, 1940. Nothing special there. Nobody's birthday. Not yet time for school. Then what were Saul and Rachel doing at his window? David had fallen sole heir to the tiny fourth-floor apartment at the top of the Ullman home in Amsterdam. True, it was laughably small, a storeroom really, but it had a fine view of the canal. Saul and Rachel were leaning far out over the flowers that lived in potted celibacy along the sill.

"Yes, you two. What's going on?" David demanded. He was sitting up now.

Saul was too engrossed to reply, but Rachel turned and as calmly as she might report events at school said, "We're listening for the bombs."

"Bombs!" David leaped to the window, sending a potted plant end over end into the dark canal below. "What bombs?" He had heard nothing. A distant mutter perhaps. "It's the sea," he said.

"Not at this distance," Saul replied. "It's Schiphol." He was referring to Amsterdam's international airport, built on drained land thirteen feet below sea level on the floor of the

30.

old Haarlem Lake. It was called Schiphol, or "ship's haven," for the sea battle that had once been fought there.

Finally David heard it—or rather, what he heard took on new meaning—and he stood in the glare of sun with his mouth wide open, like someone caught by a flash bulb. No surf this time, but staccato thunder that forecast a different sort of iron storm.

"The Germans are bombing the airport," Saul repeated, "with those Stuka dive bombers that look like gray wasps." He had a pack of airplane-spotting cards. He knew them all.

"Who says?" David demanded.

"The radio," Saul replied like a telegram, "since 4 a.m." With German precision, exactly on the hour, Dutch neutrality, which had been maintained throughout World War I and Germany's recent attacks on Poland, Denmark, and Norway, had at last been violated.

"But the English and French are coming to help," said Rachel, always the optimist.

"Why us? Why attack us? It's France they hate."

"According to Uncle Daniel, it's simply because we're in the way."

David looked out and upward. The window, designed in former years for hoisting goods by pulley, leaned out over the canal, one of fifty-odd waterways in Amsterdam. The view gave him a picture of springtime: empty blue sky, facing rows of steep-gabled, red-brick, four-story houses, elms and poplars lining the canal. The bright sky threw down inky-black blotches of shadow into the water and the narrow cobbled sidewalk below. A sparrow cocked its head, throat pulsing quicker than any heartbeat. Cormorants and gulls soared high over the rooftops down toward the docks, but the sky was empty of planes. A canal barge swung around the bend and

vanished briefly under one of Amsterdam's four hundred
bridges. When it appeared again, the barge was bursting, not
with soldiers or anti-aircraft guns, but with tulips and hya-
cinths, bound no doubt for the flower market that was held
beside the bank three bridges and half a square away. The
old woman with her basket of pretzels and poppyseed cakes
appeared as she did each day, rain, snow, or shine. A husky
organ-grinder followed, pouring out a torrent of sound. Cy-
clists swarmed over the bridge, as though nothing special
were going on, as though it were just another spring day tast-
ing of summer. Even as he scanned the sky, David found
himself thinking of Moses. "Snap your fingers and it will be
summer again." But never the same summer, David sensed,
though the household would conduct itself as usual. The family cat would lazily wash down its twitching tail in a patch of
sun while just as lazily considering the family canary high
and safe in its cage.

How strange war was. They had been half-expecting it for
months, ever since Uncle Daniel had wakened them at the
cottage on September 1 the year before with the news that
the ancient German battleship the *Schleswig-Holstein* had fired
on Poland. It had been a dry, clear day all over Europe,
despite the warning in Moses' bones. Commentators in the
West had predicted that there'd be rain, that the German
armor advancing into Poland would bog down in the mud.
Day after day of brilliant sunshine followed. Britain and
France declared war on Germany. World War I seemed to
have risen from the dead. By September 14, the first day of
Rosh Hashana 5700, Warsaw was under siege. By the end of
Yom Kippur, with greedy help from Soviet Russia, Poland
had ceased to exist.

Uncle Daniel had been in his element, predicting doom for the civilized world. It had not come true, though Russia and Finland had fought. The valiant Finns had been overwhelmed by sheer numbers, and in that spring of 1940 Hitler, who was forever declaring an end to his territorial ambitions, marched his troops into Denmark with scarcely a shot being fired. Norway had fought back with Britain's help, but Norway had fallen all the same. Now Holland?

It was not a complete surprise. Important buildings had been sandbagged for months. The army had been mobilized. Stalks of steel asparagus guarded all the frontier highways to repel tanks, and there were always the dikes as a last resort. David had often heard in school that the opening of the dikes had saved Amsterdam from Louis XIV of France in 1672. Of course, later, French invaders had come over the frozen ice, but it was spring now and there were plans to create a water barrier between Holland and Germany. This would not be a wild and suicidal letting in of the sea, but a scientific directing of clear Rhine River water, which would produce a shallow band six or seven miles wide, too deep for vehicles, too shallow for sizeable boats. This "New Holland Water Line" was to run from Muiden on the Zuider Zee inland northeast of Utrecht and Gerinchem, and on south. Surely it would defy German tanks where the sun-baked plains of Poland had failed. Though David said this to Saul and Rachel while they parroted back reassurances, though the sky remained blue and empty and the vendors moved as usual on the canals and streets of Amsterdam, though the cat licked down the tip of his tail and the canary sang, creating a cozy air of domestic tranquillity, which the Dutch call *gezellig*, all knew that desperate things were happening beyond their limited horizon.

The day progressed, an ordinary seeming day, except that David was surprised when Saul appeared with his book bag in hand.

"School today?" David had said.

"Why not?" was the reply. School was something dependable to which Saul would cling. They went together, only to be advised by the headmaster to return home. There they heard their mother singing in the kitchen. This was her last redoubt, and she would not surrender it to war, pestilence, or earthquake. Rachel helped out, scrubbing the parquet floor with pads of fine steel wool, which she strapped to her feet, skating back and forth until the floor gleamed. As long as the household went on as usual, how could Holland fail to keep in step? They were forgetting about school, and Abraham further broke the pattern by returning early from the hospital with so many rumors in his head that he wouldn't discuss any of them. The only thing he knew for sure was that the airport had been bombed.

"I don't understand these Germans. They're the people of Bach and Mozart and Goethe."

"And Wagner," Moses reminded him. "Don't forget Wagner's fire music."

Was there anything to be done? Should they hide in the cellar? Run out the Dutch flag? The discussion was largely between Abraham and his wife while the others listened in bewilderment. Nothing was resolved, though the eminent surgeon revealed himself to be, rather, a little boy lost in matters beyond his surgery. He wanted Rebecca to tell them what to do, which could only mean wash up for dinner, keep life as usual. This was her domain where she polished the brass, dusted the books and furniture, scoured the pots and pans. This was home, safe and sacred haven, as it had been for generations of Ullmans. In the dark red study squatted Moses' massive desk, gigantic as a mastodon, bearing on its back the old bronze lamp, a pirate with an upraised sword. Let German tanks try to move out that desk, or anything else.

"Supper's at six," Rebecca said. The discussion was ended as far as she was concerned and she began to set the table.

"Will the water really keep the Germans away?" Rachel asked.

"Of course, dear. Now clean up for supper."

They all felt better. David studied the canal and observed that the water level had risen, a sure sign that the fields were flooded.

"No, I think the water's down," Saul insisted. "Look there at the seaweed. Still, it comes to the same thing. It's been drawn off to stop the Germans." Then the barrier of Saul's usual reserve let down. "It's got to stop them, David. I can't imagine being a refugee, can you?"

"I hadn't thought about it," David admitted, hugging his arms close to his sides. He would not think about it, not yet.

"If the water doesn't work, we haven't a chance." Saul began to cough. Tight and controlled, the touch of asthma sounded strangely like laughter.

Listening to the radio only added consternation, a hodge-podge of hopes and fears. Winston Churchill had become prime minister in Britain and was sending great armies to Holland's aid. German paratroopers were sneaking into the country clad as nuns: brawny, blond, wimpled nuns with hand grenades hidden under their robes.

"That might qualify as a pilgrimage," Moses speculated dryly, and shut off the radio. "They won't come for a while yet. Meanwhile, it's suppertime."

"Why isn't Ruth here to help?" Rebecca protested. But mealtime was mealtime and, as Rebecca often maintained, the stomach was a warehouse from which good health was supplied to the body. She was as adamant as ever that all such warehouses in her charge would be filled to bursting. For all of them there was a quality of reassurance, of warm vitality, in sitting down together as a family with the rest of the world shut outside. If only Ruth were home, but she didn't always return for dinner now. She had her theater friends.

Though neither Vera nor Rebecca kept a kosher kitchen, Moses said the Kiddush as though this day was sacred. "Blessed art thou, O Lord, King of the Universe . . ." and then they ate the solid Dutch *groentensoep*, a consommé loaded with vegetables, vermicelli, and tiny meatballs. From the marrow-bone stock yellow moons floated on its surface, each one reflecting a golden universe.

Rebecca tried to keep the conversation going. She spoke of opening the summer cottage, then broke off to insist, "Now eat. The soup's good. Eat, all of you, while it's hot." But the atmosphere was charged with excitement and for once even David found it difficult to choke down his food. Only Vera was eating in her customary fashion, and that was with help from Rebecca. Everything Vera did now required help. She was too weak to dress herself, too weak to lift her still-thick dark hair to the comb. Rebecca held each spoonful to her lips and the old woman swallowed painfully. She had, on returning from marketing the winter before, gone into the kitchen with her bundles. Then David had been startled by the clatter of parcels falling, followed by the hoarse, inhuman sound of strangulation. He had found Vera clinging to the edge of the table. She had had a stroke, though Moses preferred to call it a vascular convulsion. In any event, it had been nearly fatal, and David could not yet believe his grandmother could look so old, shrunken down to a little old creature with a face no bigger than a child's, gone short in the chin, long in the nose. Her memory had been affected as well, which had one merit: she could read the same novel over and over without losing enjoyment. The outside world had virtually ceased to exist for her.

"Why isn't Ruth back?" Rebecca said again. In her voice was a quality of indictment.

"I know I'm nothing but a burden," Vera said, "but I'll be gone soon. Then you'll no longer have to bother with me."

"Vera, don't be silly. I'm worried about Ruth, that's all."

Her worry was presently relieved. Before the table was cleared, Ruth burst in through the front door. Uncle Daniel was with her, and they brought with them the huge blackness of what was outside. Daniel wagged a long finger. He was grimly knowledgeable about the day's events.

"German paratroopers have seized most of the bridges," he told them.

"What about the water barriers?" Abraham asked.

"Crossed in rubber boats. All useless."

"Surely it can't be that bad."

"It will be soon," Daniel reported, his voice heavy with foreboding. "Holland will fall in a month."

"No!" from several voices.

"It's true. Yes, it is," Ruth confirmed.

"The Dutch make brave soldiers," Daniel said. "They seem born to lose courageously, but they're so outnumbered and outtrained, the whole thing would be a farce if it weren't so damned tragic."

"Surely they aren't near Amsterdam," said Abraham. The Germans were becoming simply "they," the nameless scourge.

"Not yet," Daniel admitted, "though of course they've bombed the airport."

Outside, searchlights swept the night sky for planes that did not come.

"But they're dropping down everywhere by parachute." At his uncle's words, David seemed to see evil blossoms falling through the dark onto Dutch soil.

"We Jews must get out or fight back," Daniel told them. He touched his forefinger to Abraham's coat button as if to underscore his remark. "Hitler is calling this the war to decide the fate of Germany for a thousand years. Do you think any of us will survive even the first ten? This is no ordinary war. If I believed in providence, I'd say Germany meant to build the future of Europe on this war, and there's no future for Jews here."

"But we're all of us Dutch," Rebecca protested.

"Don't you suppose there are plenty of good Dutchmen waiting with their tongues hanging out, ready to answer Hitler's call? It's fight or run away, and nothing in between." The conversation was punctured. The Ullmans had always thought of themselves as Dutch first, Jews second, reformed in their beliefs and lax in their practices. "I for one," continued Daniel, "intend to fight. I owe these Nazis some pain. A Nazi is not something you kill with kindness. You must kill him as you would kill a mad dog."

"We don't talk about killing people in this house. We don't speculate upon it," said Rebecca.

Daniel looked at her, his face like a knife. Then he

laughed. "My dear sister-in-law, you talk about not killing, while your country is being invaded. Personally, before I'd be eaten by those Nazi dogs, I'd poison my own dying body for them."

"All right, Daniel, but how can we fight back?" Abraham asked. "I have no gun. Do I charge with a scalpel in both hands? Does Rebecca arm herself with a kitchen knife?" Violence distressed him, his own most of all. Except for his surgery, where he practiced with detached skill, Abraham disliked involvement, was always by preference a spectator rather than an actor.

"Listen to Holland's hope," Daniel replied scornfully.

"Brother, there's no good sneering at me. I have no weapons." Two thousand years of tradition had ingrained in the family respect for the word, not the sword.

"Then get out now. Go to Palestine, where there's still hope."

Daniel's attitude was unsoftened by doubt. His audience was stupefied by the alternatives. Saul coughed softly into the back of his hand. He's afraid, David thought. Maybe he knows more than I do. David felt the ground sliding away from beneath his feet as though the pilings that held Amsterdam aloft were melting into the mud.

"But we can't leave everything just like that," Rebecca spoke for all of them. Her voice sounded as though she were exhausted from a long uphill run and, if she faltered, the family surely would fall. "This is our home." The gilt-clawed furniture, the towering highboy that seemed always about to fall, the porcelain clock on the mantel with its playfully wrestling cherubs, the ottomans, the hard wood sculpture, the silk screens brought by Moses from the Orient, a polyglot made up of years of family living. All had been enjoyed with love through many generations of marriage. "This is our home," she said again, more firmly now.

"Hear me out," Daniel replied. "Rebecca, hear me out this once." He gave the impression of a man with at least five lighted cigarettes in each hand. "If I could only help you wake up from your beauty sleep! My dear woman, how often must I remind you, I stayed too long in Germany. I lost my wife. For God's sake, learn from my mistake. If you insist on staying, do this one thing. Make your will." He laughed, a bark of despair that died falsely and was followed by the dry retching of metal lungs, his tobacco cough.

"But if we go, what happens to the canary? And the cat? Can we take them?" Rachel broke the silence. "We can't leave them."

"Don't worry about them," David told her, but attention had shifted now from Rebecca, from Daniel, from the intruding warring world, to Vera, who was pushing small white tablets between her lips because she was frightened and having trouble with her heart.

"Help us," Moses said. With Ruth and Abraham, he maneuvered his wife to her bedroom.

"I'm not really weak," Vera protested. "I only need a little support under my arm, Moses dear." She leaned on him, hanging her head. Her bedroom had been moved recently to the ground floor after she had said, half in jest, "If I die here, you won't be able to get me down the stairs. You'll have to cremate me right in the kitchen stove."

So they put Vera to bed and Moses sat with her until she slept. In the dining room, the atmosphere had calmed. Daniel had taken hold of himself, but he had not changed his opinion. "Rebecca," he said, almost sadly now, "if God listened to housewives, we would all rot away in a doze of easy living. I wish things went that way. But when you're alone, think over everything I've said. I've been through it all before. I may be a bitter, pessimistic man, but I love this family. I don't want anything to happen to it."

They were like arm-weary boxers, too tired to raise their gloves for a knockout punch. When a fresh contender entered the ring, they were no match for him. It was Moses, coming from Vera's bedside. He began as though he only meant to exercise the old man's prerogative of philosophizing. "History is becoming a nightmare," he said. "I can't seem to wake up from it, but I can't escape it by running. Vera and I will stay here, regardless. She will go in her sleep one day sooner or later, but it would kill her to move." No one could argue this. Vera had the sunken death sleep of the very ill already, but while she lived, Moses was bound to her. Marriage was more than a paper contract. It was loyalties and shared experiences. It was a weave of memories, laughter and tears, a web of communication beyond language, of habits understood and accepted, born of living side by side for over forty years. He would die with her here rather than drag her off to perish in an alien land.

Rebecca had been listening, her head cocked to one side, like a puppy hearing odd sounds. Now she rallied behind this unexpected ally. The Ullmans must stay together. "We have always seen things through as a family. This is no different." So it seemed finally settled.

Saul breathed a very audible sigh of relief. David put his arm around Rachel, who managed a hesitant smile in return. Her pets were safe for the moment, but the family discussion was not over. It would still have to pursue that vaguely geometric pattern of most Ullman family conferences, in which the shortest distance between any two points was a circle, or perhaps even a figure eight.

"At seventy," Moses went on, "I feel I'm much too old to lie to myself or to any of you." Here he cleared his throat, a sort of monologue of sad sounds, "Arrumph, hurrumph." They were the noises, thought David, that might be emitted by a lonely old sea lion abandoned on a rock in the silent frozen sea. "I wish I didn't, but I agree with Daniel about the rest of you. Maybe I'm just a sentimental old pessimist, but I've been to the edge of this world and looked over. I've met men like this Hitler." Again he cleared his throat with great delicacy, as if the membranes were made of rice paper. Then in a very deliberate tone, one that sank to the depths of their relationship and seemed to assert an authority he had long abdicated: "I want the rest of you to leave Holland while there is time."

Again the questions, with Rebecca the beleaguered spokeswoman. "Go where? Palestine? We have no friends there."

"I was thinking of England, my dear, where we have relatives."

"Whom we scarcely know."

"I have done them favors. You'd be more than welcome for as long as need be. Perhaps only a few weeks. If longer, well, England will need surgeons then."

"And I suppose we're to swim the Channel?"

"I had in mind a ship," Moses went on doggedly.

"A ship! I wouldn't put my children on a ship from Amsterdam, going out through the IJmuiden locks. Think what the Germans would do to it."

"Of course not," Moses agreed. "I was thinking of Rotterdam. At night. Van Walsum's a friend from the old days. I've already been in touch with him. It will be just for a while, until things settle down here."

The force and surprise of Moses' proposals had quelled all opposition. The family sat in wonder as he went through his trouser pockets and his jacket, flattening scraps of paper until one yielded up an address and phone number in Rotterdam. Getting the telephone call through was another matter.

"Hello? Hello? Operator?" He spoke into the cold, black, unresponsive ear. "Operator . . ." Finally Moses hit the receiver on the table to give the operator's eardrum a shock, and the line hummed back at him. "Operator!" The lines, it seemed, were overloaded. Some were down. If he would be patient, they would call back. Moses returned the receiver to its cradle. He waited. They all waited. Outside, searchlights swept the empty sky, and only after all expectation of a response had evaporated did the telephone suddenly ring. Moses jumped as though from sleep, suspiciously said, "Hello?"

"The late Max Van Walsum here," came a voice through heavy static.

"Ah, Max! Old friend. Moses Ullman speaking."

There followed a series of yeses, then an emphatic no. Finally, from Moses: "You're certain that's the best you can do? Yes, Max, I know how hard it is. Well, thank you. I knew I could count on you."

Again the phone was put to bed. "Well," said Moses, "all Max could do was book four tickets on a boat leaving the night of the fourteenth. That isn't all of you, I'm afraid." But the allocation seemed obvious. If the tickets were to be used, the bearers would be David, Saul, Rachel, and Ruth.

None of the four regarded the tickets as a privilege. Ruth

even threatened rebellion, saying, "I'm old enough to make up my own mind," and Rachel, her voice a pitch higher than usual, asked if she might at least take the cat. Saul hunched his shoulders and silently left the room as though he had just received a death sentence, but Moses had made the arrangements methodically, immutably, as though he had chiseled them on stone tablets. Only three days intervened. Three days of uncertainty and vacillation.

The news on the following day came as a torrent of Job's messengers. The German Eighteenth Army under General Von Kuchler, reinforced with the Ninth Panzer Division and Von Reichenau's Sixth Army, was closing in on the central bastion of Holland, the triangle of The Hague, Amsterdam, and Rotterdam. They were cut off from France and their allies. At dinner on the evening of May 12 Rebecca suggested, "I think it would be a good idea if you each packed a small kit." With this the future seemed to fly toward them on black wings. "Of course, if you don't go, you'll simply unpack, that's all."

On May 13 Queen Wilhelmina called on Britain to send clouds of fighters to defend her country. They sent, instead, a destroyer, and that night the Ullmans heard their queen broadcasting from her British exile. "Our hearts go out toward our compatriots who, in our beloved country, will have to pass through hard times. In due course, however, with God's help, the Netherlands will regain their European territory." The Ullmans heard her with tears in their eyes; her voice came to them like a kind of death knell.

No damage had yet been done to Amsterdam. There war remained an invention of rumor and the radio, but that was sufficient. Abraham and Rebecca in private conference agreed that their children must go. Rebecca wanted to escort them to

Rotterdam and the ship, the *Texel Queen*, which Moses described as a small black tramp steamer, used to carry spices, raw rubber, pickled pigs' feet, and occasional passengers in accommodations somewhat less lush than steerage. But it was hard to get permits to use automobiles, and there were only four bicycles available.

"If we have to do this," said Ruth, "it's senseless for Mother to take us and then return alone. If I must go, I'll go as an adult who can be trusted completely. I know, Mother, you don't think I can tie my own shoelaces. Well, I can. In a lot of ways I'm older than you."

This was a challenge. A muscle in Rebecca's cheek flexed, but she said nothing. She stared at her elder daughter, and Ruth stared back, unwinking, her well-shaped face firm of lip and chin. David could feel the tension between them like static electricity.

"I do trust you, Ruth," Rebecca said finally. "More than you know. I'm only worried that the trip will be too much for Rachel."

"Rachel can make it," Ruth said. "Can't you, Rachel?" She had been riding her bicycle to and from school for the past year, but, if Ruth's appeal was to pride, it failed.

"I want to stay home," Rachel answered.

"But you must go," Rebecca implored, "because of the war. Dear, what do you know about war?"

"It means that people kill each other."

"And I don't want that to happen to any of my children."

From this entrenchment Rachel moved to the bird and the cat, and when told they were not allowed to go too, she cried. Finally, with her mother's help, she packed, preferring her teddy bear and crayons to the necessities her mother set aside.

They all packed on the evening of the thirteenth with slow deliberateness, each being very careful not to stare at the others, but at the same time sneaking glances, appraising, evaluating, folding their belongings into bundles in the best tradition of fairy tales.

When the time came for bed, David could not sleep. Rather, he felt as though he had been asleep and dreaming all the time. He had never been farther from home than a long day's journey by bicycle to The Hague or the summer cottage. This sounded like one of his grandfather's stories of sailing over shining horizons into the bright unknown. Adventure called to him, but still he was afraid, and Saul, who had never shared his fascination with maps and globes and names like Mogador and Rangoon, was even more depressed than he was. David could tell by Saul's stony silence, and the way he occasionally coughed softly into the muffling lump of his pillow. "Go to sleep, Saul," he whispered. "It won't be so bad. Honestly, it should be exciting." The coughing had stopped and David left him. Presently he applied himself to sleep, flat on his back, rigid as the effigy of a dead knight. It was long past midnight when he succeeded, only to toss in dreams of ships beset by storms and sea serpents. He was awakened in the dark before dawn. Rachel was blowing her nose. So was Rebecca, who was trying not to show it. Ruth maintained an aloof dignity and David, looking at Saul, didn't know whether to be gallant or join his younger sister in tearful chorus.

Then his grandfather appeared in an old bathrobe, saying, "Isn't today Shavuot? I can't remember." The feast of the first fruits. With this David lapsed entirely into unreality. He was dreaming. He witnessed without emotion his own movements and the fact that Rachel was wearing her navy-blue skirt and jacket with silver buttons and white cuffs, the one she liked for outings. Then Rebecca began to set out food, as she would come hell or high water: jam and gingerbread, sliced cheese and hot chocolate. His father handed out guilders to all of them, and Moses presented an envelope of papers to Ruth in case they had trouble along the way. Vera had not been wakened.

At last the front door, oak carved with leaves and beasts and bearing a brass lion-headed knocker, stood open. David felt his feet descending, the bicycle bouncing beside him, into the cobbled street. It was still dark. Better to go quickly now, David thought, before I wake up, before Mother or Rachel begins to cry.

"Nothing will happen to you," Rebecca was imploring, and Ruth replied crisply, "No, nothing will happen to us, I promise," while all the time the world was turning upside down.

Their street was said in the tourist brochures to have old-world charm, though electricity had replaced gas in the globes, which were now blacked out. The Westertoren clock tolled five as they mounted and began to ride, Ruth leading, then Rachel, the two boys bringing up the rear. At the bridge they waved, but it was too dark to tell if their gesture was returned. Then they were steadily pedaling south over the vast web of concentric canals that had grown and spread throughout the centuries with Amsterdam, the Venice of the north, held up by stilts. They rolled down narrow medieval Kalverstraat, crowded with shoppers by day, where now a solitary stray cat held dominion.

"I wonder, will they be opening school again?" Saul spoke wistfully.

"There are good schools in England," David assured him.

The sun was glowing below the horizon by the time they had reached the open, more modern suburbs of Amsterdam-Zuid. Here the streets were broad macadam, easier for pedaling, and the terrace homes on either side had big windows that seemed designed for looking in rather than out.

Dew still sparkled on the fields as they entered the polder country, and their bicycles threw long spears of shadow before them. Forty kilometers to go, so they took a first break for Rachel. Forty kilometers was a long ride for a girl of eight, but the cyclist association had built well-marked, flat cycling paths beside the highway with many rest areas. They were not the only ones to seek a temporary refuge. Traffic on the path and highway was far above normal, though seemingly aimless. Many who were trying to escape were following conflicting rumors, and they were as confused as rabbits surrounded by a forest fire. To David, none of it seemed real. They might have been on some wild picnic jaunt, for under the spell of warmth and humidity the polders were a rainbow competition of growing and flowering. There were square fields of clover for acre upon acre, and massed tulips were ranked like grenadiers. Cyclamens and anemones glittered as brilliantly as fresh-fallen snow. The windmills turned like slowly revolving crucifixes as they neared the flower-market town of Aalsmeer.

Here they were stopped at a check point where many refugees were being turned back.

"I hope they stop us," Saul said. It was a wish they all shared, but Moses' papers saw them through. They continued south, though the general torrent of refugees was headed straight for the coast, on foot, on bicycles, in autos, carts, and trucks. Even a fire engine clanged by as though it expected the Channel to open, like the Red Sea of old.

The sun had long since risen high overhead and Rachel was beginning to pant and complain. "Oh, it's hot. Ooh, I'm so thirsty." David's fingers had the cramp of rigor mortis on the handlebars, but pride contained his protest. Fortunately Ruth presently called a halt. They were just beyond Gouda, two thirds of the way, she estimated, and they would picnic before going on to Rotterdam. They settled down on a low hillside covered with wild tulips, their petals blown out like thin, clear bubbles of blood. Far to the south they could barely distinguish the spires of Rotterdam, that sane seaport on the Neder Rijn which had been the last in Western Europe to extinguish its lights, months after France, Belgium, Britain, and Germany had gone black for fear of air raids.

Rebecca had prepared them a picnic of cheese, cold cuts, and thick homemade bread, which Ruth sliced recklessly, drawing the knife toward her chest through the round loaf. It remained a handsome day, clear and breezy. The luminous blue well of the sky contained an occasional puffball cloud, and the sunshine made it hard to worry. If this was to be an adventure, David concluded that it was starting well.

Ruth complimented Rachel on her sturdy legs. "I wasn't really sure you could keep up, at first."

"My legs hurt. I still wish I were home." Rachel was always honest.

"Of course you do. We all do," Ruth replied. She looked so boyish and athletic on the bike, so feminine now in repose. "Anyone for more cheese or meat? It'll be hardtack and wormy crackers once we're aboard ship."

In complete non sequitur Saul replied, "I hear planes."

"You've been hearing planes all day," David told him.

"Maybe he's got a bee in his ear," Ruth joked. She pretended to peer with concentration into Saul's ear as one might scrutinize below an iron grate for lost coins. "What have you got down there?" She beckoned David over. Both looked, listened. "Sounds like a whole hornet's nest." Ruth was in a good mood now. "Can you believe it? Tomorrow we'll be in London. Rachel, you've always wanted to see Big Ben." But for all her hearty, confident, and appealing manner, for all the soft dreaminess of the sky, England with its cold rains and dense fogs seemed smaller and farther away than ever.

"I do hear planes," Saul insisted.

"Hornets," Rachel said, "inside your head."

Then, like a quick touch of summer lightning that even from far away can lift the hair on the head, they all heard it. The sound of mechanized doom began to fill the reverberating sky. Black squadrons, birds of ill omen, swept down the wind, so low that the crosses on their wings were visible. Their racing shadows cut sharply across the fields. The propellers were disks of fire in the sunlight.

The picnickers cringed close to the earth as though these great predators might sweep down with spread talons.

Only Saul stood up, transfixed with wonder. "Stukas," he said. "They won't be wasting their time here. My God, just look at them all!"

Refugees scattered from the road as wave after wave of bombers flew on toward Rotterdam.

Then the first bombs fell, wagging their fins like schools of metal fish. An incandescent flame shot up from downtown Rotterdam, and the entire center of the city burst open with rapid orange flashes. A turbulent wave of orange and gray smoke churned upward, and David could feel the ground quiver. Ruth stared at the inferno with outraged eyes as though its sole purpose was to thwart her well-laid plans.

How long the raid lasted none could say. Not long in minutes, but endless in terms of human cruelty. Never before had a Dutch city endured such a a raid. What had been a prosperous seaport on the Neder Rijn now appeared to be a pillar of black and oily smoke.

"Well," said Ruth, "I think it's time we look for our ship."

"If it's still there," Saul said pessimistically. "They'd go after the ships."

Now it's time to go home, David thought. Now's the time for Rachel to cry and call for Mother, for me to wake up, but none of them did wake up from a nightmare that was just beginning. It was too much for tears, and even Rachel climbed stoically onto her bicycle as they all did, relying on Ruth to bring them through.

Forty-five minutes of steady pedaling brought them to the seaport. The sputtering throb of dive bombers had given way to the tinkling of ambulance bells and the screaming gears of fire engines. An acrid odor from fire bombs filled the air as flames raced down block after block. The area worst hit was the Binnenstad, the old town and port. It had been crowded during the lunch hour. Now it was a wasteland. The victims were past counting, many dismembered or burned beyond recognition, others drowned in shallow basements where they had hidden from the bombs only to be found by flooding canal water.

The fifteenth-century Groote Kerk pointed the gutted arm of its black steeple toward the sky, and Ruth made for it as a point of reference. When they pushed their way inside, they saw that the church was being used as an evacuation and first-aid station. Its dark interior was lit by acetylene flares placed on the ground. Antic shadows contorted on the walls, and there was a low chorus of agony. Rachel broke into tears. Saul lost his lunch as he turned back to the steps outside.

David closed his eyes and tried to tell himself it was surely all a dream. Sternly, Ruth led them away. "We must find the *Texel Queen*. No nonsense, now. Just don't look and don't waste good food by being sick." But it was impossible not to look at what bombs had done, impossible not to stumble over the ruin of a city and its people.

They came to the famous old windmill "de Noord." The turning of its sails evidently had warded off the flames and flying sparks, but little else remained of the old city and the port, and of the few vessels floating there none bore the name the *Texel Queen*. Even Ruth began to look weary and beaten when a sailor who was hosing down a smoldering pier said that he had seen the *Queen* early that morning and believed she had slipped downstream with the tide before the raiders came. Evening was already in the air; the ship would presently be sailing if she was still afloat. The young travelers were all exhausted. Only Ruth's adamant determination to fulfill her pledge of getting them to England kept them going. Always smiling, as David felt convinced she would smile in pain or despair or even in death, she cajoled them on, hauling Rachel's bicycle up the slightest slope along with her own. So they progressed slowly toward the Hook of Holland, hoping that their ship, any ship, might be moored downriver. Their cycles had generator-powered lights that glowed only so long as they were in motion, a problem on the dark and crowded road where the flood of refugees from burning Rotterdam was scarcely larger than the backwash from The Hague. These newcomers brought fearful rumors of German paratroopers, some disguised in Dutch uniforms, who had landed at The Hague to capture Queen Wilhelmina in her palace there. Prince Bernhard had been among the guard firing from the palace roof. They had held off the invaders until the queen had escaped to London. All this had happened two days before, but since then the fearful "ifs" had accumulated. More and more Germans were said to be landing in and around The Hague. Refugees had scoured the coast for boats. At Scheveningen, they had trampled one another. At IJmuiden, a ship had been set aside expressly for Jews, but only those with cars and special permits had arrived in time. The coast was said now to be peopled with despairing watchers gazing out to sea. A few had actually plunged in, swimming straight out into waters that no seasoned Channel swimmer could hope to cross.

Finally Ruth admitted what they knew already. "We won't be finding a ship tonight." The only thing to do was to leave the main road with its confusion and find a place to spend the night.

"How far to the summer house?" Saul mused.

"Too far," Ruth said. "Maybe tomorrow. If we're lucky."

They took a wandering side road where the trees seemed bigger and older. Here the weathered farms had overgrown, mossy roofs and the canals were lined with swaying roads and willows, a night scene of peace after a day of total madness.

They were about to settle down in the lee of a shed, for the breeze was fresh and cold from the sea, when something large and heavy lunged toward them through the thick dark reeds.

"Germans!" shouted Saul, spreading his arms as though to protect them all.

Undergrowth and bushes gave way.

"An elephant!"

"A tank!" wailed Rachel.

Then Ruth's calm voice reported, "It's only a cow. It's only a cow parading around naked. Ought to be put in jail for not wearing a bra." This collapsed them all into helpless, rib-aching laughter, painful convulsions of mirth. David ground his knuckles into his damp eye sockets and could not stop for thought of the tank turned into a cow without a bra.

Finally exhaustion caught up with them and they slept, curled together like lion cubs with only a chorus of frogs to disturb the soundlessness. Somewhere a village clock struck the hours of the night, but none of them heard it.

David awoke with a blade of early sunlight striking his eyes. Ruth was already up. She had wangled milk and eggs from a farmer.

"Oh, I'm stiff," Saul said. "I can hardly stand up."

Ruth insisted they all drink the milk and raw eggs. Rachel promised to vomit if she was forced.

"If you try that trick," Ruth said, "you'll begin again at the beginning."

Rachel kept the slithering breakfast down.

Soon they were pedaling again in the hope of reaching the summer house before nightfall. There they could rest and decide what to do, but the going was slow. They avoided main roads and any others that radiated from The Hague, with its Peace Palace and its cobbled squares. They had once attended a wedding there on Java Straat, where snow-white horses had pulled the bridal couple in a coach. Now the city was said to be entirely in enemy hands. To the north of The Hague was Scheveningen, popular for its beaches in summer, but rumored now to be held by the enemy against a possible British landing. It, too, had become a place to avoid.

They did not entirely circumvent contact with the war, however. About noon they had just passed through a clean little town of bright orange-tiled roofs and particularly clean windows and were heading north toward the summer cottage when they found the road blocked by three Dutch soldiers. One was a tall blond Frisian with dark-yellow hair and a tight, weathered face. His anxious green eyes bore a clever and knowing look, and he adjusted his mouth to a smile as he held up his arm in a signal for the riders to halt.

"Our papers are in order," Ruth told them.

"Actually, miss, it isn't your papers. You see, we've fallen a bit behind our regiment. We're on the way to the front, and . . ."

"Yes, go on. What's your problem?"

"You see, we need transportation. In the interest of national security, that is."

"I smell a rat," Ruth said, "about six feet tall."

"I'm afraid we'll require your bicycles, all but the little girl's, miss." He was still being polite.

"Go to hell." Ruth spoke arrogantly. She had the fine high cheekbones for arrogance. "You're three deserters on the run. Be honest, at least."

One of the soldiers made an end of the farce by drawing back the bolt on his rifle, then cracking it forward. David felt his chest grow too small for his heart. He did not resist as his bicycle was taken. None of them did.

Ruth looked bewildered for the first time. "Oh, how funny. Isn't this hilarious?" She was close to sobbing as she shook her fist at the rapidly retiring trio of deserters. "Cowards!" she yelled after them. "Did you see what a mess that one had made of his pants?"

Except for Rachel, they continued on foot, still hoping to reach the summer cottage before dark. With Rachel pedaling ahead, then resting while the others caught up, they moved on steadily through an area of reclaimed land, chicken and goat farms, then sand dunes and the year's first dandelions.

They crossed several canals where men sat obliviously fishing. German planes flew high overhead.

"They'll be landing troops at The Hague," observed Saul, who had read a good deal about the campaigns of Napoleon, Caesar, and Alexander the Great. There was something about conquerors that fascinated him and he liked to speak about "the art of war." The expression seemed incongruous to David, but no doubt Saul had a better idea of what was going on than the rest of them.

By late afternoon Rachel had pedaled to the front door of the summer cottage, which was locked, as they had left it. The little fishing boat sat on its wheeled cart against the side wall away from the sea.

"Now what?" Saul was the first to ask what they were all thinking.

"Now," Ruth told them, "I'm afraid we break in." A small stone was all she needed. They climbed quickly in single file through the window and began scouring about for canned goods. Sardines and peaches turned up. There was bedding put aside in moth balls and no one objected to staying the night.

"But tomorrow, do we go back home?" asked Rachel.

"We'd better look for a boat," said David.

"I doubt there are any boats left," was Saul's opinion. "Even if there are, the Germans will have planes out."

"There's our boat," David reminded them. "It has a sail." That would be his grandfather's way.

"I'm not a good sailor," Ruth admitted, "and it's miles and miles to England. I promised to get you there alive, not drown you like kittens."

"It's not that far. Sometimes a thin gray line at dusk gives you the feeling you can see England from here," said David.

He felt himself caught up finally in an adventure that had seemed only a bad dream.

"That's impossible."

"I know, but it really isn't far. Two days. Saul and I have done plenty of sailing."

"On the canal," Saul admitted. "Where it's always flat calm."

"What if a storm came up? You can never be sure of the Channel. Grandfather would tell you that," Ruth objected.

"But he'd risk it," said David, knowing Ruth had made up her mind, not because she was afraid, but because she was not a romantic. Common sense told her that the chances were too slim. She would have her way, he knew, particularly with Saul and Rachel on her side. They were all exhausted, too; tired of talk. "There's nothing left to do but go home," Ruth concluded. "Home has to be faced. If there were any sane way to get to England, I'd take it, but there isn't."

Resentfully David walked outside. Dusk. He was sick of them all just then. At least he had hoped for some support from Saul. Strange, he thought, how different twins could be. David followed the serpentine path past pink scrub roses to the beach. The sea beyond the dunes was flat as a parking lot and vibrant with sunset. The only sound was that of the small waves lapping at the shore. The tide was low. David threw stones into the pools to frighten the fish while the interrupted gulls tilted on the slight breeze. Sweeping high above, they caught the falling light as they gained elevation and finally left the land's grasp and soared out to sea. They at least had escaped.

Finding an old gin bottle, David scrawled on a scrap of paper. "To whomsoever in the world this may concern, I am a fifteen-year-old Dutch boy standing on a beach south of

Zandvoort on May 15, 1940. My name is . . ." Setting his name and address adrift on the vast Channel tide was melodramatic, though he suspected conditions of breeze and tide were such that the bottle would return to its point of origin as soon as he turned his back.

That evening they ate sardines and peaches without turning on the lights. Rolled in blankets, they could hear the mutter of distant war.

"Listen," Ruth whispered. "Don't you hear it? Somewhere we're fighting back." She still seemed to resent the three deserters more for their cowardice than for the theft of the bicycles. They slept under great shrouding mosquito nets that night since no one had sprayed the canal this year. The nearby village was fast asleep. Overhead, bright stars flashed like swords.

As usual Ruth roused them early. She had already assembled the leftover scraps from supper for their trek home. It remained for Saul to board up the small pane of broken glass. As an afterthought, the boat was hidden in a thick patch of brambles, just in case.

"I'd rather face the sea in any kind of boat, than face them," David said, but that argument was over.

With bicycles they would have been home by noon, for they had completed the greater part of a fruitless circle. As it was, Ruth calculated a day and a half of plodding, with Rachel darting ahead on her cycle.

A blue egret stood on one stilt leg by the canal as they set out. Ruth walked fast, as though leading a parade. It was good to be free of uncertainty, good to be going home, and no one could hold Ruth responsible for missing the *Texel Queen* under the circumstances. The sea breeze brought them the tintinnabulation of a church bell. They ought to drop in and surprise Father Lebbink. It might be ages until next time, but Ruth propelled them on through the sunlit marshes. The broken mirrors of water multiplied the old windmills.

"It's the best thing, David. Honestly." Saul put an arm around his brother's shoulder, trying to console him. "Things'll settle down, you'll see. We'll get back to school."

"I don't care about school. Anyway, what about the Germans?"

"They've won. What more can they want?"

Perhaps Saul was right. David felt a certain relief. They were going home, and home was sacred. How could anything really bad happen there?

At first none of them interpreted Rachel's pell-mell return flight toward them as anything but exuberance. "Hide!" she yelled, still pedaling hard. "Hide! They're coming!"—as though the devil and his demons were in hot pursuit. The facts when finally understood were hardly less spine-tingling. Above the side of a stone bridge, German helmets moved smoothly and steadily, at unnatural speed. A better view as they swept down onto the dike road explained their motion: motorcycles. Stick bombs hung from their belts, carbines swung from their backs, and they moved two by two until more than thirty had passed down the road.

David found himself sweating, panting with the curious rage that was panic's postscript. Ruth stared after them until the roar of their motors had died and even the dust had settled. Then, as though breaking from a reverie, she said, "Let's go. We can't worry about Germans any more."

It was quiet.

They walked and walked.

Finally they heard the putter and thump of a diesel truck overtaking them. "Keep going," Ruth told the others. She herself had stopped. Taking out a small mirror, she considered her face before going on. The truck had almost caught up. "Just keep on as though you didn't notice," she ordered.

"But I think they're Germans," Saul protested.

"And I can make them do what I want," Ruth replied. By "them" David knew she meant men. In this case, German men. The truck honked, but it did not seem in a hurry or disposed to run them over. In fact, one of the soldiers in gray-green leaped down. He had a fair face and a stupid one. At least, it was open and lacked cunning, in David's opinion. He cracked his great boots together and said, in immaculate, school-marm Dutch, "Would you care for a lift, miss?"

"Very much," Ruth told him with a throw-away smile, "but I can't leave my friends."

"But of course not," he continued gallantly. To Rachel, who seemed to cower in his presence, he squatted low, as if to befriend a timid dog, and spoke jokingly: "We won't bite you until we know you better."

At a nod from Ruth, they climbed into the truck and pulled Rachel's bicycle after them.

Georg, as he identified himself, the only Dutch-speaking member of the truckload of soldiers and hence the officer in charge, was not German at all, but Austrian. He had been an orphan of World War I, reared by a Dutch family. Because of this background he had been selected as part of the liberating vanguard. "The war is over," he told them. "The Netherlands are free."

"Free?" David asked in confusion.

"Yes, of course, free from the British, who intended to turn the Netherlands into a battleground." Now that danger had passed, it required very little effort of the imagination to picture these intruders as Holland's protectors rather than its captors, unless, of course, one let memory wander back to Rotterdam after the bombing.

Ruth tilted her head back, rolled her eyes slightly sideways at what Georg had to say. She stretched, placing her hands behind her head, pushing back her fair hair and thereby revealing a dangerous curve of body. Such conduct seemed to David a hazard to them all. He had never doubted that Ruth belonged in that fantasy of every conqueror who sees himself dominating a beautiful woman. Laughter fairly radiated from her eyes as she explained that she was a dancer who appeared in nightclubs in Amsterdam. Of course now, with the war, all that would be different. A poor dancer would be out of work.

"Oh, not at all," Georg admonished her. "We Austrians always encourage the arts," and he made a joke in German with his comrades as they motored along toward Amsterdam's outer suburbs.

David was aghast at being suddenly thrust into the midst of the enemy. He hated Georg's handsome stupid face, for which he would have gladly exchanged his own intelligent one. Georg was just the sort he disliked, cocky and self-assured, with golden hair and polished boots. He almost hated Ruth just then, and could make nothing of the sudden wink she directed at him without in the slightest changing the expression on the other side of her face.

With a look of deep regret, Georg dropped them off near Amsterdam's flattened airport. He had no authority to enter the city.

Once more he clicked his heels. Taking Ruth's hand, he bestowed a kiss of mock solemnity. "I hope I may see you dance one day, Miss . . . ?"

"Salome," she told him. Her smile was dazzling. It could

make an ordinary man forget everything. "I will look forward," she said.

Finally the truck was pulling away and Ruth was rubbing her hands together.

"Why did you act like that?" David demanded.

"So beggars could ride, of course."

"But flaunting yourself . . ."

"I'm naturally a show-off."

"And this Salome. Will you dance for them?"

"Yes, in my way, with Hitler's head on a platter. The swine! Destroying Rotterdam and then saying how they saved us from the British. And that ass, he believes it, every word."

David felt better. She had not changed inside, but was merely more adept at assuming masks than he had reckoned.

Amsterdam had not been touched in the three days since they had left, but evidently the NSB, the Dutch Nazi party, about one percent of the population, had been parading. The NSB was led by Anton Mussert, who was married to his own aunt and whose shoes were built up so that he might seem of normal stature. The NSB were still milling about in uniform, waving flags, swilling beer, snapping each other's picture. They were too flushed with victory to be ugly. The four young people made it to the old quarter of the city, the Jewish quarter where Rembrandt had lived and painted, without incident.

They came to the bridge from which they had waved a last goodbye. How fine it was to be home! And then they saw a small group of uniformed figures, their faces scrubbed pink as babies, their uniforms silver-trimmed but otherwise black as night from head to foot. They were something new, something more than soldiers, and David felt, though the afternoon sun still shone, that somehow it had already set.

"Who are they?" he asked suspiciously.

"SS," Saul said mysteriously. "Hitler's elite bodyguard."

"What?" asked David again.

"You'll find out soon enough," Ruth informed him, and her words were not spoken as a joke.

THREE

EARLY OCCUPATION
1940-42

Usually David found it hard to be physically demonstrative with his mother, but upon returning home he easily overcame the barriers of reserve. He flew into her waiting arms and kissed her soft, cool cheek with clumsy force. It was kissing, hugging, and tears all around. "Never such a welcome since Lindbergh landed in Paris," Moses exclaimed. Then came the questions: "What's all this? What's going on here? Will somebody tell me?" This from Vera in her confusion. They told what had happened in snatches, with interruptions from Rebecca, who admitted through her tears that she feared they had all been drowned on the *Texel Queen*.

"Yes, she went down in the raid, and we couldn't be sure whether you were aboard or not," Abraham explained.

"My God, if I'd been responsible for sending my grandchildren to their deaths . . . my God." Moses' voice was not quite steady.

"Well, you didn't. We had a very exciting time and we're home again good as new." Ruth flung comforting arms around the old man's neck.

"You might have telephoned, reassured us somehow," Rebecca replied. "I'm not accusing you"—and so of course Ruth stood accused—"but you put us to terrible worry. Your poor grandfather! I don't think any of us has slept a wink."

Ruth seemed to turn her head at each thrust as though to let the blows glance off.

"Now, Rebecca, we're just relieved to have them home."
Abraham stood there in his shirtsleeves and black office trousers, adjusting his spectacles and beaming. "Ruth did very well." He threw a loving arm around his elder daughter.

"I think I did, too," Ruth acknowledged, but presently she had vanished from the family group, and when David found her she was in her room, face down on the bed.

"You did just fine, Ruth."

"Oh, leave me alone!"

"What's the matter? Don't worry about Mother, she's just upset." Ruth didn't answer or look at him. "Ruth, do you remember that rich art dealer, Mijnheer Goudstikker? Just now Grandfather was telling us how he got onto one of the ships to get away to England, and fell into the hold by accident and was killed. Well, anyway, I think you were right about coming home."

"I wish we'd gone in the skiff," she retaliated. "You were the right one, David."

"No, I wasn't."

"Oh, go away and let me sleep!"

So they had come home to occupied Amsterdam, where no bombs had fallen. Anti-Nazi newspapers were burned, as were some English dictionaries, and in the Jewish community an immediate pogrom was expected. Mass suicides took place, but all that happened was that street signs were replaced with ones in German. NSB men began selling Nazi newspapers.

There was a parade down Raddhuistraat, with the paukpauk-pauk of treads on cobbles, the bronze of eagles, the trumpets and the flags. "Count the eagles. Not even Napoleon's army could match this," Saul said from the street corner. Hitler's army was certainly well fed and well drilled.

"What marvelous uniforms!" Girls twined ribbons in their
hair, moistened and bit their lips, and waved at the passing
conquerors.

"Pinhead gladiators—ant soldiers," Ruth said, for in her
eyes still raged the reflected flames of burning Rotterdam.

"Wouldn't it be nice," said Saul, "to think that this was like
a stage set, and they"—he gestured toward the marching
troops—"were really only a few actors going round and
round the block." But even as Saul spoke, David sensed that
this was a changed moment in history, an end and a beginning. Here was an army that must win and hold its victory
forever and thereby change the world, or accept instead ruin-
ous defeat. There would be no half measures. Great and terrible days lay ahead, and David felt a compulsion, as the
ranks went by, to keep a record of some sort lest he forget.

"*18 May 1940*. Reichskommisar Seyss-Inquart has been
put in charge of the Netherlands. He's an Austrian. The
weather is good."

That was his first entry. On the twenty-seventh he recorded the fall of Belgium, just as it had fallen in the other
war. On the twenty-ninth he wrote, "After the radio barked
at us, 'Achtung! Achtung!' Inquart said"—David was copy-
ing now from a later edition of the newspaper—" 'I have
today taken over civilian authority . . . the magnanimity of
the Führer and the efficiency of our German soldiers have
made it possible to restore civil life quickly. I intend that all
Dutch law and general administration shall continue as usual
. . . Though 5,000 Dutch and German soldiers' " ("mostly
Dutch," David added in parentheses) " 'have been killed,
there is no animosity in our hearts.' "

"It has the simple beauty of a liar's speech," Uncle Daniel

commented at the time. "The voice of the serpent hissing as
he hands out apples in Paradise."

"I don't see why he should lie," Rebecca told Daniel across
the dinner table the evening after Inquart's speech. "If we do
nothing to offend them, they'll treat us like Austria."

"As part of the Thousand-Year Reich? Oh, splendid!"
Uncle Daniel gave a sad laugh. "But I seem to smell something in the air like the wind from a garbage dump. You'll
pardon a cynic, Rebecca. Perhaps it's just that my electric
train was derailed and my dog was run over when I was a
boy. Perhaps that's why I think it might have been a good
idea if Noah had pulled the plug out of the Ark."

"But Inquart sounded sincere," Rebecca persisted. "I really
do think he wants to be a friend to Holland."

"Of course he does, just as the bear made friends with the
man. Then one day, when the man lay sleeping with a fly on
his nose, the bear, out of sheer love, mind you, swatted the
fly away. Unfortunately, he knocked off the man's head as
well. Of course, this made the bear very sad, and when the
man wouldn't wake up and play, the bear wandered off to
look for new friends. The moral, my dear—and I hate hurt-
ing your tender ears with the facts of life—is that the bear
was named Inquart and the man was Dutch. Undoubtedly a
Dutch Jew. Frankly, I don't imagine there will be very many
Jews left in Amsterdam to enjoy next year's tulip crop. Particularly those with foreign passports like myself, living in
exile."

"Then what do you propose to do?" Abraham asked his
brother.

"Join the underground, of course!" Daniel thumped his fist
on the table, propelled his chair backward so that it nearly

fell over, then stood up. Anger kept his words going at high speed. "Before the German dogs eat me, I want to get in the first bite."

"What are you talking about? You're no assassin, Daniel," Abraham protested.

"Look again, Abraham. I never forget. They have left me destitute, taken the only life I loved above my own, but I'll pay them back, tenfold." If the words seemed excessive and melodramatic, it was Daniel's face that made David afraid. It was like a wild animal's, thinking not of itself or of any other animal, but only of the kill.

"But what underground?" Abraham questioned. "There may be one, I grant you, but where? And what Jews are there in Holland with guns? I don't even know anyone who goes hunting."

"Somewhere there is an underground. As long as Holland has a heart, there must be one. People are confused now. They've lived so long at peace that they're not yet able to believe in this war. Give them time, Abraham, and they'll learn to kill Germans."

"Yes, Daniel, and for every dead German there'll be ten dead Hollanders in retaliation."

"Better ten dead than one living as a slave. But I've ruined supper for you, and I've upset my stomach."

"I'll get you a soda mint," Rebecca offered.

"No, but thank you. What I really need, I think, is a good brisk walk."

So Daniel departed after dinner, and David did not believe for a moment that his uncle was simply going out for a stroll. He went too much like a man with things to arrange, with weapons to cache and plots to spin.

"Daniel's talk about an underground organization worries

me," Abraham said when the door had closed after Daniel. "The truth is, he can't forgive himself for having failed to save his wife. I think in a way he despises us because we represent what he lost. He sees me coming home every night, opening my paper, being with my family, and he wants to destroy everything."

"Dear, your stomach's rumbling, too."

"Yes, I hate these arguments. If someone handed me a pistol, I'd probably throw it among the Germans and let them fight each other to get it."

"Here are the soda mints," Rebecca offered.

"Thank you, my dear. And now, would you care for a spot of chess? And do you mind my smoking one of these new cigarettes? Rolled artichoke leaves, or so I'm told. Curious smell—almost like singeing flesh."

These early days were days of hope in Holland. Life did indeed go along almost normally. David's diary had sparse entries, such as "Today all Dutch prisoners of war were released!" A few days later *"4 June:* The English soldiers have been driven from a beach at Dunkirk. Father says France must fall."

But in Amsterdam, Jews and Gentiles took up their old occupations. On June 29 many celebrated Prince Bernhard's birthday by wearing white carnations. Though German uniforms were common in the city, the occupiers did not challenge this act of defiance. There were no pogroms, as some pessimists in the Jewish community had predicted. The only hardship was that Jews were told to leave the coastal defense area. According to the joke going around, this was because the Jews refused to give Hitler a rod to divide the Channel to England as Moses had divided the Red Sea. At night, hundreds of bombers rumbled over Amsterdam, and it seemed to all they were safer in Holland than they would have been in England, the planes' destination. The Ullmans yearned for the peace and quiet of the now-forbidden summer cottage on the beach.

"*25 July:* A law was passed today [wrote David] against cruel practices in slaughtering. I don't think this is bad, though of course its only purpose is to hurt the kosher butchers.

"Jews of foreign nationality have been told to report. I guess Uncle Daniel was right about that."

It was not until autumn, when David, Saul, and Rachel were back in school, that the real restrictions began. They did not at first affect students, but David duly recorded in his diary the events whose implications were beyond his grasp. At first there were only rumors that the Constitution of the Netherlands, which allowed for public service by all Dutch citizens, was to be circumvented. Forms attesting to Aryan background were mailed out. Many schoolteachers, Jews, Protestants, and Catholics alike, refused to sign.

"*22 October 1940:* All firms owned by Jews are to be reported. Why?"

On October 25, David wrote: "Now it is clear that Jews are being fired from government jobs." By mid-November all Jewish university professors were "temporarily" suspended. Professors at Leyden University spoke out in protest, as did students at Delft, and the university in Amsterdam closed early for the winter holiday. But the law stood, and the word "temporary" was deleted.

"*1 November 1940:* Today a boy in school asked me if it was true my uncle was in the underground. I didn't know how to answer and he said, 'What's wrong with that? I say good for him. If you want to know, I have some cousins in the Black

Hand.' That's a terrorist group for the resistance, by the way. It isn't the only one. There's been one since last summer called Order Dienst and another called Organisation der Geunzen. The Germans say they are mostly Jewish, but this isn't true, I think. We Jews are under such close surveillance that the partisans don't want us. It's very dangerous for anyone to join or to say anything against the Germans. My father used to joke about throwing books at them. A professor at the university got so mad he did just that. They shot him dead. I don't miss Uncle Daniel, he was always so angry and sort of frightening, but I hope he's well wherever he is. I hope Ruth is well, too. We don't see much of her."

It worried David that his sister seemed to be fraternizing with the enemy. She had never before been in such demand as an entertainer, and this was odd, since places of entertainment were being denied to Jews. When Ruth came home, it was usually very late, and she put aside his questions with "Oh, David, can't it wait? I'm exhausted!" But she didn't seem so much exhausted as preoccupied, with some secret excitement he couldn't share.

"Grandfather doesn't bother much," David wrote in his diary. "He just says he's obsolete and the world's crazy. Grandmother never goes out any more, and doesn't know a thing. It's so awful, but maybe, as Mother says, it's for the best. Father keeps busy at the Israelitisch Hospital. He's been asked to join some kind of Jewish council which will try to deal with the Germans. So far he's refused the honor.

"*1 January 1941:* We had a family party last night. Father brought some special alcohol from the hospital. I had a small drink at midnight. Even Ruth was there, and Grandmother perked up and sang along. It was good, all of us being together. Father told a joke about a Gestapo agent who climbed onto a tram. No one made a sound until an old lady sneezed. When the Gestapo man demanded, 'Who sneezed?' everyone hung his head and finally pushed the old lady to confess. Then the Gestapo man smiled and said, *'Gesundheit,'* and got off the tram. We laughed, but of course it wasn't really funny when you think about it. We're getting like that—afraid to sneeze.

"*6 January 1941:* Three bad days. Two days ago signs were hung out in Leyden where we used to go for lunch, 'Jews not wanted here.' There's some talk that all Jews are being herded into Amsterdam and then they'll make a ghetto. Yesterday most of the cinemas put up *'Für Juden Verboten'* signs. Today everyone with even one Jewish grandparent has to register as a Jew.

"*9 January 1941:* Now all the cinemas are closed to us. I think this is hardest on Saul, who is really our big movie fan. I worry about Saul sometimes. He gets so moody. I caught him looking in the mirror the other day and he asked me straight out, 'What do you think? Do I look like a rat?' Of course I told him no, and then he sort of profiled and added, 'With a nose like that?' So I told him what Grandmother used to say, that big noses were a sign of intelligence, except that he informed me I remembered it wrong. 'What she said was, big noses are signs of virtue,' and then he looked at himself again. 'With a nose like that, I don't think I can avoid being virtuous,' he said. Finally it came out that what was really bothering him was a new Nazi film they're showing at all the 'Aryan' theaters, *The Eternal Jew.* According to Saul, it makes us out a horde of rats overrunning Europe. But to start staring in the mirror because of a stupid thing like that!

"*11 February 1941:* The universities won't accept any new Jewish students; that's the latest German law. They haven't said anything about preparatory schools yet, but I'm worried.

"*12 February 1941:* Now Jews are supposed to hand over their weapons. 'What weapons?' Father asked. The Jewish Council has finally been formed, but he says he still isn't interested in joining, that it will only be a tool of the Nazis.

"*18 February 1941:* This really is funny. We can't be blood donors any more! Better to let people die than for them to be contaminated!

"*26 February 1941:* I don't know where to start, so much has happened in the past week. Father likes to talk as though it's some kind of play. 'It's just a stage,' he said, 'and some of us are desperately unrehearsed.' The trouble is, the Nazis are beautifully rehearsed. There's a curfew because they say we're black marketeers at night. We're kept out of theaters because we're supposed to start riots. But getting back to these last few days, I guess it all began on the nineteenth. In south Amsterdam there's a chain of ice-cream parlors run by Jews. I guess some Nazis threatened to close the places up. Anyway, some customers set up an ammonia flask to protect the place and it went off in the faces of the German police. The owners were arrested, and will probably be shot. That was just the beginning. The SS began to take hostages, four hundred young men, and they're supposed to be sent to a camp in Germany, I think it's called Mauthausen or something like that—anyway, some sort of work camp, and most people say they won't come back alive. Only one good thing happened. The whole city was so shocked that there was a general strike in Amsterdam. Just for a little while, with everyone marching and singing the 'International,' we felt we were really Dutch again. That was good. Now the strike's over and the Nazi newspapers are crying over a Dutch storm trooper who got himself killed while breaking into a Jewish shop. This is really what the paper said: 'Judah has finally dropped its mask. Murdered? No, cut down with sadistic lust. Crushed beneath the heel by a nomadic race of alien blood.' Speaking of blood, they didn't dare put such an idiotic idea in the papers, but in school I heard someone saying that the Jews had ripped open the poor storm trooper's arteries with their teeth and drunk his blood. Sounds like Dracula or something. Anyway, school goes on pretty much as ever, and with all the family together, I guess I can't complain.

"*1 March 1941:* Now something really bad has happened. It happened to Rachel and me. At least, we were there when it happened, and Rachel has looked strange ever since, with the sort of expression you see on little kids' faces at the zoo when they keep expecting the lions to roar at them. We were coming back from school (Saul was home with asthma or a cold or something) and there was an SS officer with a submachine gun who was making all Jews who went by take off their hats out of respect. Well, all the kids began going back. We'd take off our caps five, even ten times, with really terrifically respectful expressions on our faces. We knew he was getting mad and we didn't go too close, but then this really old Hasidic Jew came by. It was beginning to rain, and the SS officer grabbed him by his beard and hacked it off. Hacked at his tallis, too, and stuffed the hair in the old man's mouth. Then he kicked him until he fell in the wet with everyone else flying away under their black umbrellas, and all I could think of was a fleet of fishing boats scudding for a safe harbor. I took Rachel away, and kept telling her not to be frightened, but it was a bad thing for a little girl to see. She has a great imagination and a very impressionable mind, and she's been upset ever since. It's different when you see it for yourself than when you read in the newspaper that some hostage has had a 'fatal accident.'

"*2 March 1941:* Father's really unhappy. He just comes home, slumps down in his chair, and doesn't say much, just that he's had a long day, and finally today he said he'd been pressured into joining the Jewish Council."

So David kept up his diary as winter of 1941 became spring. On March 15 he wrote: "Since people have been leaving cafés and restaurants as soon as a German comes in, an order went out that they must stay at least fifteen minutes after a German arrives. Now the Dutch customers sit with their watches on the table!" His entry for April 11 was less amused. "Yesterday Amsterdam's Jews were told they couldn't move from the city. Does this mean a ghetto? We've heard terrible stories about the ghetto in Warsaw, Poland. As of today there are no more Jewish newspapers, except for the new *Joodse Weekblad,* and that's just a way for the Nazis to publish their decrees.

"*1 May 1941:* From now on, Jewish doctors can treat only Jewish patients. Maybe Father will get some time off.

"*13 May 1941:* Lots of excitement. Hitler's secretary, Rudolf Hess, has flown to England. Everyone's saying the war will soon be over!

"*4 June 1941:* Now that warm weather's coming, we've been forbidden to use the public parks and bathhouses. But we can still go boating on the Amstel, Father says.

"*11 June 1941:* The resistance set off a bomb in the German naval officers' club. Three hundred Jewish hostages have been arrested. They'll be sent to Mauthausen camp and die there, Father says. He's had a serious talk with Saul and me, since it looks as though all those not 'usefully' employed are going to be sent to work camps. It would be a good idea for us to take some special training. At first Father talked about masonry. When bombs are falling, there's always need of bricklayers, but now it seems we'll probably go to the A. B. David metalwork school this summer. It's at Valchenir Straat, and not too far from our house.

"*15 June 1941:* They say Jewish musicians will soon be dismissed from orchestras because they pollute Aryan music, and trumpet players are forbidden to sway their horns when they play or hit a note over C, because both these things imitate Negro music, which I guess is even more infectious than Jewish.

"*22 June 1941:* Good news. Hitler has made the mistake of attacking Russia and everyone says he will lose, just like Napoleon. It's said thousands of Dutch soldiers have volunteered to fight against Russia. I don't understand this. Maybe they just want to get away from the anti-aircraft guns booming all night when the British bombers fly over. It's impossible to sleep.

"*1 July 1941:* School's out. The last day someone wrote on the blackboard: 'Roses are red, violets are blueish, if it weren't for Jesus, we'd all be Jewish.' Is that a joke, an insult, or a compliment? One little boy asked me once whether the little spots baked into the matzoh crackers were blood. Queer ideas! There's some talk we won't be going back to school, that we're beginning a long summer vacation that will last all winter.

"*5 July 1941:* Father says it's probably true about school. I don't care much, but Rachel cried. She had a lot of 'Aryan' (I hate that word, but everyone uses it) friends there. Instead, there's to be a new Jewish lyceum. Saul's looking forward to it. As long as he's got something to study, I swear he'd be happy no matter what. The metalworking classes are to continue in the late afternoon, so we'll keep busy. I'll have to do more with Rachel. She really is downhearted. Just the other day she said to me, 'It used to seem as if everything nice would come true, and now it hardly ever does.' We often do drawings together, starting a figure, say, with her putting on the head, then me adding an arm. We tried that yesterday, and when we had a figure done, she put a bandage over its eyes and gave it a pair of scales to hold. Justice, except that I gave the figure wings, like the pictures of angels, and that made it look more like blind victory or some kind of monstrous goddess of the hunt.

"*15 August 1941:* The summer hasn't been too bad. We're all getting used to the new wooden-soled shoes after a lot of aches and blisters, but good food is hard to get, especially for those who try to keep the dietary laws, because Jews are allowed into the shops only in the late afternoon after other customers have picked things over. Sometimes there's black market horsemeat. The way this works is, two horses come into town pulling a cart, and only one goes out. Mother and Rachel won't eat it; Grandmother will, ground up, but she doesn't know what it is. I don't like talking about her now. We used to call her the Old Dragon, and now all her fire's gone out. She used to scare me, and now she just sits by the window to look at people going by. She hardly talks any more, though her lips move and she makes little grumbling noises. Grandfather says it's good for old people's gums for them to talk to themselves! And then sometimes she'll shout in her old voice, as if she's calling us to dinner, 'Bring the pan! Bring the pan!' which is funny, but awfully sad, too.

"*13 September 1941:* One hundred more Jewish hostages have been sent to Mauthausen. It's supposed to be for sabotage near Enschede. Everyone knows they won't come back alive.

"*22 October 1941:* Lots of Nazi decrees today. Number 198 says that Jews can be employed only if they have a special permit, and Number 199 that Jews can't be part of non-profit associations such as bridge and tennis clubs if there are Aryan members, and 200—this one made Mother laugh—that we can't employ Aryan housekeepers any more, as if she would let anyone else handle 'her things.' Rachel has promised to help more, maybe she will. She's a good sister right now, and nice to have around.

"*5 December 1941:* All non-Dutch have been called to the Zentralstelle for 'voluntary emigration.' What does that mean? I know Uncle Daniel won't be there, even if he's still in Amsterdam.

"*8 December 1941:* We celebrated the good news of America coming into the war. With the Nazis doing badly now in Russia, we're bound to win in the end. There are signs up all over the city—'V for Victory,' and 'Orange Will Win,' but 'Victory' written over '1918' makes the Nazis maddest of all. They grab Jews in the street and make them rub off the signs, but it takes time. The Germans are supposed to be calling this year '1941-A,' because Hitler promised them the war would be won by 1941.

"*7 January 1942:* I haven't written for a while; we've been waiting for something to happen. Food has been hard to get, especially fish. One of my teachers has two cats, and when we can we take him the fish skins. Of course, our cat has to eat, too. Father came home late tonight and said the Jewish Council had been told to supply a total of 1,400 unemployed Jews to be sent to some camp. They take away our jobs and then say, since we're not doing anything, we might as well go and work for them! Not that the city is emptying out. They take some from Amsterdam and then cram in twice as many more from other parts of the country. They say all the Jews from Zaandam will be coming here.

"*1 February 1942:* There are planes over the city almost every night. Searchlights and anti-aircraft guns flash and boom.

"*20 March 1942:* We can't travel by automobile any more. Father's afraid Jewish patients will soon be thrown out of the hospitals. All this seems unbelievable. I think we'd explode if it all happened at once, but it's one thing after another until all you want to do is hide in school or hide at home. Still, people get married, take violin lessons, are tutored in French. Saul is going in for Latin. He's building a model catapult, the sort Caesar used. As long as he's busy, Saul doesn't seem to worry. I'd like to take more art. Rachel is getting better than me. Mother hardly ever goes out now except to shop. Maybe soon they'll just lock our doors from the outside and throw away the key.

"*29 April 1942:* I don't know that I want to go on keeping a record after today. I know I won't ever want to read this. It's been a day like winter back again, with hail and sunshine all mixed together. Rachel and I were drawing in the living room. Mother was getting supper when Father came in. He never was one for hiding any kind of news, and he was holding up these yellow patches as if with tongs. Then he dropped them on the table and said. 'They cost us four cents apiece. A real bargain,' and he prodded them with his finger as you'd prod a rat to make sure it's dead. They were big stars made out of yellow cloth with the word JOAD written across them. 'The official announcement's not until tomorrow,' Father said, 'but we're supposed to wear these things when we go out.'

"I was too stupefied to talk. It sounded like the Middle

Ages. Rachel picked one up and said she thought it was sort of pretty. 'I suppose it is. A kind of special decoration, because we're special,' Father said, but he looked awfully sad.

"When Grandfather came in, he said, 'I'll be damned before I sew on one of those things, and nobody's putting one of those on Vera, either!' Of course, Grandmother doesn't go out any more, not even in her wheelchair. She's had another 'cerebral incident,' as Grandfather puts it, and the left side of her face has slid down as though she were made of wax and that part of her was out in the sun too long and melted. I don't really feel sorry for her. Father says she's sort of locked away in a time womb. She smiles nearly all the time now and her eyes are glittery. I won't say so out loud, but I try not to be alone with her. The one I am sorry for is Grandfather, when he says things like 'When you're twenty years old you think you'll be twenty forever, and then you blink your eyes and you're seventy-two and that little old lady in the wheelchair has eaten over fifty thousand meals with you.' I don't know what I'm going to do about wearing that yellow thing. I'd like to say, 'Father, I don't feel very well, I don't think I'll go to school any more.'

"The biggest trouble over the stars was from Ruth. She came home after we'd eaten supper and said, 'Here I am, late as usual.' I think she looked beautiful, but Mother said, 'Take that stuff off your face, you look like a geisha,' and 'What have you done to your hair?'

" 'Does it show that much?' Ruth asked. She'd used some sort of bleach, and she pirouetted around to show it off.

"Then Mother told her if she wasn't hungry, she could begin sewing. Ruth was hungry, of course, she always is. Not that I'm picking, because she brings home lots of things

Mother can't get in the shops. 'Well, then, eat, and you can help me sew these on when you're finished.' For some reason it hurt Mother that Ruth was in such a good mood.

"Then Ruth picked up one of the stars. 'Just lovely,' she said. 'This would make me a star overnight, but no thank you.'

" 'It's not a matter of choice,' Mother went on.

" 'I'm aware of that,' Ruth said, and then she pulled out something she'd been holding back: Aryan papers, fake parents and everything. She looked the part anyway, without lightening her hair, with her fair skin and sort of pert nose. The rest of us, except maybe Rachel, couldn't get away with it, and then with us men there's that business of circumcision. Father says it's something you can't undo surgically, and the Nazis aren't above hauling a man's pants off right in the street. It may sound ridiculous, but I've seen it done. It's lots easier for a girl to turn into an Aryan than a boy. And I don't blame Ruth. She couldn't keep her job otherwise.

"But I guess a whole lot had been building up in Mother because she said, 'As long as you've mentioned it, do you mind if we talk about that job of yours?'

" 'No, if you insist,' Ruth said, obviously minding very much.

" 'Dancing for Germans! I don't see how a daughter of mine can do such a thing, whatever kind of papers she has.'

" 'Well,' Ruth said, and she looked as if she were laughing at Mother, 'I happen to do it very well. You should hear the applause. Too bad you can't come to the Silberin Spiegel, Mother. It's such a cozy place, and you'd like Tante Wies, who runs it. She's a huge, fat, jolly widow.'

" 'I'm sure the Gestapo men sitting at the bar love you

both, but let me give you some advice, young lady. Decent
men really don't like girls who flaunt themselves. After the
war, when it's known that you and these Gestapo . . .'

"I think both of them wanted a fight that night, because
otherwise Ruth wouldn't have said what came next.

" 'Know what, Mother? I've always heard that kisses leave
no fingerprints.' We all sort of straightened up at that, and
just so there'd be no misunderstanding, Ruth added, 'I'm an
adult now. I do what I want out of choice, but if you think
I'm a collaborator, I'm not. If I had the power, I'd conduct
every swine of a Nazi straight to hell!'

" 'Ruth, you needn't curse in my house,' Mother said.

" 'What are you supposed to say when something's dam-
nable?' Ruth was really warmed up now, but she got hold of
herself, and the next thing that came out was very casual, like
an old secret that isn't worth keeping any more. 'By the way,
Uncle Daniel sends his greetings. He's very well, but of
course there are reasons why he stays away.'

" 'Then he is in the underground?' Father asked. Ruth
nodded. 'And you, Ruth? You, too?'

" 'Not in the same way. I'm in no danger, I assure you.'

" 'You don't assure me of anything. You're making me a
nervous wreck!' Mother threw the words at her and Ruth just
stared back with an awful expression on her face as if she had
just killed someone. 'Would you care to hear my opinion?'
Mother demanded. 'Would you?'

" 'I suppose I have no choice,' Ruth replied, very cool now.
I won't go into it all word for word, but the gist of it was that
while Mother was drudging away trying to keep the Ullman
family safe and together, Ruth was out trafficking with both
sides and thereby putting us all in danger, and if she was
going to keep it up it would be better for her to move out al-

together. After Mother's speech was over, they stood there
looking exhausted, like a couple of tired fighters waiting for
the bell.

"Then Ruth said, and she sounded very agreeable and
sweet now, 'Yes, you're right.' It seemed too important a
decision for just a yes or no, but there it was. Father tried to
say that Mother wasn't serious, but Ruth wasn't listening any
longer. She went off and began to pack and the rest of us just
stood there and no one said a word. By the time she came
back with her suitcase, Mother had changed around. 'You're
breaking up the family. You can't go!' But Ruth just kissed
each one of us, and when she got to Mother, she said, 'Now
it's my turn to give some advice. You don't belong here any
more than I do. It isn't safe.' The last was for all of us, but
somehow this house seems the only safe place left. It's home.
Every creature, every blade of grass, has a spot where its
roots and strength are, and this is ours.

" 'Please don't go, Ruth,' I said as she passed on her way to
the door.

" 'It's best. You'll see,' she said.

" 'You mustn't do this! Ruth!' Mother was crying now, but
Ruth had done it. The door stood open and she was going
down the street, her body moving from side to side under her
dress. Maybe that's the way Eve looked when she packed up
and left Eden.

"I probably shouldn't be writing all this down. What if the
Germans found it? Well, the walls would have to be torn
down first, I have such a good hiding place. And if I'm going
to bother at all, I want to tell everything, so I'll never forget,
the way you quickly forget a nightmare once you're awake.

"*15 May 1942:* Saul and I are getting used to the star. It
was a shock. I always thought of myself as just Dutch, and

now I have this thing on my jacket, and it's like a physical deformity, like an eye in the middle of my forehead or something. Saul calls us the Tattooed Men. We could hardly look at each other at first. Some people try to make it up to us. Once I had cigarettes forced on me, but most people look away as if the sight of us was painful, or as if they'd been looking at a wall and suddenly noticed an obscenity written on it.

"There is one good thing, though. I haven't mentioned sailing on the Amstel. It's probably an oversight by the Germans, but Jews can still rent boats, and Father is passionate about it. He says he wants to turn Saul and me into salt-sea sailors—sounds like Grandfather, doesn't it? Lots of boats are out weekends, old fishing types with brown sails and leeboards, and thin racing shells that skim over the surface like water bugs.

"*30 May 1942:* I thought for a while that I wouldn't keep up this journal, but anyway here I am back again with the month of May to talk about. More and more people are being called up and sent to Westerbork. That's where most German Jews went before the war. Now it's called a police transit camp, a place to collect Jews and send them on to God knows where. Until now, Jewish doctors were deciding who was fit to go. Now only Aryan doctors make such decisions, and they don't give a damn. I know of a soldier who was taken there who had lost both legs in the 1940 fighting. What work can he do? Then one day at our school a Nazi showed up and explained that one of the students' parents had been caught illegally buying eggs from a barrow, and they were to be transported and the boy had to go, too. 'So we can keep families together' was the explanation, and when the boy asked to get his coat first, the Nazi said, 'Of course, but if you fail to come back, the headmaster will have to go in your place.' Classes are getting smaller.

"*30 June 1942:* Now there's a curfew from eight at night until six in the morning. We keep our windows closed no matter how hot it gets. More and more people are being called up for forced labor. They get a notice to report and to bring a rucksack, and if they don't go, they're hunted down and sent to Mauthausen, which everyone knows by now is a death camp. Mauthausen is supposed to be in a very pretty Alpine setting, but there's a rock quarry there and prisoners have to carry the rocks up 148 steps and then slide down on the loose pebbles on either side. It sounds like Sisyphus in hell, but it doesn't go on forever, because when their strength gives out they're killed. One day, it's said, ten prisoners linked hands at the top and jumped to their deaths. The guards actually applauded, and those ten are now called 'the parachutists' in jokes. This is what I've heard, but I don't know if it's true any more than the story that the camp commandant gave his son fifty Jews for a birthday present to use them for target practice. That sounds far-fetched, but what does it matter? Jews who go to Mauthausen don't come back alive.

"The Jewish Council can exempt from forced labor only those who are vital to the community. With Father's position at the hospital we feel fairly safe, but how long can that last?

"*17 July 1942:* Special trains are going every night to Westerbork. Supposedly, Jews are given ordinary work there, and families are kept together, but I'm not sure I believe it. The bureau for aid to displaced persons puts out bulletins about what one should take along. Books, postcards, etc., but hardly any cards are sent home. Father has special identity cards for us with the 'Bolle Stamp' (Bolle is the General Sec-

retary of the Jewish Council), so we're supposed to be immune, but still it's frightening. People aren't going when
they're called, and a lot go into hiding, so the security police
tour around snatching substitutes off the streets, or they
break into houses after curfew when they know people are at
home. Yesterday they went after a woman who was pushing
a baby's pram on the street. Rachel and I were looking out
the third-floor window and saw it. She tried to run, butting
the pram along like a battering ram, and got over the canal
bridge and out of sight, but just when we couldn't see any
more, we heard two shots and a scream. I couldn't even say
for sure it was the woman, but it must have been. After a
while the 'Greens,' that's our own Green Police, took something away wrapped up in a bag, and then Mother came into
the room with her hair on end and pulled the curtains.

" 'There,' she said, as though she'd erased the whole business outside. But you can't, of course, especially toward dusk
when the real hunting begins, and you're always afraid.

"Let me tell you about any night. Even with our special
papers, you can't feel secure. People have been taken right
from their homes, so about now, with dinner over and dusk
coming on, you begin to feel that creeping fear, like a snake,
winding up from the canal and coiling itself slowly around
you. The streetcars are fewer and fewer. The sky goes red
and then loses color. It's nearly curfew time and the streets
are deserted. There's not a sound. And you wait, until finally
the big clock in the hall gives a wheeze and counts the hours.
Eight o'clock, and time for the hunters to wipe the gravy
from their chins and get into their trucks. At first all you hear
is the clock ticking. Now the street is black. A truck comes,
buzzing its tires on the canal bridge, and a film of moisture
forms on your hands. The truck goes on, but you wait. It's

become windy now and the wind plays tricks. You wait, listening, while your whole body goes stiff, waiting for a lull in the wind to tell what's happening outside. There are running feet. If the doorbell rings, if there's a knock, will you run for the fire escape? All these homes are on fire with terror and you know why people scream because you feel like screaming, and the clock goes on tick-tocking, only thinking about what time it is. After what seems like an eternity, the clock clears its throat and strikes twelve times, and it's midnight. They usually don't come after that, and by two in the morning you can sleep. Such relief; it's like being drugged. You're still alive, you're safe for a few more hours. You can sleep like a baby until morning, and then you'll find out who was taken.

"*28 August 1942:* Big celebration tonight. The security police are guarding Seyss-Inquart, who's seeing a performance at the Dutch Theater, so no roundups. Saul went around swatting all the flies in the house. He was in a passion, as though each fly were Inquart himself.

"*3 October 1942:* We are calling yesterday Black Friday. They said 14,000 Jews were rounded up. We were sent home from school at lunchtime. When we went today, half the desks were empty.

"*15 October 1942:* The roundups go on, but people aren't being taken to the Zentralstelle any more, but to the Dutch Theater. Besides taking people, they are now taking things. The Nazis may come into your house, say, and paste a requisition stamp on your piano to be picked up later. And of course, once a house's occupants have been sent to Westerbork, 'action groups' come around with wagons or barges and haul off everything of value. It's all taken to Lippmann, Rosenthal and Co. to be used for the 'war effort.' Supposedly, unofficial looters are sent to concentration camps. I'm describing this because of what happened last night. It didn't involve Nazis, only our family, but it wouldn't have happened except for the Nazis. Grandmother has been really sick for over a year now. About all Grandfather has hoped for is to spare her the confusion of being torn from familiar surroundings. He hoped she could sleep away her last few months in the quietest corner of the house, but last night he began to worry, or maybe he'd been worrying for a long time without saying so, that if the Nazis showed up here they'd want Grandmother's rings. She's always worn these really valuable rings, and Grandfather wanted to get them off because he was afraid the Nazis would break her fingers to get them. This might sound a little crazy, but it has happened. He tried soap, and you'd think they'd have slid off those little hands with all the work gone out of them, but the problem was, Grandmother didn't understand, and she didn't want to let them go. She'd hardly said a word for days and then only whispers, dry as cracker crumbs. Now it was her old imperious voice, 'Moses! Moses!' with her eyes blazing and bright with resentment and confusion. It was awful. I think Grandfather was crying, but maybe it had to be done. With Mother's help, the rings were finally off and Grandmother was lying back with Grandfather stroking her face because he couldn't explain. Once she fell asleep he put the rings in a leather bag with some other valuables and pulled out a tile beside the fireplace. He made us all watch when he sealed it up again. 'Remember this,' he said, 'but never talk about it.'

"That ought to have been enough for one night, but it wasn't. That was a night that didn't really end at all. The ring business must have been a kind of last straw with Grandmother, because she began breathing loudly, like snoring, and Grandfather and Father went to her. I never heard snoring like that and after a while Father came out and said, 'She's going.' They didn't even know for sure when the breath went out of her. It was what people call a lovely death, I suppose. I couldn't look at her. I could hardly look at Grandfather, who was blaming himself, of course. His eyes weren't wet, but he was crying in a way, and his head went from side to side as he wailed, 'Aiee, aiee,' very softly, so he wouldn't disturb Grandmother.

"*18 October 1942:* I'm going to tell about these last three days and then finish. I wouldn't even do that except this journal's the only friend I've got who doesn't already know. Thank God for Mother. The rest of us were no good at all. She closed Grandmother's eyes, combed her hair and washed her, and put the mattress on the floor and lit the candles. Even with all the horrible things that have happened, this is the hardest. I can't get used to it.

" 'She just looks asleep,' Rachel told me, and dragged me in. I was glad Grandmother's eyes were closed. I'd been dreading their glance. Her right hand was on her bosom and held a little yellowed photograph of Grandfather in the uniform he wore as a ship's doctor. She did look peaceful, but she also looked dead, and I couldn't stay in that room full of shadows and candlelight and death. I guess it was the first time I really thought about death without anything to take my mind from it.

"This morning the rabbi came for the funeral. The coffin was so black it seemed to suck down the daylight, and Grandmother lay in it like a sad stuffed owl. Moving it out was a problem. Grandmother always said it would be. For a while it looked as if they'd have to stand it in the corner like a grandfather's clock, but finally it went out, head first and canted over so you didn't want to think about what was happening inside.

"It's been a miserable day, raining and very windy, and Amsterdam looking ready to sink into the sea. It was a long way, following the coffin, with Grandfather and the rabbi up ahead. Grandfather was shattered, but he knew how the rest of us were feeling and he wanted us to be as dignified as he was. He'd picked out a special headstone with a little drinking well cut into it, because 'my Vera always loved birds.' My face got stiff trying not to cry.

"Ruth surprised us by showing up. I don't know how she'd found out, and I stood beside her with the rain soaking her hair and the ribbons on the flowers while the rabbi spoke. 'Blessed art Thou, O Lord our God, King of the universe, the righteous Judge.'

"Grandfather said, 'She didn't want to be buried at all, just thrown into the sea to travel the waves as she did as a girl,' and then Mother surprised me by saying, 'When my time comes, just dump me in the canal. No stones over my head or wilting flowers.' I can't honestly say it would matter to me. One way or another, you're dead. That's the bad part, which I can't shake off. Everything ending.

"When it was officially over, we started for home. Ruth went along with us. What she said may have been in bad taste. Mother thinks so, but with life so topsy-turvy, I'm not judging. Right away Ruth was after us to leave home, saying things like 'You were born with feet, use them! I think you all prefer your knees.' She wanted us to become 'onderdunkers,' or 'divers,' which is what people who go into hiding are called. 'You don't think the people who were taken first are resettled in quaint little work camps, do you? They've been liquidated, cremated, and nobody has said a thing. The

Nazis have the impression that they're doing the world a favor, and we're next. You just have to listen to the British radio. The deportees are being gassed!' Her eyes blazed with terrible certainty, and her words seemed to fall as heavily as the sod on Grandmother's coffin. 'It's madness to stay in Amsterdam!' But Father shook his head. 'We've done no wrong,' he said. 'I'm still needed here. Besides, I remember in the first war the reports of German soldiers tossing Belgian babies onto their bayonets. It was all propaganda, of course. All this horror talk is probably just the underground trying to drum up support.'

" 'No testimonial from the Jewish Council will help,' Ruth replied, grabbing Father by the shoulders right there in the street. 'In God's name, don't you realize you're putting Mother and your children in danger? Look'—and she pressed something into his unwilling hand—'look at these, if you don't believe me. I have postcards sent back from a place in Poland called Auschwitz. Read them. How cheery it sounds. But Father, why is this word in Hebrew? Yes, there, you see? It means "All is up with us," does it not?' Father seemed staggered, but still kept walking. 'And here's another card from the same place. "All the others are happy," it says. "They are with our sister Hanna." Father, are you deaf? This Hanna died as a baby years ago. You know the family.'

" 'I was the doctor who tried to save that child, I remember. It was a premature birth; she lived only a week,' Grandfather admitted.

" 'Come home, Ruth,' Mother insisted. 'We'll have something to eat and then we'll talk. It's been a hard day for all of us.'

"But Ruth wasn't going any farther. She was shaking her head. Though I guess she saw nothing but tragedy ahead, she was ready for it. She'd never had a taste for everyday life, but she'd said to me not long ago that she was ready for a last dance on the crater's rim just before the eruption.

" 'Ruth, come home to your family.' This was an honest appeal, not a command, from Mother, who had tears in her eyes. Ruth, too, was having a hard time. I could tell from the way her voice had gone husky. 'I can't, Mother. I'm worth more to you now as an Aryan.'

" 'I want my daughter back again. You're my daughter only if you come home.'

" 'But I'm worth more to Holland this way,' Ruth said, and she straightened up and made an end of it by turning and walking away. The rest of us just went home. It was getting late, and in spite of the sadness about Grandmother and Ruth, I felt the fear of night coming on as usual. Rachel took my hand, but she wasn't too scared to ask some difficult questions.

" 'What does "cremate" mean?' she asked me, and I told her, 'Well, it sort of means, when monkeys get married.' After a while she wanted to know what "liquidated" was, and I explained it was a fancy word for going to the bathroom. That seemed to make sense to her, and she said it was so cold and wet she wished we'd all hurry up and get home so she could do some liquidating.

"Well, that was our day, and now it's after curfew and I'm listening to sounds in the street. I don't think things can go on as usual much longer, but the more afraid you get, the more tired you become, and you want to hang on to what you know. Except that we can't much longer. Which is about all I have to say, and as far as I'm concerned this journal is finished. I'm not going to write in it any more."

FOUR
LATE OCTOBER, 1942

Abraham Ullman, competent physician and surgeon, contented in his work and in his family circle, endured a mental struggle such as he had never before experienced in a life of success and recognition. Recent events had etched lines of bewilderment on his otherwise smooth face and he had taken to swallowing valerian pills every day against depression. Though his patients needed him more and more, there was less and less he could do for them. If one called him up during curfew and said he had pneumonia, about all Abraham could say was "Stick out your tongue and cough." Then he'd observe, "Well, it doesn't sound that serious," and he'd write out a prescription which the chemist wouldn't be apt to fill. Was God really so embittered against the Jews? Had they indeed sinned more than other people? He knew better, yet there was the look now in his eyes of a man who had been locked in a closet by God without any explanation.

Rebecca, who had always taken the lead around home, lost her habit of command. Apart from scrubbing and dusting what was already dusted and scrubbed, she seemed to watch the others with a luckless gambler's air of desperate calculation. Saul constantly surrounded himself with books as though the sober and sane words he studied could serve as bricks to wall him off from the mad, threatening world outside.

Only Moses among the Ullmans remained sure of himself, moving about the house in his tattered bathrobe and slippers like an old stork, walking carefully so as not to betray his weakness.

"Abraham," he said without hesitation, "you must hide—all of you."

"Hide? Well, yes, I have thought of it." Abraham pulled at his lower lip, but only qualifications, not words of decision, were forthcoming.

"If I had my old strength," Moses said, thinking of his youth when he'd had the strength of seven, "I'd drag you out of here." But only the power of his brain remained. That gave him no joy; it was as hurtful as a box of razor blades. "I may not be a qualified judge, Abraham, but it seems to me a Jew in Amsterdam has four choices: commit suicide, surrender to the Germans, hide, or depend on the council. You're too young for the first, and I hope not fool enough for the second. I'm afraid you're taken in by the council. We Jews have always relied on the law, but the law here is gone. The Jewish Council's only a shadow, handing out worthless stamps that we trample each other to have. It's a clever Nazi device to break down our resistance and fill us with false hopes until it's too late."

"The council does what it can. We play for time. The war will end some day."

"Yes, but not soon enough. There'll be no Jews left in Amsterdam when the war ends." Moses lit his pipe, his eyes staring sadly through the first cloud of smoke. "It's an awful thought, but true."

As far as his own intentions were concerned, Moses was equally adamant. He was old and obsolete. He'd lived a good, full life. "The Nazis can't harm me. I'm too old. I can stay here with nothing to fear, but not the rest of you, Abraham."

And Abraham lowered his head into his arms. David could see his father was really in trouble, and it frightened him. "I don't know what to do," Abraham admitted softly. "With the best will in the world, we may both be wrong. Let me think it out, Father. I need to think some more."

So the days of autumn passed, with inaction the only response to the opposing tensions. Somehow, the longer they lived under this anxiety, the more it seemed to sap their courage to act. It would almost have been easiest to go down to the Gestapo headquarters and say, here we are. David felt this, knew that his parents did, and still he sensed they were wrong. If they would only listen to Ruth and Grandfather. They must not sit mute and helpless with fear, like rabbits caught in an auto's onrushing headlights.

Then, without warning, everything changed on an early evening at the end of October. It would be remembered briefly as the Halloween Raid, a minor affair in the history of the elimination of Dutch Jewry. Saul and David were hurrying home from their machinists' class. David frowned slightly to explain his haste, but it was fear of the lengthening shadows that drove them up the big Jodenbreestraat in the old quarter where Rembrandt's house still stood. Few people were abroad in the Jewish Quarter, with the dangerous hour of curfew only fifty minutes away. They hastened past the big Portuguese synagogue, a brooding mountain in the gloom but glorious inside, and it was there that David first noticed the car parked at right angles to the street ahead. He glanced quickly to right and left, felt the rootlet of every hair on his head rise. The narrow street and the canal bridge were blocked. Green Police! It was a trap. Those with stars or lacking Aryan identification were being seized. Saul urged him toward the synagogue with the hope of losing themselves in its intricacies, but the doors were bolted. They were like fish caught in a net as the street became a floundering confusion of wide-eyed terror. A truck arrived. You could climb aboard with help from the Green Police or be roughly hurled aboard if you resisted. Saul and David entered together. The interior smelled of stale sweat and fresh fear. A young woman shook papers at one of the guards. "My baby! He's up there!" she cried, pointing at a tenement. When she would not climb up voluntarily, the police knocked her down and then yanked her like a sack into the truck, where she lay sobbing.

This was a one-truck raid. The barriers were down in minutes and the prisoners were driven directly to the Dutch Theater. People were calling it the Jewish Theater now, but there was no entertainment except for the guards, who presided over as many as fourteen hundred captives at a time. Corridors, foyers, balconies, and stairways were packed. Some had been living here for over a week.

The newcomers were lined up for presentation to the Nazi interrogator. A Jew with the right papers or an irresistible bribe might be waved left, back into the relative freedom of the street. Ahead of Saul and David was an old man, his hands full of testimonials.

"You see, I manage a home for the aged . . ." he was explaining.

"For how long?" the interrogator shot back.

The old man, shuffling his papers, produced a date.

"Do you call that an established home?"

The old man produced more documents.

"All right, to the left. Next!"

Next was the old man's wife. She only helped out at the home. "To the right."

"But she's very old," her husband pleaded.

"If she can work for you, she can work for us. To the right!"

The old man hesitated for a moment, could not bear to be left alone. He took his wife's hand and they entered the theater together. David and Saul soon followed. During the day, chairs were set up theater-style. Now, with night coming on, straw mattresses were brought out from behind the scenery and fitted into a kind of jigsaw arrangement. The prisoners were settling down among their meager possessions. Some, like David and Saul, had only the clothing on their backs.

Before the lights were extinguished, a couple were married while the crowd watched dully. Lemonade and little cakes were produced for the wedding party and some of the prisoners joined in song. The new couple were allowed to occupy a small room behind the stage under the threat that, if they used the window to escape, their entire families would be sent straight to Mauthausen. They were present the next morning when breakfast, a thin gruel of cold potato soup, was passed out.

"I can't eat this," Saul said. "It's gone bad."

David forced it down stoically. When afternoon came, with nothing better to eat, Saul also choked his portion down.

"Poor Mother," he said. "She'll be frantic."

"They all will be," David replied. He was thinking about Rachel. He'd promised to do some drawing with her. "I suppose they must know what happened by now."

"Do you think Father can do something through the council?"

"I wouldn't count on it. I wouldn't count on a damned thing." David didn't want to raise false hopes.

That night, after the lights were put out, came a distraction. An SS officer with a flashlight appeared. There was to be a foot inspection. The officer was pale and his lips were slightly pouted as though he'd been raised on fish food, but his pale-blue eyes, staring blankly right and left, had the look of a killer. Those who slept were prodded awake. Convulsed with mirthless laughter, the officer shone his beam on one set of bare feet after another. "Disgusting! You animals!" To Saul and David he said, "Your feet are filthy. We can't let you go home to Mother like that." The inspection went on for hours, and in the end a handful of "clean" Jews were released as an example to the thousand others that they should make better use of the choked and soapless plumbing.

"We've got to escape," David said. The only escapes they had heard of so far had been by way of suicide. A man hung by his belt from the balcony. Saul, who usually had good ideas, was now despairing. His imagination was too vivid. He could see beyond the escape to the painful moment of capture.

"David, I've lost my spunk," he admitted.

"You can't lose it now. Help me think of something," David urged. "They say we're all to be shipped tomorrow."

"I'm tired. I can't think," Saul replied, and that night might have been the end of it had they not later been shaken awake. David stared into the beam of a strong flashlight. "My feet are clean," he said automatically.

"Ullman?" a voice said from behind the light. "Both of you, come with me."

The light was part of a rather stout SS uniform, black, with the usual tinfoil decor. The voice belonged to a round, pudding-faced German who looked as if he indulged too liberally in fresh eggs, cream, and country butter. "I have orders. Come, and do not smile." He spoke in the harsh unfriendly tone of a man who does not much like his task.

They were led behind the stage and there were told in whispers, "The others are to be taken tonight. You will hide—there." He unlocked a small trap door that led under the stage, then shoved them inside. "Not a cough; not a hiccup."

"But why us?" David managed as the small door swung into place.

"You have friends," came the whisper, so faint they could not even be sure there had been a reply at all.

Time passed. No light could penetrate to where the twins lay in hiding, and it was only by the sudden tumult above that they knew the time had arrived for the prisoners to move on. Cries, blows, the insistent rhythms of anguish, beat above them, and David felt more than ever the deathward flow of Amsterdam. Finally absolute silence returned. Fear and hunger were a blend in the stomach that kept sleep away, though David fell prey to continuous trembling yawns that seemed about to dislocate his jaw. He was half drowsing when a hail of footsteps rang out above. As his blood seemed to distill itself into separate icy drops, the key turned and they were ordered out.

"Hurry! *Schnell! Schnell!*"

The theater was once again dark. Stumbling, barely able to straighten up after a night and a day in such cramped quarters, they were pushed to a stage exit and outside. There stood Ruth, her teeth gleaming at them.

"Surprised?" she said, and, turning to the German, "Once again, thanks." She gave him a kiss on his soft, cowlike cheek.

"Yes, thank you," David added, taking the German's hand. For one of the few times in his life, he too felt like kissing a man.

"Go with God," said the German, already dipping back inside.

Ruth led her brothers down the long, dark alley.

"Who is he?" they demanded.

"He's something very rare: a Nazi with a conscience. They say he's helped dozens of children escape from that place in crates and potato sacks. His name is Zundler, and in the end he will be caught and killed."

"Does he know that?"

"I think so," she answered, "but he will die with a clear conscience. Now brighten up. Don't look so funereal, you two. You don't want to be caught again, and believe me, gloom is a Jewish identity card. So are those stars. Get them out of sight. Coats inside out." David did as he was told and felt for a second strangely criminal, for the star had come to signify his compliance with the law. Only now did he fully realize that to Jews the law gave, not protection, but a sentence of death. "Hurry. Down this way. Give me your hands so I don't lose you. Nice hands, hard. I used to try to hold Mother's hands, but she was always pulling them away." Her own grasp was dry and firm as she drew them under an archway where they waited for booted feet to pass, then on faster and faster so that she seemed to grow, the twins to diminish. They crossed a well-lit square. "Look businesslike. Eyes straight ahead. The Germans call it *'dienstlich.'* They don't expect it from us."

The time was past midnight when a tramcar slammed through the soundlessness, threw up sizzling sparks as it cannonaded around a corner. It was packed with Jews, like a runaway aquarium full of fish.

"A living hearse," Ruth called it, and David felt the gooseflesh rise on his arms. But for a conscience-stricken Nazi and his sister's love, he and Saul would be there.

They had passed now into a street from which all the residents had been removed. Doors were padlocked. It was absolutely silent except for a distant carillon that played "Pure in body, pure in soul."

Home. They stood outside the familiar stout door with its brass lion's-head knocker.

"If we knock, we'll scare them all to death," said Saul.

"If we don't, we'll freeze," Ruth replied, and let the knocker fall. Minutes passed before the door opened a crack. There was Rachel looking out.

"David? Saul?" she exclaimed. "Is it really you?"

"Look hard," said David. "Touch us. We're not ghosts."

Suddenly she was through the door and his face was buried in her hair, and she was kissing him, then Saul, then Ruth.

Rebecca appeared next. "Thank God," she said.

"You can thank Ruth, too," David said, and Rebecca did. Through her tears she kept saying, "You were right. You were right all along." Now Abraham was there with his hands held out. He gave an inarticulate growl of delight as he enveloped them, all his children. Finally Moses came down the stairs to lead them inside and to say, "Now, my family, it is time to talk of escape."

Many had already gotten away. Some had hiked, depending on luck, all the way to Spain. Others had relied on money, giving gigantic bribes. Holland had no mountains, few forests. It was not a hider's land, and still many were in hiding there.

"How much time have we to get ready?" Abraham asked Ruth.

"Now! Only now!"

She spoke crisply, crossing every *t*, dotting every *i*, for she had won. Ruth and Abraham talked for a time in private and then, while it was still dark, she slipped out as though she was well rehearsed in passing rapidly through doors.

"I think she'd like to be reincarnated," Saul said. "Then she'd have the chance of being a general."

Dawn was in the sky when Abraham reassembled his family. He looked assured, with the air of one who has successfully overcome a long illness. "I want to give you your instructions and answer any questions about the course I've adopted. We must pack immediately. Dress heavily, for we dare not take big suitcases. We must be ready to depart at a moment's notice." His face as he talked was fixed, his speech remained measured and cool despite the turmoil of thoughts behind it, for at last he felt sure of himself. The decision might, for all that, prove fatal. Who could say? But it was made without regrets. For good or bad, the Ullmans were going into hiding.

FIVE

HIDING

Abraham had not yet totally divulged his plan, but David was packed and ready. "Ready" really meant only that the yellow stars had come off with his father's razor, leaving him with an odd sensation of naked vulnerability. "Packed" meant he had pulled on all the layers of clothing he could stand: three pairs of pants, four shirts, two sweaters, socks until his ankles bulged as if with elephantiasis. They all looked like deep-sea divers. Was that where the expression for hiders, "divers," came from, he wondered.

Rebecca had prepared one final family meal, a makeshift rice table. Thanks to the Japanese victories in Malaya, it was based on potatoes rather than rice, and therefore scarcely an infringement on what had been Vera's province. All insisted it was as good as past rice tables. None praised it more than Moses, but, even with food short, none had a good appetite and all attention focused upon Moses, the only one who radiated calm. He relished the food.

"Grandfather, you have to come—we need you," Rachel pleaded, which opened the gate to other voices. Rebecca's: "Moses, I beg you to come. Do. It is the last time I shall ask you for anything. Try it with us. You can always change your mind." Only Abraham refrained. He knew the old man. They were talking to a rock. A glance of silent significance passed between the two men, and Abraham remarked, "I want to leave a note indicating we've gone to Spain." Thereupon he departed, leaving Moses to finish the discussion. "I'm old enough to make my own decisions. You must remember the nest egg," he said, nodding toward the fireplace tile, "if I'm not here when you return."

"But, Grandfather, what will you do here all alone?" Rachel persisted.

"I'm an old sailor and a doctor to boot," he said. "I can look after myself." He put his hand over hers, covering it completely. "When you grow up, Rachel, you'll look exactly like your grandmother when she was young. Beautiful. So watch out for sailor men with roving eyes."

"But, Grandfather . . ."

Rebecca pulled her away, saying, "We must make arrangements for the cat and the bird."

"Won't Grandfather look after them?"

"That wouldn't be fair, leaving Grandfather with all our jobs. And, besides, they have the right to look after themselves just like us."

The canary was first. Startled out of its sleep, it sat long on the window ledge and finally flew to the bare branches of a tree beside the canal. Fortunately, for late autumn it was a warm night.

"Tomorrow I'm sure he'll fly to the Canary Islands where he belongs. Isn't that nice?" Rebecca's voice had raised an octave. "And now the kitty. He likes to go out hunting at night. Oh, how fat he will be." And the cat passed from the house like a shadow, into streets where stray cats were being sold as rabbit meat in the shops.

Everything was said, everything done. The Ullmans waited; waited until the old clock proclaimed 1 a.m. Soon after that came the sound of a car, the screech of brakes outside. David peeked through a crack in the shutters, saw an official-looking car, black as a hearse, with the Nazi pennant standing stiff above the hood. An SS officer moved from behind the wheel.

He ran to warn the others, but Abraham laughed at his panic and threw open the door. A figure in a dark uniform stood in the frame, performed the rectangular salute beloved by the Nazis, and smashed booted heels together. It was Uncle Daniel.

Moses saw them off. Rachel presented him with flowers. Where she had found them, nobody knew. He put his hand briefly on David's shoulder. "I must admit to you that I've saved your journal. It shouldn't go out with the trash, and I will make sure it doesn't fall into the wrong hands." He smiled as though he knew something about his grandson that David didn't know himself. "Look after yourself. I have a feeling you're the one who will remember and tell of these days." David said nothing. The old man looked suddenly so sad and proud both at the same time that David felt foolish, but, as he entered the car, he was glad of that last moment. He would not forget his grandfather.

The car backed, turned, screeched over the bridge. Moses stood watching until it had gone, then he went up the stairs carrying the bouquet of flowers. He closed and bolted the door, an old man in an empty place. "I must put these into water," he said, speaking aloud to himself, a habit he had learned at sea. With the flowers in a vase, he went to his study, where he saw himself in the silvery glass of the old mirror. "I'm a ghost already," he observed. The place smelled of morocco leather bindings, fine books he had collected over the years, books marred with use, the pages marked with observations.

From the enormous desk he took a bottle of hoarded port wine. Liquor by now scarcely existed in the Netherlands. What an odd sensation to uncork a bottle for the last time. Methodically he set the bottle and a fine crystal goblet on the desk, adding to these a faded portrait of Vera on their wedding day that until now had hung like an ectoplasm over his desk. It left a light patch on the brain-gray wall. "This place ought to be painted. It's a disgrace," he told himself, and took a long sip of port. That was good. To the portrait he added a photograph of an old-fashioned ship with masts and furled sails. Behind it was a beach and palm trees, and he yearned to feel the tropic sun on his back once more. Such heat spoke of life stirring everywhere. He put on a sweater, the elbows of which were gone. Then he sat down, wanting no outside ripple to disturb the sea of his sentiment.

"Now," he said, producing from an upper drawer the diary that David had abandoned. He thumbed the pages as though they were familiar, and at the end he took out a fountain pen and began to write. Finally he closed the book and rose. How had his legs become so like brittle ivory sticks? Stiffly now he bore the notebook to the fireplace, removed the tile with a knife edge, and placed the book inside. "There." Now everything was done. He returned to the study and poured another goblet of wine. Before drinking, he extracted a pillbox from the desk's top drawer. It contained eight translucent brown capsules. He would need but one. Since the capsule was rather large, he placed it deep in his throat, then washed it down with wine. Through some optical trick, he seemed to see the square-rigged ship rocking there in the amber fluid in the glass. It sang to him of long and salty voyages, of scudding south with the forceful trade winds driving them night and day, the Southern Cross a jeweled sword at night, and the sails painted ghostly white by the moon. Deep in the heart of the glass he saw dolphins dancing round a phosphorescent bow. "Clue the skysails up!" he said aloud. "Clue up the royals!" The crash of canvas on the wind was like the beating of a great bird's wings as the ship buried her bow in the foam, laughing through the drenching southern seas. "Oh, God," he said, murmuring like an old shell cast up on the beach. "Oh, God." He would do it all again, but the robots had the future. All he wanted were the oceans, horizons not seen before, and someone to enter in the log "Half past one. Ship's doctor gone overboard. Moderate sea, steady winds from the west." He seemed to swim now in that tinctured ocean toward a tiny harbor lit up like a Japanese fairy tale. The sun was setting. He could feel the sea pulling him, an irresistible current, and then a far-off cry of hurt made him sit up straight. He felt his heart beating like the clock, striking the hour, and like the good doctor he was, he tried to go to the side of his patient, to respond to the cry of the injured. It was beyond his strength. Besides, the patient had come to him. "Vera," he whispered, "it doesn't hurt any more." The golden ship dipped once in the amber sea. The glass dropped from his hand.

Meanwhile, the black car with its official pennant sped through Amsterdam, heading west, with Daniel at the wheel. His passengers felt safe with him, for he was no hero expecting victory but a vicious fighter who could not comprehend defeat. They were heading toward the coast. It was a night for hard thought. Stars sparked above, sharp individual pricks of light. The moon was full, cold, and supreme. The car, despite its hooded blackout lights, leapt forward, presumptuous as a blind man on a tightrope, threading the narrow dike-top roads. It was Daniel's habit to do dangerous things calmly, and it did not seem fitting or even likely that their odyssey would end in an auto accident.

Rachel was the first to break the hypnotic silence of that black and rocketing ride. "What will my friends think when they call and Grandpa says I've gone to Spain?" She pondered this a moment, then came back to the cat. "What will he do if Grandpa doesn't feed him?" The old canary, she seemed to feel sure, would have no trouble making his way to the Canary Islands.

Apart from their imaginings—pursuit by massed motorcycles, a grenade ironically thrown from hiding by partisans—there was a road block and a check point as they neared the coast. Sudden zebra-striped gates barred the way and a soldier with a Mauser rifle shouted, "Out! Check point!" That was enough. David nearly leaped into the canal, though Daniel had prepared them for this. Actually, he alone left the car for the small wooden guard shack, and he returned in a moment. The zebra gate rose, and with an exchange of "Heil Hitler's" they were off. "One of these nights," he informed his passengers cheerfully, "that post will make a rapid ascent. It will rise almost all the way to heaven and then it will come crashing down."

At a spot that seemed uncomfortably close to the guard post, they came to a stop. "You'll have to walk from here," Daniel apologized. "You know where you are." David had no idea. "With luck, I'll see you tomorrow night." Then he said to Abraham, resuming a conversation previously audible only in the car's front seat, "Think about splitting up. It will be much easier to place you." Then Daniel drove away.

They were in the seaside zone long forbidden to Jews, very near their summer cottage, to which Abraham silently led them in single file. This was a prime Nazi defense area. Hitler's "Atlantic Wall" spread out from The Hague. Scheveningen had long since been demolished as a summer holiday community; pillboxes and bunkers had replaced homes and cafés. Such fortifications were continually being enlarged, but here, evidently because the area was difficult for vehicles, there were only the usual beach defenses: barbed wire, tank traps, and the posting of sentries. That was enough to make the Ullmans walk softly, to blanch at the snapping of a twig or the dry rustle of beach grass.

Had the summer cottage been haunted, they would not have approached it with more apprehension. The windows listened; the key turning in the door was like a gunshot. Abraham pushed the door gently open and still it screamed a warning. Moonlight winked from an oilcloth-covered table; a chair seemed to leap at them. "Not a sound, now," Abraham warned in a whisper that seemed to invite danger in with them. "And no light." Something scurried under the house. Field mice? "Take off your shoes, everyone. And walk close to the walls so the floors don't squeak." All this in murmurs, followed by a harsh whisper from Saul: "What's that noise?"

"The wind under the door."

"And that?"

"Only the wind." The autumn's last crickets were cheer-cheering outside in the moonlight while the Ullmans settled down. The house slumbered through the night, still as the halls of death.

Not until morning did they dare talk at all, and then still in whispers, although the upper windows gave a good view of all approaches. The subject of course was, what next? All of them, even Abraham, opposed, if possible, the idea of breaking up the family unit, though it would make their placement with sympathetic Christian families easier. Another thought, which had evidently smoldered long in Abraham's mind, brought David to attention: escape to England in the boat. So that was the reason for all the sailing excursions on the Amstel. Abraham admitted as much, but now he quickly dashed any such hope. In midsummer it might have been worth trying, but this was the season of sudden storms when the big ocean swells rolled fifty feet up the beach. They would be lucky to launch the boat, even if there were not barbed wire and a sentinel who paced the beach so methodically that he repeatedly stepped into his own footprints. Besides these barriers, there was another. Rats and mice had been at the boat's sails. They were in tatters. "But I think it's important," Abraham said, reviving hope, "that we mend them against some future contingency."

All this solved nothing, so they waited with diminished food supplies for Daniel's return that night. But the uncle whom they had all begun to regard as an infallible guardian angel failed to appear. If he sent a message in the flight of sea gulls, it was beyond their powers of augury to interpret. Only one thing was clear by the following morning, and Abraham summed it up: "We can't stay here." It was evident that the house had been entered more than once. Its location suggested periodic checking by Nazi or local officials as well as by vandals.

"We can't all hide under the boat like elves," said Rachel.

"But there is a mill," Saul said hesitantly. "Remember, David?"

"Of course!" David agreed, wondering why he had not thought of the secret room before. By evening, when Daniel had still not appeared, they began their trek cautiously, in stocking feet. In the stillness, David's heart was a drum in his ears. Then the rain began just as they were passing the bone-white slabs of Father Lebbink's cemetery, and it hushed the rustling of brown leaves underfoot.

The mill loomed as a refuge. They were cold and damp.

Rebecca, who suffered most from winter, was shivering uncontrollably as they pressed inside the millhouse. A twitter and a shudder in the darkness told them bats were in residence. They fumbled for the millstone, rolled it heavily aside, and by the light of one sputtering match after another the Ullmans crawled down the brick tunnel to the secret room.

Somehow, with all of them pressed inside, the room beneath the dike looked smaller and dirtier than David had remembered.

"I don't like this place," Rachel murmured, rolling her eyes up to where a last bat detached itself and vanished into the shadows. "It's not nice."

"Now it's coming," David thought, "it's coming, and there's nothing I can do about it."

"I don't like it here. It smells bad. I want to go home to Grandpa," Rachel said, her voice beginning to crack.

Rebecca held her close. "If we were only bats, there'd be no problem, sweetheart," she said, trying to joke.

"We're lucky to have it," Abraham added.

"We're always lucky," David agreed, but he didn't, with all that wood around, knock on any. He was relieved that the only hiding place he knew of had been so easily accepted.

"Now, as soon as it's light, we must begin by tidying up. At least it's dry, I'll say that." Rebecca was taking charge. "Only I don't quite know how we'll eat. Though mushrooms might do quite well here."

"Don't worry," Abraham replied, "Daniel was in touch with Father Lebbink. We may not eat well every night, but we'll eat. He promised. It's just a question of letting him know we're here and not at the house."

So the new life began. They kept quiet during the day, sleeping much of the time, for their living space was beneath a canal road much frequented by military traffic. At night, still quietly, they worked on improving their new home. First they divided the territory, like Gaul, into three parts: the parents' section, the twins', Rachel's corner. A pipe was found leading to the canal that at low water could be used to discharge waste. At other times it had to be plugged. Rebecca cleaned every inch thoroughly. After a week it did not shine, but it no longer smelled of bats. Abraham had met with Father Lebbink and they were receiving enough food to keep them going. They had prayer candles in little glass jars for light, and four buckets that they could fill with fairly fresh water from the canal. When Rebecca finally stood back and surveyed their achievement, she looked tired. All she said was "Is this all we've been able to do in a week? God built the world in that time, with a day to rest at the end."

In fact, the days dragged when sleep did not oblige, but David found excitement in the nights. Then he could sneak out to see the glow of a distant town and count the uncountable stars. How could the Wise Men ever have sorted out just one to follow? And of course there were the occasional air battles, more often heard than viewed.

On the ninth of November came splendid news. The Americans had landed troops in North Africa. This information was received via the steadfast Lebbink, who had, however, no word of Daniel. Still, it was news to celebrate, and the Ullmans decided to do so boldly with a raid on the summer cottage. It was important, on this as on all occasions, to stick carefully to the stone path that led to the road, for they could not afford to leave footprints and give the mill a used look. The summer house was still well equipped with wicker chairs and a variety of old tables, beds, and dressers, most of it too bulky to move down the brick corridor to the secret room. They were obliged to limit themselves to bedding, which created a vaguely Bedouin tent effect. A few cans of jellied fuel turned up, which made smokeless cooking possible for special occasions. There were also books, some with uncut pages, enough to keep Abraham busy for hours. The wall of the hideout became a library from floor to ceiling, and, after several such nocturnal raids, Abraham could say to his children, "If you read one of those every other day, by the time you finish the war will be over." So they read with avidity, as though they might push the Allied tanks faster through African sands by skimming the lines of print.

The books were mostly too old for Rachel, and she spent much time wondering whether her cat was well fed and whether the canary had yet reached his island home. She talked, too, of Moses. What must he be doing alone? Wouldn't he be happier here even if it was crowded? David had long ago guessed the truth about his grandfather. So, he knew, had Saul, though they had never spoken of it. In fact, Rachel's dark, searching, always honest eyes, by begging David for the truth, drove him to lies. He pictured for her, Grandfather scrubbing the hearth, feeding the cat, even tending the canary, who had undoubtedly found his way back home. It was a torment that Abraham, in his unbending honesty, had to end.

"Your grandfather's with your grandmother now. He was a great man, the last of his kind." And when he had put across the idea of suicide to his daughter, he had to answer her question, "But why did he kill himself, Father?"

"Because it seemed the right thing to do. Rachel, he'd had a fine life, and he just wanted to be with Grandmother. You can understand that."

"Do many people kill themselves?" she wanted to know in a tiny voice, no more than a spun thread of sound.

"Not often, dear, but sometimes people see it as a remedy."

She began to cry, and he put his arm around her so that some of the sorrow might be absorbed by his nearness. Finally he said, "He wouldn't want us to mourn for him. We make it difficult for the dead if we cling to them. Just remember how he was. Remember all his grand stories."

But the shedding of tears must have been contagious, for Rebecca, too, was crying, not so much for the old man as for their slightly less than human condition.

"This can't last forever." Again Abraham was the comforter.

"But it can!" she insisted. "For all of us, it can!" And she began to cry really hard, not hiding her face. The family had never seen her cry before. David and Saul were struck dumb.

With a shuddery breath, Rachel began again to worry about her cat with no one there to feed him, and David, feeling suddenly vindictive and frustrated, had an impulse to blurt out, "He's in cat heaven by now. Some animal lover has made rabbit meat out of him and a little girl just like you is using his skin for a fur cap." That would have done it. What a howl then! But he managed to keep the words inside and retired to his portion of the room with a book as though there were a wall and not simply a sheet for privacy. From behind it, he could hear his father: "Now it's time for bed. I want you to think of the fairies, yawning under the autumn leaves. Now sleep."

Rebecca's complaining voice: "It's so damp and cold it's like living in a grave," and then Abraham's voice again, murmuring, "Now sleep. Sleep, both my pretty girls."

Life in hiding had begun.

SIX

1942-43
WINTER IN HIDING

David lay back on his cushions with his hands folded behind his head. He had been lying down for an hour, but sleep refused to come. It had been difficult for him in these early days to give up the habit of thinking as a free man, to realize that he was a kind of prisoner. He watched a tiny black varnished beetle scuttle up the wall on some errand vital to insects, and felt envious. He pondered the worms burrowing out there in the soil. If they were down below the frost level, they could go wherever they pleased.

Close quarters had necessitated the forming of certain routines. One could get lost in routine. At least fear had left him, but in its place had come the endless repetition of habits which seemed to imply that if each day was fulfilled as the day before had been, all would be well.

Abraham had pushed studies at them all. "No one can be overeducated," he said, "only wrongly educated. And when you have that feeling of being in prison here, remember no locks or walls can capture your mind. When we get out of here, think, with all these books, how far ahead you'll be in your education. The Germans want to turn us into animals, but books can help us stand erect." To David, looking at all the old heavy leather books with gothic titles, this sounded like a prepared speech, but in truth there was little else to pass the time. Saul could read all night and never tire of it.

He coached David in physics and biology, and David in turn taught Rachel, who found it hard to concentrate and often distracted the others from their lessons. She thought a great deal about her lost pets, insisting that animals were her best friends. Since the cat and the canary were gone, they had to be imaginary, so David would tell old stories while Rachel listened, her eyes wide open, showing the deepest concern. "Did you know that once upon a time in this very mill there was a miller who at midnight every night was frightened by three great black cats? They hissed at him from the shadows until he threw a pot of boiling broth at them. Then they vanished screeching into the night, and the next day, when the miller went to the village, he saw three old crones, one with a burned hand, another with burned legs, and a third with a blistered face."

"You're making that up," she said seriously. "Once-upon-a-time stories are always made up."

"It's true. Honestly."

"And did the cats come back?"

"Never," he said. "And the miller disappeared, too. Now sometimes at night you'll hear a dog howling high up in the mill, though some say it's only the wind stirring the old wooden gears."

They all had problems adjusting. Rebecca yearned for a window. "We're boxed in. Beams and bricks all around us." Of course, a window was impossible, but Rachel remembered the yard of pipe half submerged in the canal. With a stick she cleaned out the old spy hole, which had filled up with leaves, so that Rebecca had a glimpse of daylight and more particularly of an oddly leaning, tipsy angel in Father Lebbink's graveyard. Sometimes there were funerals, with country mourners in dark clothes and black armbands.

"Mother, do you really enjoy watching funerals?" David asked her once.

"What else is there to see?" she asked. Rebecca was not one for reading, either.

A principal distraction for all of them was Father Lebbink's regular visits to bring them food and candles. That was one thing about country hiding—food was always available. Hiders in the cities were said to be having a hungry time, but the priest never failed to come three nights a week, just after dusk, smelling of horses, cows, and fresh air. They were his captive, eager audience now, and Lebbink was a tongue-wagger, gratifying their urge for news with stories about his congregation and their problems, great and small. Obtaining food was everyone's principal occupation. Half a pound of tea now cost 350 florins. Everyone was dealing on the black market, and he apologized for the tedium of their diet, which went through phases of one thing or another: endive, then kohlrabi, seldom meat. "It could be worse," he told them, "though they say that in Amsterdam the raids against Jews have let up. Did I tell you that Princess Juliana is expecting a baby next month? That came over Radio Orange from London. Oh, and before I go, there's a new story going around. It seems an SS officer banged on someone's door and told the owner he must leave at once for a forced labor camp. The owner got down on his knees and pleaded to stay, so the SS man agreed to oblige if the home owner could guess which was his artificial eye. The home owner said, 'The left one,' and the SS fellow wanted to know how he could tell. 'Because it has the more sympathetic look,' came the answer."

Once, because it was her birthday, Father Lebbink

brought Rachel an illustrated copy of *The Little Flowers of St. Francis*. He said that he wasn't doing missionary work but that the pictures of animals might be fun to copy in a notebook, which he'd brought along as well. The priest had long ago abandoned discussing religion with the Ullmans, though he had once enjoyed debating theology with Moses. Now all he said was rather apologetic. It seemed to him very sad that St. Paul, himself a Jew but unable to convert his own people, had turned against them. In Lebbink's opinion, this was the initial reason for today's persecutions.

The priest's nocturnal visits really began the hiders' day, for then it was quiet and dark and they dared stir from their lair. It was a time for which all of them yearned. "Look at the moon, Abraham! Will you just look at it?" That was Rebecca, gazing from the mill windows at what had become their sun. Sometimes they saw shooting stars, said to be angels repelling evil spirits from heaven. A barge might chug by on the canal, bound with milk and eggs for Amsterdam. More often came the British Blenheim bombers, flying from the Channel in V formation. Sometimes they flew terrifyingly low in a long sweep to catch the German shipping at Rotterdam's harbor by surprise. Usually they were just passing over on clear nights under a bomber's moon. "Hear those motors," Abraham would say. "It's music to my ears." Then the searchlights would waver across the sky, intersecting, striking back and forth as though to entrap the planes in webs of light. The tracer bullets would go drifting upward, and they would see the flash of the anti-aircraft guns before they heard the sound. Some planes fell. One had burned near the mill on the edge of the canal, which it filled with oily flames, but the planes seemed always to reappear in greater numbers. Did it signify a turning of the tide? Father Lebbink said German armies were trapped in the Russian snows, and it was rumored that the English and the Americans were steadily moving ahead now in North Africa.

The end was not yet near, but it was moving closer, if they could only hold out. "We have to hold out," Rebecca said, "and once this war is over, surely people will give up hope of success by means of war. I feel sure there will be some sort of rebirth, a renaissance of the spirit. This terrible lesson will change the world. It must!"

Old ideas, and noble ones, but Abraham, standing beside his wife in the abandoned mill, could only wonder if the circumstances fit them any more. She had such trust in her eyes. He longed for faith himself, for behind his skepticism lurked a darker speculation, one with which he dared not contend. What if man was neither good by nature, as the Jews said, nor bad, as the Christians believed? What if the universe was ignorant of man's presence? What if there was no God?

"Do you think Hitler will be happy when he sees himself with God's eyes?" Rebecca was saying. "I wouldn't be that man on the last day for all the gold and all the laughter in this world."

"No, I suppose not," Abraham acknowledged. Would that day ever come?

These vast speculations were suitable for a starry night, but everyday problems took up more time. A yellow paper star had appeared, tacked to the door of the summer cottage. Had someone guessed? In any event, the Ullmans did not return there, even on foggy nights. The first December snow came, and the thought of tracks made all excursions impossible. Their confinement intensified. Little irritations were magnified, such as Abraham's snoring. Sometimes the whole room reverberated. If someone strolled overhead, what would he think? Trolls? Hardly. So Abraham was forced to sleep with a hard ball of paper tied between his shoulder blades to keep him from lying on his back.

For David, Saul, and Rachel, who were growing fast as toadstools, there was the problem of clothing and moving buttons, cuffs, and hems until they could be moved no farther. The boys took turns with Abraham's razor, tearing their chins because the blade was dull. The only shoes available through Father Lebbink's intercession were the all-wooden *klempen*, which galled the feet of the uninitiated. "That's one good reason for not walking very far," David observed. The real problems were the lack of privacy and boredom. David sat in the "music room," that section of the passageway large enough to accommodate a makeshift toilet, and applied himself to an old crossword puzzle, the answers rather inadequately erased by Rachel. "A kind of hernia, 7 letters." On returning, he found a notice pinned to the curtain marking off the area he shared with Saul: "Preoccupied." David entered. Saul was behind a dog-eared volume that had split down the back, and his posture implied: "I do not wish to be spoken to. I am reading. You bore me." As David well knew, Saul could go on in this way for days, absorbing everything from Plato to Hemingway, while a stray finger explored independently to see if a pimple had raised itself in the night upon his forehead. To see him so content infuriated David. He too picked up a book and pecked at the pages in hopes of finding something new, but the words came at him like a swarm of gnats. His eyes ached in anticipation. He grabbed a magazine, kissed the picture of a pretty girl advertising soap: the faint taste of ink. Saul did not stir or look at him, so David flung the magazine with rumpled creases beside his brother.

Saul gave him a dull introspective stare. "Shush," he said. "No one's deaf, not even the Nazis."

"But I'm dying of boredom!" David protested.

"Fine. Die a little."

David hated his self-satisfied twin just then. How could anyone lie here, reading, forever? But they would have to stay in this hole for as long as the war lasted, and he grimly remembered learning in history class of wars that went on for a lifetime. He yearned to be outside, to be in the sun. The slur of rubber tires on the icy dike road above set his imagination behind the wheel. The gas pedal pressed to the floor, the clang of milk cans, the cackle of chickens, the hooting of a canal boat, all called to him. Even in sleep, he could no longer escape a sense of boredom. It was as if his sixteenth and seventeenth years were still waiting inside him, howling to be born. Soon I'll be eighteen, and still down here. Through the spy tube, he viewed a dry autumn leaf bejeweled with melted snow. How bracing it must be out there; how good to trot beside the canal, to slide down the dunes to the sea. If Saul was content to exercise his mind, David's body yearned for expression. Running, skipping stones into the waves, even to hit the walls with closed fists; anything to break the awful quiet. "I wish I were a circus performer," he said aloud. "The one who gets shot out of a cannon."

"If the Germans find us," Saul replied above the edge of his book, "who knows, you may get your wish."

"Saul, what would you do if you suddenly had a million guilders?"

"Go on reading."

"I'd buy a fast car, maybe an Auto Union, maybe a Mercedes. I'd drive a hundred and fifty kilometers an hour on the dike road."

"Why not buy yourself a harem and keep them all in the mill?"

"And I'd get some food that tastes good, some red meat and some chicken."

At this point, Rebecca brought them a fifty-pound bag of parsnips to clean and go over for rot. They would be scrubbing and scraping all week, and, because of the snow, there'd be nothing much else to eat. At least the cold kept food from spoiling quickly. There was some bread left over, too. The week before they'd been lucky. Two Germans had been fishing in the canal with grenades, and some of the fish had drifted up next day.

"Maybe one night when the snow melts we could forage," David suggested. "We've had so many vegetables I'm turning green."

"You mean steal?"

"Not so it would be missed," David replied. "Just an egg here or there, maybe a cheese."

"I don't know," Saul said; but the idea was planted, and faintly on the air came the luring sound of life outside: a farm boy whistling for his dog, calling his cows to return to the barn; cows full of milk.

Though it lay now only in deep and shady places, the snow hung on for a week—a week of living on parsnips, which had taxed even Rebecca's powers of invention. The priest had finally brought more food; apologetically, only beans. By this time Saul was won over. They sneaked out at first dark without telling anyone. The night was pure and icy, full of stars. The village was dark and shuttered, the farmers asleep. Down the path, then up the road, their feet wrapped in rags to leave no sound or human print. Frozen grass stroked their ankles like thin rapier blades, and it was exciting in the same way that it was exciting to run and jump. Along a sea mole slippery with spray, all was stillness. No owl hooted, no dog noted their prowling. Soon they were near those polder farmhouses which clustered around the older town on its high ground. Clouds were piling up, and David was reminded of El Greco's nightscape of Toledo. Too bad Rachel wasn't along. She'd like this, he thought, and she had a sort of primitive talent for finding things, the way a bee knows how to fly to the sweetest flower. She'd sense where the hens were laying. They waited for a growing cloud to catch up with the moon before crossing the road into its shadow. A sea breeze had sprung up and they approached an isolated barn from the leeward side so as not to alert the dog, if there was a dog. Somewhere a cow coughed gently, but neither of them knew how to milk even the most willing of cows.

"We'd better hurry," Saul hissed. "I think it's going to snow again." The sea air was cold enough to cut to the lungs, and, as if in confirmation, the first snowflakes began driving in. They had no choice but to raid this one barn and then return. No padlock on the door. A cow, round-eyed and curious, stared at them from a dimly seen stall. Two more cows and a horse, but no chickens, no eggs, nothing tempting hanging from the rafters, only a bin full of old, dry corn, unhusked and ripe with the seminal smell of rats. So that their errand would not be wasted, they stuffed their jackets with corncobs, a change from beans, anyway, and then, forgetting to close the barn door behind them, they were off, loping through the hard-driving flakes, leaving marks in the snow that were erased almost as soon as they were printed.

They arrived back, winded and proud conquerors, expecting their stolen hoard to overcome any anxiety their absence might have caused. To a degree they were rewarded, for Rachel at least applauded the food. Rebecca was only glad of their safe return and Abraham admonished them with his eyes, saying, "I don't want you young idiots doing that sort of thing again. It isn't just your own lives you're risking." There was more he had wanted to say to them, but in the end he whispered it only to Rebecca after they had gone to bed. She was one who listened more to tones and intonations than to words, and, since he spoke so calmly, she must not have heard him at all. Indeed, he was not talking so much to her as to himself, to the effect that war was debasing. It corrupted, in the end, the conquered as surely as the conquerors. And now "our boys" . . . but Rebecca slept. He could feel her warmth leap up beside him and he envied her the sleep that came so easily, envied against his own will the adventure of plunging out into the night, of plundering the enemy. He had to catch himself and say, "But that isn't so." It might be that farm, that very farm, which was keeping them alive.

The snow, borne on a western wind from the sea, fell all that day, so that the problem of excursions was solved for a while. Traffic was muffled on the road and voices were lost in the white world above.

Then Saul came down with a sore throat and fever. For the first time Abraham was called on for doctoring. He had very little medication, but it proved no more than a cold, with a cough that had to be muffled in a pillow.

"You see what comes from running around at night," he said, but they lived on the corn the better part of the week until Abraham and the priest worked out a way of swinging food over from the road by means of a rope secured to the mill shaft.

Snow was not the only reason for added caution. The Germans were augmenting the coastal defenses, which had already caused the demolition of thousands of buildings along the coast from Scheveningen north. Where seaside resorts had once stood, now were miles of concrete and stone "dragons' teeth," tank barriers, some of them fashioned, it was rumored, from Jewish cemetery headstones. Barbed wire and guns lined the coast. Sandbagged trenches were said to be in progress on the high ground seaward of the summer cottage. The Ullmans could only hope that the house itself was far enough inland to escape destruction. It seemed a more likely spot to serve as a German outpost, which in the long run was just as final.

December 5 was St. Nicholas' Eve, and David wondered if the bearded old man in the red robe with the gold miter and crook would still parade in Amsterdam. Father Lebbink brought them ginger cookies and a small carafe of communal wine, knowing they would want to save it for Hanukkah. They had only a few candles to spare, but Abraham, standing before his family, began the rhythmic prayer, "Praised be Thou, O Lord our God, Ruler of the universe, Who has sanctified us with Thy commandments and bidden us kindle the Hanukkah lights." Then they drank the wine and whispered the song of jubilation, but all save Rebecca seemed to lack conviction. When no one else would carry the occasion, she said, "We are told to look for God's will in all things. I like to think that even behind this war, and what it has done to us, there is a benevolent purpose at work, that we are being shown by terrible example that the only hope for man is to live in peace. I think that time is coming soon, and I believe that when it does, it won't matter which color a man's skin is, or with what songs he worships God. When that time comes, I like to think, we'll stop using words like 'enemy' and 'stranger.' " She was hoping to live something that could only be sung, and though Abraham no longer believed in the song, he raised his glass to his wife's words, hoping somehow against his own pessimism that they bore more substance than a wisp of smoke on the wind.

"L'Chaim! To life!" said Rachel, and they all touched glasses. At least they were still together. They had hope. They were alive.

They did not toast again until New Year's Eve, 1942, the year 5703 in the Jewish calendar. This time Father Lebbink was with them, for they had solved the problem of footprints in the snow by putting out a white plank between two stones when they knew he was coming. The priest was cheerful as always, burying the bad news beneath the good. The bad was simply more of the same. His parish was now officially *"Judenrein,"* that is, free of the Jewish poison. Of course there were the hiders, and *Algemeen Politielblad,* the police gazette, was publishing lists of missing Jews and rewards for their apprehension. Even the Jewish insane were being shipped off from mental institutions, supposedly to labor for the Reich. Soon there would remain no acknowledged Jews in Holland, so the Ullmans must be doubly careful. Then the good news: victories for the Allies. A great German army was said to be trapped at Stalingrad. Britain and the United States would soon invade the Continent. With luck and God's will, 1943 would end the war.

So the cold new year began with continued hope, but it was not this that changed the nature of their hiding; it was another arrival. Day had come, and the Ullmans were sleeping, or trying to, when David became aware not so much of a footfall as of a vague sense of intrusion. "I think someone's in the mill," he whispered to Saul. "It sounds like . . ."

"Like what?"

"Nothing. Just my imagination."

But he had scarcely gotten the words out when a curse echoed down the brick passageway. Someone had stumbled or hit his head. Police? They were hopelessly trapped. But when the truth burst upon them, Uncle Daniel's flesh-and-blood reality after three months of silence was almost more startling. He wore a high-necked sweater, breeches, and tall-laced farmer's boots. He looked fitter than ever, a man to be held in awe by his friends and feared by his enemies.

"David, my boy," he said. "God, you've grown another ten inches." "And Saul!" He embraced them all, inspected the hiding place with the thoroughness of a dog exploring new quarters. David could almost hear him sniffing out loud. "I've seen worse," he said, adding, "Abraham, how would you care for some horsemeat?"

"Are you serious? I could devour an entire Percheron myself. How many have you?" Abraham replied.

Daniel produced a package tied in brown paper, large enough for a night's feasting. With saliva churning in his mouth, David checked the snow outside, erasing Daniel's tracks as best he could. It was odd how his uncle seemed to have no concern for the risks involved. He maneuvered the millstone back into place, then returned to listen with the others to the bloody and brave doings in the outside world. Daniel told of the Palestine Pioneers, a group of Zionists who led Jews and fallen Allied aircraft crews over the Belgian border. The Belgians had many Jews in their underground organization, the Dutch very few, but Daniel and his comrades had received an air drop of RAF plastic explosives. He cleared his throat and leaned forward, talking in a low voice, but with grand gestures, of the deeds they had done. David and Saul listened open-mouthed.

"Remember that guard post on the way here? We took care of that!" he said, simulating with his hands the roar of explosion and the shack rising in the air. "We finished off a train on Christmas Eve. The engine rolled over like a dead elephant."

"You enjoy all this, don't you?" Rebecca asked.

"I have no other pleasures left," Daniel admitted. "To get close to a German, to put my sights just beneath the button on his chest where his heart is beating and then feel the gun buck against my shoulder . . . yes, I must admit it's a passion with me. Yes, I enjoy it immensely."

"In the end you'll be killed," Abraham said.

"Of course. We'll most of us be killed, but not defeated, Abraham. As long as I can hate, I'll know I'm still alive."

"Then may God forgive you for your hatred," said Abraham.

"May He forgive you, brother, for not hating enough."

Rebecca held up her hand. They could not afford loud arguments, especially in daytime.

"Well, I have other news for you." Daniel accommodated them by lowering his voice to a whisper. "About Ruth." He was silent a moment, glaring about to freeze their questioning tongues, then plunged on. "She's well. She's still dancing at the Silberin Spiegel. Did you know they have seventeen Jews hiding there in the attic, right over the heads of the Gestapo customers?"

"Do you see Ruth often?" Rebecca asked.

"When I'm in Amsterdam. She's one of the best. She has absolutely no fear; never worries about the risk."

"What risks does she take?"

"After hours she . . . how shall I put it . . . she lures German officers. She lures, and our people dispose of them, for their uniforms and their papers and, of course, for their guns. You remember my beautiful SS uniform? Well, thank your daughter." As he talked, he joined his fingertips into an open tent. "Not long ago, a British plane crashed near here. The crew bailed out. I nearly took the liberty of hiding them here—oh, only briefly," he hastily added at the look of alarm on their faces. "Now I wonder how you would have reacted."

"I'd have been damned upset," Abraham admitted. "We've hardly room to breathe as it is," and then, forgetting that extra excuses only serve to weaken an argument, "Besides, we live in real hazard here. This is hardly a safe place for British airmen."

Seemingly undeterred by his brother's unreceptive manner, Daniel pressed on. "Sometimes one gets into more trouble by trying to avoid trouble. And think, brother, of those who have risked their lives already to keep you here."

Abraham bowed his head slightly, having no answer. "Should the occasion arise in the future," Daniel asked him, "and I'm not saying that it will, can I tell my organization that you'd be willing to help them?"

There was a long silence. Ashamed to act the coward, Abraham still could not be brave on behalf of those he loved. He looked at them, at his wife, and Rebecca nodded. So Abraham put out his hand and Daniel took it. "Sometimes a man has to hang on with his teeth, if need be."

"My teeth aren't all that good," Abraham said.

"I have confidence in them," replied Daniel.

"I haven't."

"Then let's test them out on some good tough horsemeat,"

Daniel said. Before he left that day, he had worked out a way of signaling danger by positioning the arms of the mill, since the blades could still be moved. "We must all be fatalists in this business," he said. "Look at me. Not a scratch, but for all I know, I'll be done for before the night ends. I don't worry about it. And rest assured, I won't endanger you people." Then, as though to call his statement into question, he added, "Unnecessarily."

David and Saul went with him to the mill as soon as night had fallen. They put out the plank. "Stay with God and the devil," Daniel told them as he walked the plank with his arms out from his sides for balance, a kind of crucifixion. Then he was gone.

The twins looked at one another. There was something inspiring and infectious about acting for the cause, and they shared a sense of elation that both knew was foolish but irresistible. "Now we're going to be part of it," said Saul softly, and their enthusiasm sustained itself through their father's gloomy prediction that Daniel would bring them only trouble and sorrow.

What did break down their enthusiasm was the passage of time. February came, and a German army surrendered at Stalingrad. Father Lebbink made a special trip to give them the news of the Russian victory and to tell them of Churchill's announcement: "It is not even the beginning of the end. But it is, perhaps, the end of the beginning." Hearing those words, they had no doubt now that Germany would be defeated. It was simply a matter of time. "The joke going around now," the priest told them, "has an angel coming down to earth. He sees a little man with a black mustache and slicked-down hair, up to his ankles in mud and yelling, 'Save me, I'm drowning!' The angel replies, 'But you're not even up to your knees.' 'That's so,' says the little man with the mustache, 'but I'm standing on Mussolini's head!' "

There was no sign of Daniel. David often despaired of seeing him again. The war would end first. Perhaps his uncle was dead already. And then, in mid-February, he came, as unexpectedly as the first time, his footsteps ringing in the passageway. This time it was night. They had put out the plank for Father Lebbink, but Daniel came instead, carrying the priest's food parcels and followed by two men in flying rig, all fitted out with pockets and white scarves and fur-lined boots. They were English, members of the RAF. One had a shining beet-red face and evident good humor, the other was wiry, a nervous pipe smoker with the pallid look of one whose ancestors had worked underground in the coal mines of Wales.

"They'll move on by tomorrow night," Daniel pledged. "I promise, I'll be back for them." The plan was to move them, via Belgium, to France, Spain, neutral Portugal, and finally home to England. But Daniel did not appear the next day, or the day after. On the third night, when their food was running desperately short, Father Lebbink showed up. In addition to a sack each of flour and beans, he brought a message. "Escape route disrupted. Sorry." One could not even be sure it came from Daniel.

So there they were. Abraham didn't even bother to say "I told you so." It was not the fliers' fault. God knows they'd been risking their lives, but the quarters were too small, the food supply too limited, for them to stay indefinitely. They would have to be moved along somehow, but the risks involved were many. Abraham discussed the problem with Rebecca first, and she made a suggestion. "You know I did mend the sail for the boat." So Abraham took the proposal along to the fliers, saying, "I'd guess it must be a hard three days' pull to England, even without adverse winds. And there's no telling whether we'd even get the boat down to the beach. The only chance would be on a foggy night."

The pilots, particularly the red-faced one, whose name was Robin, thought it was "a jolly idea." Robin had tried out once for the Cambridge crew and been rejected, but still he felt he had a way with boats. Bill, who came from Nottingham, not Wales, admitted he could hardly swim, but he was willing to take a chance if the fog came before the underground.

The weather stayed clear. The hiding place, though crowded, was cold as an ice plant, and food was short. Robin tapped his teeth with a pencil, rolled it against the brindle bristles of his small mustache, and considered a chart of the Channel. "With luck and a following wind, we could make it in twenty-four hours, and if the boat's as big as you say, we could take the little girl along, if you like." Rebecca looked shocked. "I think you can count on us making it safely." But Rachel was frightened and Rebecca couldn't face the idea of surrendering another one of her children to hazards seemingly greater than the ones she knew.

So Rachel's fate was quickly settled, even though Abraham felt there was wisdom in the pilot's suggestion. After ten nights of icy sparkling stars and a growing moon, fog rolled in to freeze solid on what it touched. Trees, bushes, blades of grass became sheathed in ice.

Father Lebbink, who'd been informed of the plan, came to see the Englishmen off. Saul had a cold, but until the last moment David had expected to accompany his father. "You can call me a nervous mother or a possessive wife," Rebecca informed them, "but I'm the one who's going, not David." There wasn't time for the argument David wanted to put up.

She was already binding her shoes with rags so as to leave no prints.

Father Lebbink prayed aloud for the departing guests. "The Lord shall guard thy going out and thy coming in, from this time forth and forever more."

"Brrr! It's a fine night for an execution," Robin said as he followed his guides out into the fog. A dull molten glow showed where the moon vainly tried to bore through the haze. They followed the canal, filled with lumps of floe ice like translucent jellyfish. The graveyard was left behind and the church loomed white as milk. They passed houses, dark and shuttered against the cold, where they could smell the smoldering peat of banked fires. The summer cottage was as dark as all the others, and it showed no signs of occupancy. The boat was still safely hidden in the bushes.

"It looks good and sound," Robin observed, but the wheels of its carriage were locked by rust. They turned with difficulty, and the three men were hard put to move it, while Rebecca reconnoitered in front in case the German sentries were patrolling. An hour of pulling brought them to the dunes, an area of brambles, heather, and gnarled, stunted trees. Here the carriage broke down entirely. They tried to carry the boat, but gave up and dragged it along like a sled until Abraham was exhausted. He panted, "We can't make it. We can't." Robin hissed at him, "We have to. We have no choice." Of course he was right. Should the boat be found by a patrol, the entire neighborhood would be aroused. "So pull, man, for God's sake, or get out of the way." Abraham, never an athlete and out of shape from months of confinement, pulled as black spots gathered before his eyes. He was bathed in sweat despite the cold, but somehow the boat kept moving. Two in the morning now. No sign of Germans, but the fliers would have to be far out to sea before the fog lifted in order to avoid the patrol boats. The Channel, when they first glimpsed it through a rift in the fog, looked like a pane of frosted glass. As they drew nearer, they could hear the waves breaking with muffled thuds upon the shore, waves of melted ice. No guards were out. Rebecca returned to help them over the great lumps of concrete with which the beach was strewn. At last the boat was afloat, and the two Englishmen, after promising to send a message via Radio Orange, "Robin and Bill send regards," were scrambling aboard. The white surf lifted them. They rowed strongly. A wave met the bow head on, threw up a shower of spray, and then they were beyond the breakers, lost in shreds of fog, seen once again briefly, then gone for good.

"If the fog holds," Abraham said, his arm around Rebecca as much to rest himself as to give her warmth, "and there isn't a storm, I think they have a chance."

Except for the drag of pebbles in the surf, the beach was silent, a bleak landscape made spectral by the light of the invisible moon moving behind the cottony blanket of fog.

"I'm cold," Rebecca whispered. She was shivering. "My legs are numb."

"Come on, then," he said. "It's a long way home." So they started for the dunes and their family, and yet part of Abraham was out there somewhere rowing, rowing toward England.

The dull thunder of the sea diminished as they wearily climbed the dunes. Moonlight coiled like a faint golden snake behind the wreathing fog. It would be easy to lose their way while trying always to keep to the bare ridges where the snow had been blown away. All went well until they reached the canal. Now it was only a matter of following its bank home.

The area of shore defenses was well behind them when Abraham heard a sound, indistinct as wind whirled in a bottle.

"What was that?"

Both stopped at the water's edge.

The snapping of a twig underfoot. Another twig, and then, on the dike above them, silhouetted against the lesser darkness, moved two figures. Light sparkled as though the foremost figure had suddenly parted the fog to let a star shine through. He was lighting a cigarette, held the match to his comrade. Pink faces were crowned with helmets. The match flared, a small comet disappearing into the canal. Amused German voices, and then something larger than a match was flung from overhead. It struck the water like a stone. Silence. Abraham and Rebecca pressed against the bank. Then the stillness was torn apart. The canal rose as the grenade went off not ten feet from where they stood. Abraham's heart thundered panic as the bank reverberated and its frozen crust gave way from the concussion. He was suddenly waist deep in the sluggish current, so cold that it scalded to the bone, taking all feeling. Rebecca was nearly swept away, but he managed to pull her to the bank, which was so undercut that the beam of the soldiers' flashlights passed over their heads. The men were scanning the surface of the canal to see if the explosion had raised any fish. Nothing but the floe ice. A curse, a gurgling laugh; they might well have been drunk; and then the Germans passed on, completely unaware of the man and woman below them, who grinned weakly at each other as they tried to crawl back to the road.

Rebecca shook her head slowly from side to side. "I can't move," she whispered. "My legs won't work. Hold me tight, Abraham. Make me feel pain." He squeezed her icy fingers.

"Harder!" she pleaded. "I can't feel my body."

"We've got to get home," he said, dragging her up to the dike road, where they lay close together for a moment, panting heavily like fish cast up on the beach. Abraham felt the bitter cold of the ice age in his bones. If he did not get up soon, his body would become one with the ice and snow. He had to tell his legs to function, first one, then the other. Rebecca was beyond this. Only her teeth had animation, and they were chattering. It was no more than a kilometer to the mill, a ten-minute walk for people in good condition, but it took Abraham until nearly dawn to move Rebecca along in agonizing bursts of effort. When it seemed the morning sun would peel away the fog and find them still upon the dike road, Father Lebbink appeared, a worried miracle, to drag them home.

Rebecca had begun to cough, and all the blankets in the room, and all the ersatz coffee they could force down would not stop her teeth from chattering. She was in severe shock from the icy water, and Abraham felt helpless. Not with the lost secrets of Solomon could he help his wife. He must leave her to God, the worst thing a doctor could say to himself. For an hour she breathed with difficulty. When she finally spoke, her voice was barely audible.

"I want to thank you for the life we've had together," she whispered.

"What are you saying?" he almost roared at her. "We have years ahead of us!"—as though he might frighten away that frozen death which seemed, even as he watched, to impose itself like a mask upon her face.

"Thank you. Thank you for everything." She spoke dreamily now from far away. He covered her hand with his. No more words, only the surrendering of a last breath.

"Rebecca," he said quietly. He looked like a man struck

blind. "Rebecca," the name almost sung. It was the sound of mourning.

For this death in the family there had been no expectation, no ritual. Yet suddenly the linchpin that had held the Ullmans together was gone. The hearth fire had gone out. It would not be rekindled.

David, too shocked for tears, pulled a blanket over his father's trembling shoulders and asked him to lie down. The older man complied obediently. Even Rachel, to whom tears came easily, could not cry. This was too much to encompass with tears. Rebecca had made their old home the comfortable place it had been. She had stoked its furnace, polished its hearth, washed windows and invalids, bought food and prepared it, stuffed poultry as well as her spouse and children. She had made a second home of this hole in the ground, and suddenly she had left them. Was it because two drunken Germans had played with grenades? Was it because Abraham had put a higher value on the welfare of the two English pilots than on his own family? There was no decent reason.

It was only a few hours before Abraham recovered himself in a doggedly mechanical way.

"There is still God in my house." He said this for Rebecca. There were things to be done, and he spoke to his children in a series of gentle, hesitant stops and starts, like someone just learning a foreign language. "Rachel . . . you'll . . . have to do . . . the cooking . . . do you think you can, dear? . . . David, look . . . after your brother . . ." Saul had retired to his bed. He was wheezing with asthma, his first attack in months. Far away, seemingly rung down from the sky rather than from any belfry, came the first pealing of the Angelus.

Father Lebbink returned to them after dark to stand in the entry dumbly appraising the scene. He was at home with death, but here! This woman he had come to think of as his daughter. Finally he knelt beside her, and murmured a Latin prayer with great glassy tears oozing down the long slope of his nose. Then for some time they sat in silence, broken finally by Abraham.

"You once tried to convert this pagan family. I wonder, would it be possible now to find a place in your cemetery for my wife?" There was no Jewish cemetery within miles, and to attempt a burial in one would be suicidal. Even in the Christian cemetery under Lebbink's administration there would be hazard.

"If you really want that," the priest said. "At night, perhaps. But I must warn you. The Gestapo with the Henneicke column you may have heard about, they've been snooping around. It will be dangerous."

"I remember," David interrupted, "back at Grandmother's funeral"—his mouth was saying all this; he wasn't speaking at all—"I remember Mother said she didn't want to be put in the ground . . . I remember . . ."

And so it was decided that night and done the next by David and Abraham alone. Saul still had asthma. It was not something for Rachel to see. There could be no coffin. In a blanket they could ill afford to spare, they moved her down the long, narrow passageway, a great unyielding puppet that seemed to resist their efforts with strong rubbery joints. I'm glad I can't see anything, David told himself. I'm glad I can't see my face. He knew it must be white because it felt so cold. Bees seemed to buzz in his ears, but he dared not faint and leave it all to his father. Finally they were in the mill itself, resting there, breathing hard, without talk. The cold air revived them. "Father, I'm ready whenever you are," he said.

Abraham braced himself. He nodded silently. They made

it across the road and down the bank without stopping. Melting snow had turned the sluggish canal into a sleek greased metal sheet that moved rapidly, with a profound, deep murmur.

"Your grandmother was lucky," Abraham said. "She died when she had no more living to do." There was no ceremony, there were no words said. With silent accord they slipped their burden into the flow, wife and mother with all her dreams of a better world. Foolishness to believe in miracles? And yet, thought Abraham, was not her faith itself a kind of miracle?

Neither one made a move to depart. A light, wet snow had begun to fall, its heavy flakes vanishing on the black water. Flakes fell on the mill and upon the lonely church where Father Lebbink kept his austere vigil. "Come along, David. We'll be leaving tracks." The road sparkled like a million diamonds, but Abraham felt suddenly old. He hated the snow. It seemed to foretell the extinction of life. Spring would never come again. Surely hell was white. But David opened his mouth, felt the burning flakes on his tongue, and knew that he was glad to be alive.

By morning, the snow had turned to drenching spring rain. For the first time Abraham neglected to shave. There was no one to remind him. No one to do the washing. Rebecca's absence echoed in all their domestic inadequacies. Somehow Rachel, with David's help, put palatable food together, a few spoonfuls of porridge for breakfast, half-sprouted potatoes for lunch, while, all along, the almost unmentioned tragedy rang in their ears like the vibrations of a great gong, benumbing their spirits. The days passed unremarked. Abraham had broken his watch, had deliberately smashed the crystal and twisted off the hands to stop the annoyance of time, but of course time went on. The priest continued to bring food. One night he brought them a message that had been broadcast over Radio Orange. "Robin and Bill send their best." It was an echo from another world, which presently burst upon them.

Quick footfalls in daylight clipped across the flagstones like a shower of nails. Their immediate reaction was betrayal, for they knew the Henneicke column was out in force. The price per Jewish head, dead or alive, had been raised from 7½ to 37½ guilders, enough to make the dirty job worth while. The footsteps seemed to advance by an interminably devious route. Had their hour finally struck? Abraham clutched a length of rusty chain. The boys had heavy sticks. All were prepared to go down fighting, but the intruder, when he arrived, was Uncle Daniel, clad as they had seen him once before, in the uniform of an SS officer.

Stepping into the room, he appeared to misinterpret the makeshift weapons, for he said, "I realize you have reason to hate me."

"We're not blaming you," Abraham said. "You can take hate back a hundred thousand years if you want to, to Cain and Abel."

"Hate the Germans, then, as I do," Daniel said, and David could hear the teeth in his uncle's breath.

"I'm not a hating man," Abraham said in a soft voice, "but I have come to realize some men are beasts and must be destroyed. I used to think I could get through life gracefully, saving as many lives as I could, but now . . . now I feel some lives must be taken. I'm not a fighter, Daniel. I'm not a leader of men, but you can count on me, for what I'm worth." He looked around. "And on the boys as well, I think."

David leaned forward in silent acknowledgment.

"To the death?" Daniel said.

"Yes, if necessary," Abraham replied.

And so they were united by the strongest of bonds. They had become collaborators.

"Take these," Daniel said, and from a briefcase he produced three pistols. "They're loaded."

David took the assigned weapon. He had never held one before, and he felt suddenly immeasurably old, yet at the same time as new to the world as a baby still bound by its birth cord.

"From now on we're one," Daniel told them. "If one of us makes a false move, the others must catch him. If one is lost, we're all lost."

"There's only one reservation I have," Abraham added. "What about Rachel? She must be protected."

"Pity you didn't pack her off to England with those fliers," Daniel said.

"How could we? Everything was against their making it."

"I think Lebbink can do something. I'll speak to him."

From the ambivalent excitement of becoming an armed member of the underground, David was thrown suddenly back into being a little boy who had lost his mother. He faced the added loss of the person he now realized meant more to him than anyone else in the world, the one person who needed him. He could not bear it, and yet he knew there was no other way.

The Ullman family would have to be reduced once more, leaving only three servants of the underground for as long as they had breath.

SEVEN

SUMMER, 1943
Capture

Daniel had spoken to them of partisans, making the word seem like a dangerous species of wild beast that preyed on the enemy, but all he seemed to expect of them was the use of the mill and their hidden room as a way station for downed Allied fliers on their way south to Belgium, France, and the Spanish frontier. With the cooperation of Father Lebbink, their meager hospitality was extended to several guests as spring, with its drenching rains, burst into early-summer bloom. From the spy hole, David watched a flycatcher build his nest, saw the cat-faced pansies lift their faces to the sun.

The question of moving Rachel along had been deferred. The prospect of sending her across occupied Europe, even with forged papers, seemed a greater risk than keeping her with them in hiding, for the life of underground action that David had anticipated had not materialized to any great extent. Fliers, an occasional Jew, came and went without excitement. Always one nagging question remained for David: if need be, could he kill a human being in cold blood? If he were more like his uncle, there would have been no doubts, for Daniel despised death and cared little for life. He was a bullet humming through the air. He had struck down ten Germans and more. They had paid for his wife with interest, and yet it was a debt that never could be canceled. In these discussions, David had no tongue, only ears. He listened.

"It's a strange sensation to wake up in the morning," Dan-

143.

iel said, "and know that day you'll kill a man, a total stranger. I can't tell you with what clarity you see the sun, every leaf on every tree; with what gentle affection I raise my gun." And he involuntarily pointed a long finger. For a moment the expression on his face was one of madness. "And still I know it's wrong to love this sort of work," he added, calling himself back. "There is much blood on my hands. I must wash them often."

Apart from his own deeds, Daniel bore tales of a bomb here, a fire there, a guard vanished from his post; sparks of hatred in the black night of occupation. On the first of March, the Nazis had cleaned out the Jewish invalid hospital in Amsterdam, lugging the old, the sick, and the lame off to certain death. A few weeks later, the underground had retaliated by setting fire to the labor exchange and, later still, to the registrar's office. An eye for an eye. That would be the rule until all men were blinded or the war ended. There was some good news. Italy had been invaded by the Allies. The Russians were advancing for the first time in summer, but the expected invasion in the west by the Allies did not come. The war would last at least another year, which was an eternity to keep the mill's hiding place secret from the enemy, now that it was a center of occasional activity.

Danger grew at two levels. First, there was the impersonal hazard, a matter of geography and that proud Dutch boast that, while God made the rest of the earth, the Dutchmen had made Holland. They had taken it from the sea, and now the Nazis were threatening to give it back. As Hitler had pledged, "If we have to withdraw, we shall slam the doors of all the occupied countries behind us." This was no idle threat in the Netherlands, where the high tide of a winter's storm raised the level of the North Sea two stories above the street level in Amsterdam. The Germans need only bomb the sea walls and dikes to achieve horrendous results. The water gauge on the dike road indicated that the level of the mill was well below that of the city. If Amsterdam were flooded, they would drown like rats.

That was the sword of Damocles which hung over all of Holland. For the Ullmans, there was a more personal threat: the country was to be free of Jews by the end of summer. That was the official Nazi goal. It had not been entirely attained, however, owing to the hiders, and because many Nazis themselves were reluctant to eradicate the Jewish community entirely—not out of conscience, but because an end to the Jewish problem would have freed those employed on it for more dangerous work at the Russian front. Even though only an official fraction of the Jewish population remained, there were still jokes to tell. It was said that the Jewish Council, on being informed that all the Jews in Amsterdam, including themselves, were to be gassed, had begged permission to ask one question. Would the council have to pay for the gas? As hiders, the Ullmans were not threatened by the official roundup. Their danger came from postmen and farmers, children, and soldiers walking the dike road. Unfortunately, it could not be denied that anti-Semitism was spreading, and for very human reasons. Many Jews had been sheltered by non-Jews, and, as these hiders were gradually apprehended and questioned, often with a supplement of torture, their Christian protectors shared their fate. For this, and for the reprisals against sabotage, the Jews were blamed. So every neighbor walking the dike road was a hazard, and the Ullmans worried in particular about the polder board of village elders who were in charge of inspecting the dikes. Rumor had it that to counter the possibility of Nazi flooding, they would try to shore up the present dike as protection. This meant that the polder board would carefully scrutinize old dike plans, which might expose the presence of the room in which the Ullmans hid and harbored refugees. Such were the portents and threats upon which their anxiety fed, and David, though he could not settle for himself the question about taking life when and if the time came, slept with his pistol under his pillow and called it his security blanket.

More fugitives came and went as spring gave way to summer. During the short nights of July, the Allies bombed Amsterdam, especially Schiphol Airport, which the Germans had reconstructed for their own use. On quiet nights David could hear the bombardment, like distant thunder. During the day, members of the nearby German garrison often fished in the canal, their long, thin poles shining like fire in the hot sun. Everyone in the stifling hideout had to wait until night for relief.

August brought splendid news from Italy. The Fascist government had fallen, and the people of Holland wore spaghetti in their buttonholes to ridicule Mussolini. By the tenth of September Italy had surrendered. Father Lebbink reported the news as he had heard it over Radio Orange, broadcast from London. Three weeks later he came with more solemn tidings. The Jewish Council in Amsterdam had been dissolved. The last few Jews who, like so many before them, had clung to guarantees of immunity, to belief in their own indispensability, were being transported to camps. Apart from a handful of Portuguese Jews—for Portugal was neutral—and Jews married to Aryans, only the hiders remained out of a community that had numbered 140,000 before the war.

Soon winter would come again, with the problem of leaving tracks on snow and half-frozen soil. Once more Abraham's prime concern was for Rachel's safety. He meant to press this issue upon Daniel when he next appeared. He came in early October, and there was something changed about him, as though somewhere his inexhaustible flow of energy had been cut off. He looked crumpled. It showed in every crease in his uniform; it was written in his face.

"Are you all right?" Abraham asked.

"Heart beats, kidneys distill, stomach rumbles," Daniel replied.

"I'm serious," Abraham persisted. "You don't look well." There was a dark silence between them. "Daniel, I want Rachel out of here."

Daniel lit a cigarette. His face flared up between his hands, his cheeks drew in the smoke. "So do I," he said, exhaling. "I want the lot of you out of here. Ruth's been taken."

"Taken?"

This was too abrupt. Volumes were being said in telegrams.

"It could be worse. The Dutch police have her. They won't abuse her."

"And she won't talk," David said.

"No. But if the Gestapo gets involved . . . Ruth's good. She's as tough as any of us, but the Gestapo have professional ways with torture. They're horribly clever. They employ doctors capable of inflicting unimaginable pain. But this is premature. The underground may get her back first."

Such was Daniel's way: brutal honesty, nothing withheld. But Ruth captured! That joyous spirit in the hands of the Gestapo! If she could be taken, then why not the whole world?

Abraham paced back and forth. His lips moved without

audible words. He faced the wall, slammed his fist against it, then turned and said in a voice that was calm, too calm, "If it's a question of money . . ."

"Money might help. It's like manure, worthless unless you spread it around," Daniel answered.

So Abraham told his brother about Moses' hidden horde in the house in Amsterdam.

"Only as a last resort," Daniel pledged. "No fear, we'll do our best for both your daughters, and for you, too. Count on me." He left them without divulging more.

That night Father Lebbink came with food. He looked harassed, though it showed less in his face than in his fingernails, which were gnawed down to the quick.

"If necessary, Father Lebbink, could we evacuate this place and hide in the belfry of the church?" asked Abraham.

"Impossible," the priest confessed. "It's the highest point for miles around, and airplane spotters are up there day and night."

"If only Rachel could be taken somewhere . . . We've talked of this before, but never with more urgency, believe me, Father. You see—"

"Yes," the priest interrupted, "I know about Ruth. May God protect her."

"And can you help me protect my youngest one?"

"I will try," the priest said. "You know, I came to this parish to live in grace. I said those very words. I wanted to translate spiritual harmony into outer harmony for the flock I served. Now, if a priest's word had the power to kill in God's name, as it should, I would kill. To these Nazis I would be as merciless as the angel of death."

"I'm not asking you to kill, Father Lebbink, only—"

"Yes, there's a way. Have you ever heard of the quarries

and caves in St. Pietersberg Mount near Maastricht?" Abraham nodded. "They're huge. The galleries have been dug out since ancient times, and now it's like a city of hiders. The Germans fear it, and pretend it doesn't exist. There may be a way I can take your Rachel there."

Abraham began the presentation to his daughter obliquely. "There is a cave, Rachel dear, very big and very beautiful, full of stalactites like flower gardens. No one's ever explored it all the way to the end, it's so big. We'll be going there, and you must be the explorer, the first to go."

"No," she whispered, lowering her eyes. The long lashes cast a shadow on her cheeks.

"But, dear, the rest of us will follow soon. It's just that for a little while longer we must help others to escape. Besides, Father Lebbink can only take one of us at a time. Now this is how it's to be done." As Abraham explained, Rachel stared at him. Her small face looked lost and terrified, certain now of disaster and unable to believe in the manner of its coming. She was to ride in the sidecar of a motorcycle, but a special sort of sidecar, designed to hold a coffin. She would go as a corpse, boxed and sealed for delivery, a technique that Daniel and the priest had worked out for special situations when an individual had to be moved with unusual haste.

They had delayed so long in finding another haven for Rachel that David had ceased to believe she would ever leave them. They had grown close in those lonely frightened months, and now at dawn she would depart. The realization was a cord that turned and knotted in his throat.

"David, are you crying?" he heard her say. The gray twilight before dawn made a blind eye of their peephole.

"No," he told her. "Go back to sleep."

"Yes, you are." She touched his cheek with her finger.

"I'm getting a cold."

She hugged her brother then, tight as a mollusk clinging to a rock in heavy surf.

"David, I feel as if I'll never . . ."

"No," he denied it. "Everyone feels that way."

They heard the sputtering protest of a motorcycle, sluggish with morning cold upon the dike road. It stopped, coughed, and was silent. The priest had arrived.

Rachel had composed herself. She embraced them all, then climbed into the black box, which the priest bolted down, explaining about the air holes in the bottom. "It's really a very comfortable way to travel."

David's eyes were wet and burning. He did not cry, nor could he speak. Lebbink kicked the starter; once, twice, three times the machine refused. David began to hope that it had died there. Then, on the fourth try, the motor roared, the priest nodded and bent to his task. They were gone into the shredding haze of an autumn dawn. David ran back inside. With a groan of relief as much as of sorrow and loss, he broke down. Crying without shame, he took great mournful gulps of air like a hurt child.

"David, David." He felt his father's hand upon his shoulder. "You'll be the next one to go. Then Saul. Now try and get some sleep. There's no telling how much we'll get from now on." But sleep came hard, and nightmares arrived which left him sweating and shivering.

"*Manrapi hevlei sheina* . . . Blessed art Thou, O Lord, our God, who makes the hands of sleep to fall upon mine eyes . . ." It was the old formula he said to himself, and this time it seemed to work, for he did not wake again until dusk was in the air.

No one came that night or the next day. There was much
military traffic upon the dike road and, so as not to be taken
unaware, they slept in shifts. Two were always awake, and
David and Saul were those two when Uncle Daniel came
blundering in on the second night, blood on his face and a
submachine gun under his arm. His eyes were secret and
alert, and behind them lurked a quality of desperation. They
were the eyes of a captured hawk glaring at his tormenters.
Across the left side of his face, obliterating the earlobe, was a
recent slash that had been gummed over with some sort of
ointment or grease. He seemed to want to keep this wound in
the shadow as a mark of weakness.

Abraham, however, insisted he come into the light. "I
should clean that up," he said, "and take some stitches. I
haven't anything for the pain, but you've lost some blood by
the look of you." Daniel's complexion was gray. He did not
protest as his brother handed him pure alcohol to drink. He
did not cry out when Abraham plied needle and thread to
pull the ragged lips of flesh together. But Daniel had things to
say which chilled them all.

"Ruth's in Gestapo hands," he began, "and there's a search
of this area going on. It's only a matter of time."

"Is there no hope?"

"There never has been. The trick is to survive without it.
You must get out of this haystack before they have time to
pull it apart. Go to the priest."

"Is he back from Maastricht?" Abraham asked.

"Go to the church, then, while I lead them off," said Daniel. He was pulling his submachine gun apart, cleaning it,
pressing back the bright shells. There were grenades at his
belt, a first attempt by some hidden armorer to make explo-

sives. "I think tonight we'll see if they really work," he said. "Now I'm going. Once it's quiet, you three go to the church."

It was hardly a clever plan, but that could not be helped. No alternative remained.

"You've lost far too much blood to go running off," Abraham cautioned him.

"Can't be helped," Daniel replied. He was doomed, had been all along, and now he would accept his fate. He had done his share to make the Germans lose, to keep them from building victory monuments over Dutch bones, Jewish and Christian alike.

"Take this," he said, holding out to Abraham a packet of dried blood and cocaine. "It'll put off the dogs, if they use dogs." And with an expression blending pain and defiance, he disappeared into the dark tunnel, a man stronger than his enemy even when his enemy seemed victorious, stronger than the death he expected to meet in the darkness.

"I think I hear dogs barking," Saul said. The night made sounds that lacked meaning. A motorcar spinning on the road: friend or foe? Dogs indeed, but perhaps only farmers' dogs, saluting the moon. From far off there came a shot.

"Motorcycle backfiring?" Abraham hypothesized.

Then someone was spraying the night with wild darting bursts of fire. The explosion of a grenade sent its echo rolling down from the church hillside. That final sound could not be rationalized away. Within moments they were ready. Anything that might help to identify them was destroyed or buried in the hard-packed floor of the corridor. This included the three pistols, for Abraham insisted their predicament would be worse if they were caught with pistols. He made a final pass with a flashlight: blankets left to mildew, tins and spoons left to rust, the mill and the secret room abandoned to winter and the tracking dogs. They waded for half a mile along the canal bank before turning toward the church. A strong wind blew in from the sea.

They had never actually been to the church before, and remembering that airplane spotters presumably occupied the belfry tower, they were afraid to go inside. The priest's house showed a light. Assuming that Father Lebbink had returned from Maastricht, the Ullmans entered, to be met by two pale nuns who stared at them from behind steel-rimmed eyeglasses. Surprise was mutual. The older nun hissed something at her companion, who, without replying, turned and vanished from the room. She returned with a robed and sleep-laden Lebbink.

"Welcome to the poor man's St. Peter's," he said. "I am just back. Rachel's in good hands. But things are bad here, I know."

"Daniel? Have you seen him?" Abraham asked, afraid of the answer.

"No, but I heard the shooting. The Germans will come here. They came yesterday. They asked the sisters if they could buy eggs. Or did they perhaps come for me? But as the sisters say, God made them ask for eggs. I don't know, but next time will come the Gestapo. Now, you two boys—choir robes. This morning is rehearsal."

Already the church bell was tolling for matins, rousing the choir, a metal voice now near, now far. The last stroke vibrated in the air as the sun climbed over the horizon, throwing a red glare along the edge of the fields. The steeple and belfry caught the first light, while down below it remained dark long enough for the priest to escort Abraham and his sons into the church without fear of observation from above.

Father Lebbink quickly led them to a recessed corner where a life-size plaster statue of Jesus hung from a cross. To David, the figure appeared muscular as a sprinter, but its fingers curled delicately around the nailheads and it gazed down with a bored and curious stare as though it had been there a long time. "Wait here," Lebbink told the boys. "There's a coffin for your father. Yes, the same one," and he led Abraham to the small crypt, which smelled of holiness and perpetual damp. Here there were two coffins, one of which held an actual corpse laid out with flowers and ready for afternoon burial in the churchyard. Unhesitatingly, Abraham stretched out in the empty one. "Quiet, now," Father Lebbink cautioned as he set the lid into place. "Don't move a muscle."

Above, boys were arriving for choir practice. They looked at the twins curiously. Who were these strangers? Too old, too tall, too dark, somehow; and yet they asked no questions. Lebbink had returned. Hymnals were handed round and practice began. Pure, shrill, prepubescent voices rose to the vaulted roof while Saul and David worked their mouths in pantomime. They were actors with something to hide. The others seemed to guess, becoming actors, too. But their knowing smiles vanished when the crash of brakes was heard outside. Then, as if wax plugs had been withdrawn from his ears, David heard voices, ejaculant and cantankerous. The front door opened wide and the morning sun flung the shadows of four figures down the aisle.

The first was a squat, toadish man, a Dutch official hovering unhappily behind a cigar and holding his hat in his hands. He did not look dangerous or even really nasty, only slightly sour. The other three were German, a man and two women who spoke Dutch with waspish precision. The women were in gray, one thin and mousy with hair screwed tightly against the back of her head, the other large, grim, and purposeful. But it was a bleached-out wisp of a man who was clearly in charge. His thin skin had recently been torn by a razor, and his eyes were pale and cold as the remembrance of a child's death. He stopped where the stained glass reddened his face, his hands on his narrow hips, to observe the choir, a figure of authority from one of Goya's nightmares.

The hymn in progress struggled to its conclusion. Only then did Father Lebbink turn to his visitors. "I'm afraid we're out of eggs," he said.

"Eggs? What is this eggs?" The Gestapo agent sent the word echoing to the corners of the church. "We are shopping today for fresh meat, Father. Jewish meat. You have it for us, yes?"

"I'm sorry, no. You jest," the priest replied, his face turning red to the roots of his sandy hair. The Gestapo agent had seen the lie and now he savored it.

"Holy Father," he mocked, "you seem to have a taste for martyrdom. I'm really disappointed. I thought you were a healthy-minded Dutchman."

Silence. The agent strode to a door, any door, and hammered on it with his fist until the echoes rang. "Jew!" he shouted. "Come out!" No one moved. David took five long, slow breaths, remembering a child's formula for countering the symptoms of terror.

"So we must search," the agent said, calling inside two armed men in SS black. The belfry first. Only tired air spotters there. Then the sacristy, knocking things about, and finally the crypt. Nothing but two coffins. "Open them, Father." Of course Lebbink chose first the coffin containing the dead man. The screws came hard. Impatiently the Gestapo agent rose on his toes, cracked a riding crop against his leg. "Help the poor old fellow," he said to an SS guard. The soldier advanced, but instead of assisting with the lid, at a gesture from his leader he sprayed the coffin with bullets.

"And now the other. Stand back, Father." The agent's voice coiled around the priest like a whip. He stood paralyzed, but Abraham, feeling his heart pound loudly inside his chest, beat upon the box.

"What is this?" the agent demanded. Again Abraham struck about in the dark.

"Quiet in there! Don't you know you're dead?" He used the German word "*kaput.*" Then he turned eyes hard and uncaring as the polished gray buttons on his coat upon the wilting Lebbink. "We Germans are a hygienic race. We don't believe in corpses lying about growing stale. You will conduct funerals, Father. Now!" He laughed, with only his lower face in motion, a mirth no deeper than his cheekbones and teeth. "And now call down your choirboys. They will be our pallbearers. Quick! Quick!" Again the riding crop slashed. "You may thank the good Lord we found no Jews to hold against your record."

So David and Saul were called with the others. They were assigned to the coffin punctured through with splintered holes, made to carry it up and out, past the bored figure crowned with thorns, past the various Stations of the Cross, which pictured events that had happened in a cruel age long ago.

The sunlight was blinding. David's eyes watered from it. His robe leaped and billowed about him. The wind tugged at his hair. It was a perfect autumn day.

Not one but two graves had already been dug and covered

with canvas; shallow graves, but deep enough. The coffins were set down, suspended over the graves on boards with ropes for lowering. No sound came from either one.

"Well, boys, lower away," the agent commanded. "Good. Now the shovels." For all that David and Saul knew, their father might be in the bullet-riddled coffin, dead, or he might be in the other, alive but silent, protecting them to the death.

Earth thudded down. The priest, at gun point, read from the Bible. "Yea, though I walk through the valley of the shadow of death, I will fear no evil." One grave was filled. "Thou preparest a table before me in the presence of mine enemies." David could scarcely hear the words; they came to him as a droning monotone, little more than a gaseous murmur. The uncomprehending chickens drew near, listened, then departed with scandalized outcries as the gusty wind fluttered their tail feathers.

"My God, my God," David thought. Ideas coming in explosions of "Why am I just standing here?" He was transfixed by fear and anguish, no more able to move than the figure on the cross. He tried to make it all go away by shutting his eyes. If only they had kept their pistols! He tasted blood, not his own but that cursed Nazi's, who watched them all through foxy eyes to see if there were any more rabbits and which way they would bound.

In the end it was Saul's asthma that gave things away. He began breathing harder and harder, while the priest intoned haltingly and the agent drew a swastika in the fresh dirt with the tip of his riding crop.

David had to hold Saul up to keep him from collapsing. This and his labored breathing had caused the others to draw away.

"Well," said the agent, "I'm a man with a heart." He looked as insensate as a pagan idol. "I have a family, too. You two—dig him up!"

So Saul and David dug in a frenzy down through the soft earth toward the only coffin that might still contain life. The priest moved to assist, only to be thrust back with the flat side of a fixed bayonet. David did most of the work. It left him dizzy and gasping, his eyes unable to focus sharply, as the coffin was hauled out and a screwdriver applied.

Presently Abraham emerged. His face was white as cold cream and the expression in his eyes was of one who had come back from the dead. Those few minutes had changed him more than a prolonged illness.

No deception remained. David took his arm. "Father, are you all right?"

"I don't know. I don't know," Abraham mumbled weakly. His knee joints cracked as he tried to stand erect.

"Well, well, what have we here? Lazarus, boys?" The Gestapo agent was directing his comments to the entire dumbfounded choir. "The lesson for today is Lazarus. Lazarus the Jew, and his two sons."

Saul and David were summarily searched for weapons and papers while Abraham was bundled into a waiting truck. "Very good," the agent concluded. "We can use strong lads like you two at Westerbork. Now into the truck. The lesson is over!" So they followed Abraham, a clumsy haggard gargoyle of a man who sprawled loosely in the back of the truck as though he might fall apart. Something had happened inside Abraham. David knew it from his empty eyes. A dream of faith had died, leaving nothing more to sustain him.

The truck's diesel motor coughed into life. It backed and turned. They had a glimpse of Father Lebbink over the tailgate. He was on his knees, his hands clasped. Then they were bumping down the hill and out onto the dike road, past the mill. I'm dreaming, David told himself. His mind was trapped in an odd serenity.

"Father," he said, leaning toward Abraham, "do you think they'll take us to Westerbork?"

"What's the use of thinking?" Abraham replied dully. He was one more step removed from reality, and he looked at his son with dead eyes. "I dreamed of your mother last night, as she was when we were young."

David watched the countryside pass. He felt strangely relaxed, even lethargic, calmer than he had been in months. Even if the guards had not been there, he might not make the effort to escape. They drove through the town that he had glimpsed only from afar. Children were making wood-chip boats with autumn leaves for sails, to float them in the canal. As they passed beyond the street of shops, he heard the thud of footballers, saw the ball flying in the fenced field. He would have liked to linger awhile and watch the game, but already it was left behind. Cattle occupied the fields now, and, fanned by the sea breeze, the meadows glowed with autumn light. How beautiful it was. Now that hope was gone, doubt and anxiety were shed as well. David could have met death in that moment with serenity, and yet he did not want to die with such beauty all around him. The country looked as peaceful as a landscape painting. How good was the warmth of the sun.

EIGHT

PURGATORY
Westerbork Detention Camp

The truck with its three prisoners arrived at Westerbork Detention Camp on the afternoon of November 15, 1943. Westerbork had begun as a place of refuge for Jews fleeing Germany. Even under German occupation, it had remained in Dutch control until the summer of 1942. Now it was a dismal, unpainted place made of scraps and leftovers. Trodden-dirt paths, brick, wood, girded around with wire. Though it teemed with humanity, it had a deserted air. Westerbork's administration had initially been organized by Kurt Schlesinger, a Jew, and run so efficiently that the Germans had not disturbed its structure and lurked only in the background, the guardians of the guards who had direct contact with the inmates. These guards were the FK, in brown uniforms, who took charge of baggage as it arrived, and the OD, the camp police, in green uniforms. They were Jewish ex-soldiers who at first had kept order in what otherwise would have been a state of anarchy. Now they were known as the Jewish SS, and they had complete charge of Barrack 51 for criminals. To this and the surrounding punishment block designed to crush the spirit of rebellious captives Abraham was taken.

The boys were directed by an FK guard to the general camp mustering square and, because there was no confusion of baggage, on to the reception department. They moved rapidly through the Tweedledums and Tweedledees of of-

160.

ficious bureaucracy, the central distribution office, the clas-
sification desk, and the accommodation bureau. To David,
the camp seemed immense. Actually, in terms of such places,
it was small, like a good-sized country town, but tightly
packed with transient humanity numbering in the tens of
thousands. Finally they were given cups of lukewarm ersatz
coffee and told that, if they worked well, they could expect to
survive. "Make it through the next three weeks and you'll
probably last a year. You know what that means." At the
quarantine barracks, they were searched for valuables by the
local branch of Lippmann, Rosenthal and Company. Saul
surrendered his fountain pen. David had nothing—not even a
gold tooth to be noted for future reference.

Passing under a sign that read EVERYTHING NOT FORBIDDEN
IS OBLIGATORY, they were directed to a barracks. It was now
early evening. Each building was 275 feet long and only 13
feet wide. There were sections for men and women to sleep
in triple-decker bunks. The twins were too late for food.

"Thank God they didn't take my glasses," was all Saul
could say. Without them, Saul had to squint as if peering
through heavy fog.

After curfew, David tried to sleep, but there was much
coming and going in the darkness lit only by the glimmer of a
carbide lamp, talk, even laughter, and women's voices. By
midnight the barracks was finally still. Then it was that his
father's face began to haunt him. He had not spoken to Saul
of Abraham. What was the use? They could only torment
themselves; but in the silence of the night, Abraham was
there, not the strong figure of their childhood years, but a lost
soul beyond help. David tried to project himself back to the
mill to help sleep come, but the sharp-pointed reality of his

unreal day cut through the images, and dawn was near before he slept.

Dawn brought frantic activity: a storming of the washhouse, a sloshing cleanup of the barracks, then food.

"What is this?" Saul asked, looking into his tin bowl. "It looks as if it comes from a cow, but it isn't milk."

"Eat or you'll die," a stranger hissed at him. Another, who must have heard him complaining about his fountain pen, offered him a pencil stub in exchange for the meal, but Saul refused. After all, food was life, and the stealing of food was punishable by death.

For some, the food began a day of lounging, but those who lounged did not last long at Westerbork. Saul and David, instructed in the lesson that those who worked were less apt to be deported to a far worse place, soon went on record as expert machinists. The shops at Westerbork provided employment for all skills: blacksmiths, watchmakers, tailors; but the biggest section was Industrial Section XII, concerned with salvaging scrap from downed aircraft. Here Saul was set to breaking up old batteries, while David was given a set of spanners and a blowtorch with which to cut instruments out of the airplanes' control panels. Here, too, radios were salvaged, which made for a regular flow of music and news. Seldom did a Nazi show his face in the shop, and when he did his interest was possible laxity, not the rooting out of hidden radios. The subject of how hard one should work proved a principal source of conversation and the only serious bone of contention. Newer prisoners dreamed of sabotage, while hard-bitten survivors maintained that life depended on serious effort. Many even seemed to take pride in their work. David could not go that far, but fear of deportation kept him on the job in the hope that his contribution would make him necessary here.

Although he was told that the food had once been better and that there had even been a token wage of ten guilders a week, there were tales of concentration camps in Germany and Poland that made Westerbork seem like paradise. From the German camp commander, Albert Konrad Gemmeker, down, Westerbork was not essentially a cruel place. Gemmeker lived outside the wire, like an English sportsman, in a handsome house, having no more hatred for Jews than a butcher had for lambs. He did his job, and if a Prussian contempt for death had permutated into a contempt for life, at least he did not inflict punishment for pain's sake. To be actively cruel would have been to hate his prisoners; this would have been as degrading as to love them. So deaths at Westerbork were relatively few, attributable in the main to disease and the loss of desire to stay alive. Eat what you are given, work as hard as you can, and endure; survive any way at all—that was the formula the old-timers taught and which David accepted as he would have his own father's advice.

So the weeks passed, and as they did, David learned the rhythms of survival as well as the regular pattern of fear. Each Tuesday brought a dread like the end of the world, which often woke him bathed in sweat. Tuesday was a German mechanism left in Jewish hands to wind. Commandant Gemmeker, with help from his assistant, Frau Elizabeth Hassel, said to be his mistress and less merciful than he, set the weekly quota, leaving the actual selection of individuals to the Jewish camp administration, the leaders of the OD. Tuesday, when the train came with its boxcars, was a kind of bogeyman. "Behave yourself or you'll go on the train without me," mothers were heard to tell their children. Every Monday, David could feel the panic rising in himself, in everyone, until the list of victims was read out by each barracks' leader. Then terror remained only for the few. A handful tried to escape the net with bribes or by finding a substitute. Most simply gave up. From the selected there were screams and tears; for the majority, a horrid joy. David felt it, and so did Saul: a reprieve for one more week. But what of Abraham? Was there any work left in their father? Could he still be alive somewhere in Westerbork? Could he possibly have escaped the transport to some death camp far away? They had no way of finding out.

The train came in the night like a bad dream that never went away with the dawn. There it was in the middle of camp, looming black and endless, its two engines whoosh-whooshing oily dark smoke. On Tuesday the camp was roused at 5 a.m., and by 7 the victims were lined up three abreast with their luggage, to be driven outside as their names were called. Then they were packed into boxcars. Once there had been coaches, and the privileged few bound for the German camps of Bergen-Belsen or Theresienstadt still had carriages, but the average transport meant a cattle car, one small vat of drinking water, a bucket for a toilet, and a small hole in the roof for ventilation. There was straw to lie upon, but each car was packed with almost four bodies to the square meter, so that it was virtually impossible to lie down. All this was managed by Jews, with the SS lounging at a distance in attitudes of belligerent casualness in case the system failed.

Each Tuesday, David and Saul observed the proceedings with ghastly fascination. They could not turn their backs, for they had to watch for Abraham. After the initial shock, the victims were silent, their faces set as they passed by. Commandant Gemmeker was on the platform with his police dogs. Many of the Jewish camp dignitaries stood within his charmed circle, including the one who had set the machinery running: Schlesinger, clad in riding breeches and high boots.

"This can't be real," David said to Saul the first time. "They can't all go quietly like this." And yet to refuse, even to faint, was to die on the spot. Luggage was thrown off to make room for bodies. Finally the boxcars were locked, the black engines exhaled great greasy clouds, and the nightmare passed for another week, its passengers bound, as Saul once quoted, for "the undiscovered country from whose bourn no traveler returns."

With the tracks empty, survivors fought over the contents of the abandoned luggage until the OD's dispersed them with clubs. Then the camp settled down to another week in purgatory.

Wednesday and Thursday were usually peaceful. There was often optimistic talk of the Russian front. In the early evening, David and Saul would stroll the camp street, called Boulevard des Misères. One could take part in athletic contests if one had the strength; look in on a class for children; visit the camp warehouse where household articles could be bought if one had money. Sometimes there was group singing. There were flirtations, fights between Zionists and anti-Zionists, very nearly the full spectrum of normal life and a sense of contained freedom that David had never felt in occupied Amsterdam or in hiding. No need to make decisions; simply live. No fear of the curfew that drove the rest of Holland home to early bed.

The brothers even joined a singing group, not through a brave attempt to hide their suffering, but through a perverse and uncomplicated desire to sing. It was only when he thought too hard, considered cause and effect, that David became glum at midweek, and this was usually when he pondered how easily the Germans were turning human beings into machinery. How easy to accept the system, become part of the automatic tyranny, and thereby deny oneself. At best one became a child, at worst an automaton; but to demand one's individuality meant transportation.

By Friday, anxiety and rumors of the chosen ones would begin to rise, and there would follow a weekend of finger-gnawing. Then, with Monday, came the spread of panic, a process that seemed to sap the strength even more than did the wretched diet. David had begun to worry about Saul. Had he become thinner? Surely they all had. Without his books he seemed to sit longer, his eyes turned inward, even on the job, where idleness was dangerous.

It was with this concern that David proposed they attend the camp show one Saturday night. Until the war, many of Amsterdam's most famous entertainers had been Jewish. Now most of them were here, protected from the transports, for which concession they were said to put on the best shows in Holland. Commandant Gemmeker personally encouraged the choir and the ballet troupe. As much as two thousand guilders came out of camp funds to costume a single ballet. Rehearsals sometimes went on through the evening, and "first nights" were big events, which the German staff attended with enthusiasm. Subsequently any prisoner might go, and so it was that David dragged his reluctant brother to the "cabaret" with its stage fashioned of timbers taken from the Assen synagogue.

"It will do you good," David insisted. Saul was tired. He'd never taken much interest in dancing. Now he even removed his glasses to rest his eyes and was nearly asleep when the chorus line made its entry. So David, who was determined to enjoy the performance, was the first to see her glide from behind the retiring dancers to hover light and ethereal as a moth above the footlights. Initially he refused the evidence of his own eyes. But surely it was her yellow hair, her fair complexion, her blade-like vitality. "For God's sake, Saul, put on your glasses and look!"

Saul focused laboriously, seemed finally to stiffen. "It can't be," he said. But it was: Ruth alive and at Westerbork, when they had assumed she was dead at Gestapo hands.

They waited impatiently for the final curtain to fall, for the outburst of applause and the reprise. Ruth stood there with her head bowed, her hands clasped, unmistakably their irrepressible older sister, looking out through darkly made-up lashes. They did not want to share their reunion with the cast, so they stood outside shivering as the players emerged.

Ruth was among the last to appear. An instant of shock, and then she sprang at her brothers with a cry of joy. David felt her warm and laughing mouth on his. Her hands were on his shoulders, pulling him toward her. She was kissing his eyes. "I love you. I love you . . . my sweet brothers . . ." It was as though a window had been broken open in a sealed room to let the fresh air stir. Finally, half laughing, half sobbing, she broke away, pushed her hair straight with one hand, clasped Saul's hand with the other to make sure he was real. "But you're not supposed to be here. You're supposed to be blowing up trains somewhere."

"You're not supposed to be here, either," David told her.

"Well, here we all are," she admitted more soberly. "Have I changed very much?"

"Not a bit," he replied.

"Oh, of course I have. We all have." She was certainly still full of something he had almost lost: life and enthusiasm. She still had the girlish texture of skin, though her beauty had taken on harder lines.

"To be ugly in this business," she said practically, "is death, and I am still beautiful." She knew her looks were a kind of guarantee, and she kept them fresh with careful disdain.

"You've certainly got the same old laugh," David said.

"Yes?"

"Only mellower. It's good to hear."

"No harm in that. But you two . . . you have changed." She looked searchingly into their faces, though her smile remained. "You're not the boys who went away. It seems like years ago. You're men; eighteen, going on nineteen. So come along. I'll have two escorts tonight. You'll come to my place, have something special."

As an entertainer, Ruth had certain privileges. She came and went inside the camp as she pleased. She had a house all to herself. In other times they would have called it a shed and believed that only a hermit could tolerate such a place, but now the privacy was dazzling. She even had her own alcohol stove on which she proposed to cook them a treat. They refused. Food was too precious. She insisted, and the smell which rose like music from never-never land broke down their resistance.

"Lord," David admitted, "I haven't eaten meat in weeks."

"Months," Saul corrected.

"Delicious, anyway. Rabbit?" David asked.

"I don't ask," Ruth told them. "I think it's cat. Go on, eat. Who cares? It's meat, you idiots."

"You heard about Mother?" David asked.

"Yes, from Uncle Daniel. I wish I could let her die." Her

voice sank to a whisper. "We were always fighting, you know. Whenever I tried to make her take me seriously, she'd ask me something ridiculous. Was I constipated? Was I catching a cold? Still, I know I loved her. I think she loved me at the last."

"She was always talking about you," David lied.

"Is Rachel here, too?"

"No, thank God. She's safe, near Maastricht," David said. "We don't know about Uncle Daniel. There was fighting at the end."

"And Father?"

"In the punishment block, if he's still alive."

"I'll find out," she said. "They need doctors here. Gemmeker takes pride in his hospital." Then she told about herself. It was true she had been turned over to the Gestapo. She'd originally been arrested for stealing a German uniform. In fact, she had stolen dozens, but, regarding this and her other work in the resistance, she had fooled her interrogators as easily as Eve had fooled Adam. If nothing else, she was a handler of men, and her success lay as much in her directness as in her pretty face. Unfortunately, like Eve, she was Jewish, and when this was discovered, she had been sent to Westerbork.

Her one objective now was survival. "We must live through this business one way or the other," she insisted.

"I should think everyone here would feel that way," David replied, but she denied it. Too many Jews had been broken in spirit by the Nazis' contempt for life. Better a quiet death. Had one train leaving Westerbork been sabotaged? Not one, to her knowledge; not even a handful of sand had been thrown into the axle boxes of the cars. About all the Jews had done was reluctantly occupy trains needed by Germany to supply the Russian front. And yet a remnant must be saved, as they always had been. They had survived the Exodus, Babylon, the Spanish Inquisition. These tenacious few, this band of brothers—the fittest would begin again in Palestine.

"You sound like a Zionist," David told her, surprised.

"I learned it from Daniel. If he lives through this war, and I think he will, we'll all meet him there in Palestine."

"But . . ." David could not organize his thoughts to plan beyond the week ahead. He could not think beyond Holland and the way things used to be. If he could work, work hard and avoid next Tuesday's transport, that was enough. Only then would he ponder the next seven days.

So 1943 ended. The year 1944 began with an icy rain and an escape that caused all the prisoners at Westerbork to be mustered out to stand in the dripping cold until the fugitives were found and shot.

January with its frosts and its four transport trains came and went, and not until it was over did David realize his nineteenth birthday had passed as well, unremarked even by himself.

In February the smuggled newspapers that went around the camp were full of invasion speculations and the likelihood that the Nazis would flood much of Holland to stop the Allies. Maps showed that large parts of Amsterdam would crumble away. The weekly transports continued, but were largely filled by new arrivals from smaller camps which the Germans seemed in the process of eliminating. David began to feel like a permanent fixture; less than an ant to those who ran the system, but at least an article of commerce, a tool with inanimate worth. In this regard he was worried about Saul, who had been coughing continually since the night of the rain. No one's health benefited from life at Westerbork. All gradually lost weight except the chosen few, but the dying process varied greatly in its acceleration. As winter's keen frosts and whipping winds gave way to a bland but wet springtime, Saul seemed to pick up. The Allied air raids intensified. Special air-raid announcements were made throughout the day. IJmuiden was flattened in late March by half a million kilos of bombs. At the end of May, Westerbork suffered its only raid; perhaps it was a stricken plane lightening its burden of bombs. Only two inmates were killed, but the SS guards made much of the accidental cruelty of the English. They brought in more dismembered British aircraft than ever as though the wrecking crews wished to revenge themselves upon the bombers.

David and Saul were able to visit Ruth regularly, and even enjoyed a makeshift Passover with her. Though never a religious sort, she had cleaned her shed meticulously for the occasion and somehow put together matzoh, the "bread of affliction," as well as the nut and apple paste that symbolized the mortar used by the Jews when they had labored for Pharaoh. These they ate solemnly in substitution for the official fare, a distillation of pork fat that the camp kitchen humorously called soup.

From time to time, Ruth had news of their father. Abraham was still in the punishment block, serving as a medical assistant.

May brought not only Westerbork's one air raid and weather as uncertain as a baby's bottom, but more intense talk of invasion. Even Queen Wilhelmina, speaking from London over Radio Orange, said, "Soon, when I am back," and the Nazis put up horror posters of desolated cities with the legend "Mama, is this the Second Front that Papa was always talking about?"

June began with a fitful shower that settled into a steady, drumming rain. For a day the earth drank up the moisture, which presently turned the walkways of Westerbork into bogs of churned mud. Black cobwebs of rain hung down on Tuesday, June 6, as the selected ones squelched ankle-deep to the boxcars. Saul and David were already at work in the shop when the news spread like a whisper of wind: "This is the day! D Day! The invasion of Europe has begun!" No one knew where the Allies had landed, but they were coming— British, American, Free French, Poles, even Dutchmen—and the revelation that the battle was joined in France, not Holland, did little to depress spirits in the camp. If the Nazis meant to flood Holland, the weather remained on their side, with rain and high seas. Instead of returning Holland to the sea, however, the Germans fought back, turning the gardens of the Peace Palace in The Hague into a launching site for secret new rocket-bombs capable of reaching London.

July brought the sun and the flies back to Westerbork. Battles raged in France, but the invasion had lost its edge. In the camp, nothing had changed except that now every inmate, in addition to regular duties, was ordered to bring in fifty dead flies a day. This was beyond Saul, who had once wielded a swatter with dexterity, but David managed to make up most of his brother's quota. "My God, that I should become faint with exhaustion from swatting flies," he thought, and knew it was a warning of his own deterioration.

A wave of joy spread throughout Westerbork on July 20. A group of German generals had revolted. Hitler was dead! This surely was the end, and there was a joke about Adolf reaching heaven and putting in a complaint to St. Peter when he saw Jesus there. "What's that Jew doing here without a yellow star?" St. Peter replied, "Leave him be. He's the boss's son."

They were with Ruth on the twenty-first when they found out most of the news was false. Hitler lived. The generals were being shot. The war went on, and yet it was a sign the German colossus was buckling at the knees. Undoubtedly they would be liberated before the year was out.

"What'll you do first?" David asked.

"I'm going straight to Bijenkorf's and get some new clothes," Ruth said.

"Rice table for me," he replied. "All I can eat."

"All I want to do," interjected Saul, "is get back to school. I haven't seen a book in almost a year."

"You'll make the autumn term," Ruth promised, "and if there isn't a restaurant left in Amsterdam, I'll cook the rice table."

They were all dreaming. When the twins returned to Ruth's shed on August 4 she had her usual smile ready for them, but somehow it seemed too practiced, unreal. The night before at the cabaret they had given Verdi's *Requiem*, performing it not so much as a lament but as a defiant hymn to freedom.

"And that was that," Ruth said, turning her fingers into scissors that seemed to cut an invisible thread. "The end. Orchestra, cabaret, all shut down."

"Shut down? What does that mean?" Saul asked.

"It means we're expendable. The entertainers go next week."

"Transported?"

She nodded stiffly.

"We can hide you. Let us try!"

There was a long silence. David noticed tiny beads of sweat on his sister's upper lip. Her temples seemed to have compressed under the strain.

"No, don't be silly," she said. "You'd just be making trouble for yourselves and a lot of others." In the beginning, escapes from Westerbork had been quite common; it was easy enough at night to crawl under the wire. But since 1943 the punishment for escape fell upon a prisoner's barracks mates, who were all immediately transported, a penalty that made each man his brother's keeper. "Not that I have any illusions about where I'm going," she continued, staring at them unswervingly, her face a mask. "But before they make an end of Ruth Ullman, I'll tell you this, I'll take one with me; one damned German to make it almost worth while!" Then her expression abruptly changed, as though something had escaped from behind her furious disguise. Her cheeks were suddenly colored with life. "And if I don't get to Palestine, you will go. Promise me!"

"You really believe, don't you, Ruth?"

"Yes," she said. "There will be a new Israel. Now promise!"

It was the least they could do, although it seemed an impossible dream just then. "Good," she said, laughing, so that David felt his heart would break. Her laughter was as haunting as a recollection of lost love. "So here's to us all in Palestine, eating rice table." She toasted them in white wine, wine with a German label. They held their cups high in the candle glow. "To all of us in Palestine!" When they departed, she kissed them both. In the heat of summer, her lips felt cold.

To David she whispered, "Love your brother a little less, and help him a little more." Then she walked quickly away. There was nothing more they could do for her, but if the situation were reversed, would she simply let her brothers climb on the train without trying to intervene? David thought not.

"Perhaps she's being pessimistic," Saul rationalized. "Perhaps they won't be shipped after all."

Monday night brought the inevitable train, Tuesday the predictable marshaling of prisoners.

"I don't see her," Saul insisted. "She isn't being taken after all. I was right!"

But Ruth was there, gallantly smiling. David pointed her out. She was dressed in her best, made up as though about to go on the stage, and her head was high. She was even swaying her hips with that old careless touch of amoral sensuality that brought tears to his eyes. They couldn't break people like that. Not even death could defeat that kind of spirit, any more than flames had extinguished Joan of Arc. Not that he intended to compare his sister to that visionary. Ruth was a realist, but they could not put out her flickering dream of liberty any more than Joan's vision had been consumed by the fire that took her body.

Six days passed, six days in which Saul brooded, doing little work. David tried to cover for him—at least the season of flies was past—but it should have been no surprise on Monday when Saul's name was on the transport list. The factory staff was being cut back, and only good workers would remain.

"I'm going with you," David said.

"Don't be a fool! Another few weeks and the transports are bound to stop."

"No, Saul. We're not going to be separated."

Saul began to cry helplessly. He made no further protest.

Never before had David felt so keenly the intensity of their relationship. As long as they clung to one another, they would survive. It was as though he had received a mystic sign.

To avoid a transport was beyond the ability of all but a few; to join one voluntarily was easily done. David simply offered to exchange identity papers with a worker who had been called. "What's your game?" asked the man in suspicious disbelief. He did not question long. The exchange was made and the man vanished immediately with his reprieve lest the madman come to his senses. David examined his new identity. "Joshua." That was his new name. Joshua, a machinist, age twenty-one. So he'd even aged a bit. No matter. Westerbork put years upon them all.

He slept hard that night without dreaming, and then it was 5 a.m. The much-discussed, long-dreaded event was upon them: transportation, beyond which David's imagination had not carried him. The OD guards were out in force. Green Police lounged on the train itself, a buffer between the SS and riot or revolt, which was always expected but which never came.

As their names were called, the twins walked out into the whuff-whuff of the engine's weary steam. Only one engine was left to do the work of two. People were climbing aboard. All was going methodically and the only surprise was seeing Abraham in the line ahead of them. Even David did not recognize their father at first. His head had been shaved, and where hair had grown back, it was no longer black but gray. He dragged one leg as though the nerves in it had died.

A guard shouted as the twins moved to catch up, but as they joined the procession again, they were not recalled. "Father!" David shouted. "Father! Abraham!" At last he had the other's attention, and for a moment David thought, "This isn't my father at all. It's a stranger."

The boxcar loomed ahead of them, a dark and devouring mouth into which humanity streamed as if into a refuge. David glimpsed the blue sky, the gray barracks, the watchers standing where he had watched, the commandant on the platform, a man of steel, yet affable, graciously chatting with his aides. Then they were aboard, confronted by rough splintered walls like driftwood, straw, a bucket of sand, a vat of water, and the agents of Lippmann, Rosenthal and Company still trying to wring the last valuables out of lost souls.

Behind them the crowd kept coming.

"My God," Saul said, "they wouldn't pack cattle like this unless they were going to the slaughterhouse."

Sixty Jews to a car. Standing room only. David found a place for his father against the wall. He feared Abraham could not stand for long, for there was the shadow of death upon him. He shivered.

"Life is seven times cursed and seven times sealed," muttered Abraham.

"Father, can I get you water?" David offered, but Abraham's words were not an attempt to communicate with his sons. He was wrestling with God. With enormous eyes, black as night, he stared at David and through him. No maniac could look that way; only an angel, or a saint glimpsing the universe for the first time and finding it empty.

Saul and David stood close to him, protecting their father from the crowd, and yet in a way he wasn't there at all. Abraham Ullman had ceased to exist.

"We've got to stay close, you and me," David said to Saul. "Anyone alone hasn't a chance."

The doors slammed shut. A bolt was shot into place, but the train did not move. On the roof the August sun beat down. The prisoners panted like animals, and to David it seemed they must breathe through the eye of a needle. The pinholes of ventilation were like distant stars. Not until 11 a.m. did the whistle blow. The single engine leaped in its traces as if trying to snap the cars in two. They were pulling out. Another seven days had begun in Westerbork, but the Ullmans were leaving Holland, bound for that dread and undiscovered country.

NINE

AUSCHWITZ
Summer and Autumn, 1944

For two days and nights of dark and moaning misery the train moved in fits and starts. Filth piled up among bodies cast down in seemingly lifeless heaps. David was no longer sure whether he was alive and the others dead, or he was dead and the rest alive. Curled up near the wall, he had given up hope of food or water, but he had more help than some: a crack in the wood that gave him air. He breathed through his teeth to keep his nostrils closed. The stench in the car was like the reek of a slaughterhouse.

From the diminishing temperature, he guessed it was early evening of the third day. The train had stopped. The Green Police seemed to be leaving their posts. German SS were taking their places: the Death Corps, as they called themselves. Then the train moved on slowly through the darkness to stand unopened through the night. They had arrived somewhere. Through his crack, David made out winking lights and the red glare of fires. Toward dawn, voices could be heard outside the cars. A few of the prisoners banged at the door and were answered by the rip and tear of machine gun bullets. Silence again except for the cries of the wounded. Then came the throwing back of bolts and shouts of "Last stop! Everybody off! *Aussteigen! Aussteigen!*"

And so the survivors poured over the bodies of the dead and dying. The old, the very young, some crushed and puffed beyond recognition, lay entwined there in the blush of

dawn like an entanglement of great pale slugs. Of the sixty-
odd who had entered the car, fewer than half emerged under
their own power. Abraham clung to David. He walked un-
certainly, as though his feet were curved, a baby trying its
first steps. With Saul on one side, David on the other, he
emerged into the light.

The following hours would be chiseled on David's brain as
permanently as the legend on a tombstone, and yet it all
seemed unreal. He lived apart from his body, observing his
own conduct and that of others with disbelieving side
glances. He even thought of himself in the third person. His
impressions were a figment of that stranger's imagination: the
cheerful little station; the chestnut trees; heaps of bricks,
beams, and lumber; the SS officers with their shiny boots and
briefcases, their cordial smiles and vibrant whips.

"The committee of deception," Saul said.

"*Raus! Raus! Raus!*" The guards barked as though trained
by the violent black dogs they held leashed at their sides.
Some, in Dutch, demanded jewelry; others, lacking verbal
communication, cut out the prisoners' pockets.

As the cars emptied, they were entered by a labor gang,
the Kommando from "Canada," as it was called, who hauled
out the dead and dying and salvaged anything they could.
There was very little this time, for this load had not come
fresh and hopeful from a ghetto.

"*Judinnen, amtreten!* Jewesses, line up to the left!" commanded an SS woman in a wide skirt, her hair tied back in
the usual "Nordic" knot. "It is an hour's march to the wom-
en's camp. For children and the sick, Red Cross trucks are
waiting at the end of the platform."

On the right-hand side of the platform, David joined a line
of men waiting with deathlike indifference. In this atmo-

sphere of doom there seemed an intangible quality about each one that said: this one will live, this other has already come to terms with death.

Cursing, raining blows because the job they did was foul, the clean-up crews were tossing out the contents of the cars— dehumanized humanity, so many broken breathless dolls to be sent jostling down the platform in carts to be loaded into dump trucks. Some, like statues, gripped one another and had to be pried apart with crowbars. Others, barely alive, were thrown aboard with the dead, while Red Cross ambulances claimed those who could still move.

"Father," David said, "remember to tell them you're a doctor," but he could not be sure his father was listening. Abraham seemed to be staring ahead at a black column of smoke that rose from a tall factory chimney; black oily clouds that stung the eyes.

"A pillar of smoke by day and fire by night," Abraham said, and David remembered the glow he had seen the night before. "Dante would blush to see this place. He'd realize that the devil had given up in disgust and left the management of hell to man."

Under a low sky the smoke was flattening out, spreading to smother the daybreak.

"Men to the left, women to the right! Hurry!" The shouted commands continued monotonously. But another, softer voice came from one of the "Canada" work details who was loading a cart with the contents of burst and abandoned haversacks. "Stand straight, look healthy, but don't look the doctor in the eye. Eyes down, or he'll turn you to stone." Then, catching the resemblance between David and Saul, "Hey, you two. If you're twins, don't admit it. The doctor would love to do an autopsy on you. He enjoys dissecting twins.

He'll have your brains in formaldehyde if you admit it."
Then, as an SS guard approached, "Move on. I don't know
you."

Up ahead, the column was again being divided, left and
right. The breaking point was a slim figure in black, Head
Surgeon Fritz Mengele, his emotionless face as reassuring as a
voodoo mask. Glancing at each prisoner, he studied him
briefly through a monocle. Then, in indifferent execution, he
moved his baton left or right with the good-natured grace of a
dancing master. David would come to know him as "the
beautiful devil," and he sensed an imminent crisis. Whether
or not the whispered warning was true he did not know, but
somehow he felt sure this man held above them all a power of
life or death, and David could not yet imagine, even here, an
end to that faint throbbing which told him he was alive.

Saul was the first to stand before Mengele. David kept his
face averted, but the doctor must have been alert for twins.
Through an interpreter, he called Saul forward.

"Twins, yes?"

David denied it.

"Have you proof?"

By inadvertence rather than design, both still had their
identity papers from Westerbork. Fortunately David was
now in possession of a false set. Skeptically the doctor tapped
each with his baton. "To the right."

Abraham was next. He walked alone, but each slow step
seemed to demand a separate resolve.

"Tell him you're a doctor!" David called back. Even here
doctors might be sacred, but when Abraham opened his
mouth, only a prayer came forth. "Hear, O Israel, the Lord
our God, the Lord is one."

The baton moved him to the left and as the lines spread

apart, David had a last glimpse of his father. His tall thin figure was hunched like a lake bird's and he was feeling for something he had lost in the pockets of his trousers. The crowd, pressing from behind, moved him along. The prisoners' detail hurried them all into waiting vans.

"Perhaps they'll be taken to the hospital," Saul said. It seemed logical. The van was marked with a red cross. Inside it, people had begun singing the Dutch national anthem.

David and Saul, with those few who had been directed to the right, walked to their destination, a camp marked out by high cement watchtowers and a double row of electrified barbed-wire fences that hummed in the wind. They passed through a heavy wooden gate marked with the German words *"Arbeit Macht Frei."*

"What's that?" David asked.

"It means 'Work sets you free.' "

Once inside, they were prodded toward a registration center by an orchestra in white suits with red caps and piping.

"None of this is real. I'm going to wake up and find I'm still fourteen years old and living in Amsterdam," David told himself.

Their first stop was before a short, very white prisoner whose bristly hair was cut close to his head. He looked as if he had lived forever under a stone. Taking David's left hand, he placed it palm upward on the table. Then, marking a number in a ledger, he began to duplicate it with a tattoo needle on David's wrist.

"Hold still!" he commanded, when David flinched at the sudden pain. "Consider yourself lucky to have a number. No name any more, but that's better than taking the heavenly express." David did not understand. "You know, the cremo—up in smoke. Most everyone goes that way these days."

These were only hints. David asked for—wanted—no explanation. His heart, his spirit were hiding, not daring to put feelings into words. It did not even occur to him to question the absence of emotion.

Next was the barber. Here they lost almost all that remained of their human identity, for they were told to strip, retaining only their shoes and belts. Saul hid his glasses in one shoe, though they had been warned that the hiding of valuables was a fatal crime. Naked, they waited in line as the barbers hacked away at heads, armpits, crotches, with dull razors; all these poor pale bodies deprived of every dignity. For some reason, David remembered his grandmother saying, "But you've got no clothes on. Come here to me." It was the only time both he and Saul had been spanked, for swimming naked in the canal. What would his grandmother, who could barely confront a fig-leafed statue in a museum, think of this?

Streaming blood from various cuts, they were prodded toward a steam bath. On the way an SS guard spread each passing mouth with his fingers to make sure they were not hiding treasure there. He did not shake out Saul's shoes. From the steam they passed under an ice-cold shower and then were issued tattered prisoners' clothing, faded stripes that had been worn, stained, washed, and passed on innumerable times before.

Registration finished, they joined the nameless herd in the camp called Auschwitz. From the outside, the barracks were not unlike Westerbork. Inside, they contained nine hundred prisoners each, twelve to each bare wooden bunk. A high brick channel down the center was attached to an oven at either end. This was for winter and was not now in operation.

The barracks' leader had a weather-grooved face and bleak eyes. The serial number on his wrist was low. He had learned how to survive, and in the process had been rewarded with good leather boots and civilian clothes, and permission to let his hair grow. Now he made a few remarks, each one prefaced by a soft, sibilant sound, on how they, too, might avoid perishing immediately. "S-s-s you are the lucky ones. S-s-s even as I speak to you, your comrades are wafting up to heaven to form a cloud for God to walk upon." David struggled to shut his father out of his mind, and concentrated on the lisp. It was not an affectation, he observed, but the result of several missing front teeth. The gums were black. Burned with a red-hot iron? "S-s-s if I make jokes, if I speak to you newcomers in fables, it is because reality is not to be looked at directly. S-s-s suffice it to say that this is a death camp. Here you will die slowly of illness, hard work, punishment, and hunger, if lice and dysentery don't get you first. S-s-s expect the worst. S-s-s leave every hope behind. Live without hope. S-s-s forget the names of your fellow prisoners. S-s-s here there are no sons or brothers. To stay alive, attract no attention. Forget escape. S-s-s no one escapes. Forget revolt. Keep your bodies clean and remember to eat. S-s-s some have come here exchanging prayer candles for food. Prayers did not save them. S-s-s if you want to die quickly, don't eat. If you want to live, eat, no matter how revolting. S-s-s if food in any form repels you, you will perish. S-s-s now you may rest. Tomorrow there will be work."

David's first reaction was a kind of relief. They had finally sunk to the depths of wretchedness. It would not get worse, or so he imagined.

After nearly four days without food, they lined up for supper and received a meager portion from a caldron of black flour soup. The first day at Auschwitz was over. Night was nearly as bright as day, for searchlights played up and down the barbed wire and the low clouds were blood-red from the incessant fires fed by human fuel, if what he was told could be believed. His own father? He put no hope in Saul's suggestion that he had been taken to the hospital. Exhausted sleep brought little relief from the day, for the same horhors plagued him. He awoke, shivering, to hear a neighbor shrieking in the grip of a nightmare, and one nightmare seemed to trigger off another until the barracks rang like an argument among debauched parrots.

Reveille sounded at 5 a.m. Rubber truncheons routed out any who hesitated and set them all on a mad scramble that preceded the day of work. The latrine had long since been christened "the temple of reflection," though only the privileged were permitted time to pause there before trotting back for the endless inspection. Each day the inmates were meticulously lined up and counted, dead or alive, as though they were a miser's hoard of precious stones. Even those who had died in the night had to be laid out in rows for easy counting, while the living, trying to avoid attention, would struggle to find a place deep in the breathing ranks.

Then the workday began. Because of their experience at Westerbork, David and Saul were assigned to the ersatz petrol factory near the subsidiary Blechhammer camp. It was considered rare good fortune, particularly with winter not many months away, to work inside at an essential task. There was no doubt that fuel would become increasingly vital, for bombers were destroying the oil fields in the east.

Certainly they could have done far worse. There was the Scheisskommando, latrine duty, reserved, it was said, for intellectuals, but of merit at least in the fact that their smell was so bad the SS gave them a wide berth.

The SS were as remote as usual. "Tigers," Saul called them, but worse than tigers because they savored the torment of their victims. He was convinced that they were all criminal sadists who would kill a Jew simply for looking at them. Most, in fact, were not sadistic, merely Waffen SS stolidly doing a vile job with total indifference, comforted by the miles that still separated them from Russian bullets.

As at Westerbork, prisoners actually managed the camp. Over each labor command was a kapo, or prisoner foreman, who drove his charges to the factories, the latrines, and the road-building projects. In some cases reminiscent of the torment of Sisyphus, men were set at rolling stones to a hilltop only to roll them again to the bottom. These were senseless, spirit-breaking tasks; failure meant instant punishment with clubs or a mangling attack by unleashed SS dogs, and when bodies were sustained day after day on thin broth, such failures were common.

Food was the key to life or death, the one preoccupation. After a day or two of discussing the outside world, with its hopes and fears, David found himself falling in with the others. To talk of home and family made for unbearable nostalgia, but food was always on everyone's mind. "If Venus came in on a platter," Saul said once, "I'd just ask for a knife and fork." Soup came three times a day in great caldrons, and prisoners along the way deliberately jostled the carriers of these huge pots so some soup would spill. Then they would lick it up with their tongues. There was a mint infusion in the morning, turnip or harsh-smelling nettle soup for lunch. In the evening, ersatz bread was added to the menu, and on rare occasions thin porridge or even two ounces of horsemeat. Never enough to keep a man alive and working. David and Saul were quick to learn this. One needed comrades, not friends but fellow sufferers, to get more than a fair share. One had to have influence if one's bowl was to be more than half-full. One had to have experience to guess where to stand in a food line, for nettle and cabbage soup floated nourishment to the top of the caldron, while potato or turnip would settle to the bottom.

"Organizing food"—that was the magic phrase. It took up all their spare time, and it was a euphemism for bribing or stealing. They lacked gold teeth for barter. The Nazis had seen to that. There were no family diamonds smuggled in via the stomach or concealed in a toothpaste tube. Only theft remained, and everyone stole without remorse. "Forget about morality," David had said. "There is morality just between you and me, Saul. We share, but with no one else." And so any crumb, any food set down even in delirium, instantly vanished.

On the strength of a bowl of mint broth plus whatever else they might "organize," the twins joined a gang of factory workers each morning. Propelled along by a detail of SS guards, they were played out of camp in swing time by the same white-suited, red-capped orchestra. David had heard rumors of a cabaret as well, which the SS were said to patronize. He had hopes that Ruth had found her way there, but the camp was vast compared to Westerbork. Men and women were segregated, and there seemed no way at the moment of finding out. What observations David made were on his treks to and from the petrol factory. There was one cardinal rule while in the presence of SS guards or vindictive kapos: "Don't see anything," and this applied particularly to the mistreatment of other prisoners. Witnesses too often became victims, so the habit was to avert eyes and walk faster, but along their return route was one spot where it was relatively safe to look around. This was a cleared field near the subsidiary camp called Birkenau. Here non-Jewish prisoners played football in the early evening, their scrawny legs pumping up and down like the needles of sewing machines. You would have thought their lives depended on winning. Perhaps they did. In any event, the guards had developed a habit of taking a break at this point, and, while they watched the game, David could not avoid discoveries. They were near the rail line. Trains, both passenger and freight, often passed through at full speed. Signs on the trains suggested that the camp was between Krakow and Vienna. Other trains took a branch line, stopped, and unloaded. These passengers were said to be Hungarian Jews, laden with baggage, expecting resettlement, but bound directly for the gas chambers. This was a rumor David dared not confirm, but with his own eyes he saw the prisoners herded from the platform without any pretense of medical selection, watched them pass, colorful patches of color, behind the trees that bordered the playing field. Sometimes he heard the cries of women calling on their men to save them. The players kept after the ball while the SS urged the travelers on. The boxcars would pull out, making room for the next shipment. With the darkness, the only trace of what had passed would be the red and yellow billows of flame from the crematoriums that looked as if they would ignite the black sky itself. Always the foul heavy cloud hung overhead, and eyes were pink and watering because of it. There were occasional references to "going up the chimney" or to the "cremo." Even a camp song made a joke of it, but there was no real talk. Only in dreams did the reality of their situation take hold of David. Then he saw corpses wreathed in fire, giving off dense choking fumes, saw faces that he knew—his grandparents, his father and mother, friends, even himself, with hair and eyes aflame, melting like wax candles in the heat.

One day, while they loitered beside the soccer field, a procession of arriving Hungarian Jews broke spontaneously into "Ani Maamin"—"I believe"— so poignantly gallant that the players seemed to miss their shots. The incident opened the lips of a fellow prisoner with whom David had formerly passed no more than grunting salutations. This prisoner knew all about it, or said he did, having the truth first-hand from a physician who had served within the forbidden compound as a doctor to the Sonderkommando, a detail of some eight hundred husky Jews who lived there in isolation amid a nightmarish luxury until their own time ran out. Most of these new arrivals, he said, were entirely ignorant of their fate. They were marched by the SS into a great shower room where poison gas dispensed from a truck marked with a red cross could take three thousand lives in fifteen minutes. It was the Sonderkommando that dealt with the dead, hosed down their excrement and blood, pried them from one another, salvaged hair and gold fillings—as much as twenty pounds of gold on a good day. The human remains were moved finally to one of sixty ovens contained in the four crematoriums. The Sonderkommando worked round the clock with each shift taking its reward from the dead. The food and much of the clothing brought for resettlement fell to members of the Kommando. So these doomed men ate off silk brocade from silver settings and drank fine wine every night for four months until their own time ran out and a fresh Sonderkommando was chosen.

"That's the way it goes," the prisoner said, "if you can believe it. Only now there's such a rush, they're burning bodies in open pits as well, trying to finish the job before the Russians get here."

"Are the Russians that close?" asked David, feeling a glimmer of hope.

"No, but they say the Germans can't hold out another winter against them. Our only chance is that there are enough Hungarians to keep them busy until then."

Later, when David tried to relate all this to Saul, he wouldn't listen. "It's just propaganda to keep us terrified," he maintained, but David had no doubt that what he had heard was true. The only part he could not understand was why the members of the Sonderkommando all went to their deaths so meekly. They were healthy, well-fed men. They knew what was in store for them. What could they lose by fighting back at the end? Did the monstrousness of the lives they led destroy all sensitivities? After four months in such a charnel house, perhaps they had more ties with death than with the life they had known before.

Superficially, the life that David and Saul led should have been a relatively safe one. At the factory, where they had expected to deal with petrol products, they in fact loaded powder increments for 88-mm. shells. There was always the risk of explosion, but otherwise the tasks were not exacting. It was the malnutrition of the prisoners that made the work killing. Cement and rock carriers often fell on the job from sheer exhaustion, which could mean a shot in the back, or, if the guards were in a more gladiatorial mood, the unleashing of a pack of dogs. In any event, the results were fatal. But death always came back to the lack of food. Hunger and its consequences made the prisoners more susceptible to lice and disease. Poor food encouraged spirit-destroying dysentery, typhus, boils, and cysts. And when the spirit failed, that was the end. One joined the damned, the silent living dead known as Musselmen. These wandering shadows were despised and rejected by all, the more so because it was a fate to which all felt susceptible. No food was wasted on them, and no pity. They were dead already.

"We must fight off that kind of inertia," David said. "As long as we keep talking and eating and looking after each other, it can't happen to us." They did not talk very much, but more than most; yet there existed a terrible need for one another, a state that seemed near telepathy. If Saul was hurt, David seemed to feel the pain. If one died, both would surely die. For the most part, they had staved off such premonitions. They had survived all the selections. They had remained useful commodities. Selections had been infrequent inside the camp. The Hungarians had kept the furnaces busy, but every so often the cry went out at night, *"Blocksperre! Blocksperre!"* Then fear rose in David's gorge. Wounds were quickly dressed, rouge rubbed into pallid cheeks, chests thrown out, for the call meant the prisoners would be lined up for inspection. Those who had passed beyond usefulness, like the Musselmen, would be hauled off to the gas chambers. David had seen these grim processions of ghosts in nightshirts. One had sung "The Marseillaise," but more often they went silently, without even the will to slip away or fight or take death into their own hands on the electrified barbed wire.

This was the dread that now touched them only indirectly, but it was the fate that waited for all Jews if the camp survived much longer. It was an impersonal thing that left much to their own capacities for staying alive.

A more immediate and personal threat to the brothers was the kapo in charge of the factory detail. A Dutch national and a political prisoner, he had reached the camp as a result of unsuccessfully harboring Jews. During the war itself, he had met bomb fragments head on, which had severed nerves and muscles in his left cheek; now his expressions were difficult to decipher. He looked happier when he wasn't smiling, and when he was smiling, he was usually tormenting his charges. Saul called him a tinpot Mussolini, and the dislike was spontaneous and mutual. He would smile at Saul with his tongue laid along his lower lip and say, "You back again? Why haven't they sent you up the chimney, eh?"

Kapos ran the gamut from humane to savage. Some were real leaders, working their gangs but preserving them, becoming buffers between prisoners and the mechanism of destruction. Most were kapos simply because they wished to survive. Suffering seldom ennobles the character. Often it drives men toward brutality, and a few of the kapos had made the entire journey. They tormented their victims with savage joy, forbidding those with dysentery access to the latrines, and plying the whip with sensual pleasure. A more common attitude was one of complete callousness to suffering as long as their own status gave them warmer clothes, better food, more leisure. They accepted the fact that some prisoners must die and they protected their favorites so that in every barracks there was a comparatively well-fed elite who struggled day by day for the energy to stay alive. Then there were those who had given up the fight, the Musselmen, fodder for the next selection.

Fortunately for Saul and David, their barracks kapo was tolerant of them and their bowls were filled nearer to the rim than those of other newcomers. At the factory, however, it was different. There the kapo was sadistic, and Saul had become his personal Judas goat.

When Saul would ask, "Jewish prisoner number 732618 most respectfully prays to be permitted to go to the latrine," the kapo might reply, "What are you smiling for, boy, with your peanut-sized bladder?" and he would take Saul's glasses and try them on. "My God, the world's upside down." Usually Saul's request was denied. "What I ought to do is whip you, boy. It would do us both good. Wouldn't it, boy?" And a few of the others would laugh their toadyish laughter, relieved that he had turned his hostility elsewhere. It was odd how this treatment upset Saul; he detested being dealt with as a foolish child. He told David he would rather be beaten like a man, and toward the end of September that finally happened. Saul had fallen asleep at his post, his head nodding forward just as the kapo made his rounds. David was too late to save the situation. The kapo saw what he long had wanted, and his rubbery cheeks were vibrant with fury. With an open palm, he struck Saul twice in the face. Saul's glasses flew off; blood trickled from his nose. "I'd have you shot if bullets didn't cost three pfennigs apiece. You're not worth it." Saul said nothing. His eyes looked naked, unseeing. Before David could retrieve the glasses, the kapo found them with his heel, coming down hard, grinding his boot back and forth. Then he walked off. David salvaged the remains and returned them to his brother, who said nothing. Instead, he sat down on a box and began to cry. The twisted empty frames slipped from his hand.

All the way back to the barracks that evening, David tried to explain that it didn't matter, that there wasn't anything Saul could not do as before. It wasn't as though they'd been allowed books. You didn't need glasses to stuff bags with gunpowder or stand in line at a latrine or soup kettle.

"I'm right, am I not, Saul? It doesn't really matter."

He received a tight jerk of his brother's head in assent. Later Saul tried to explain his feelings. "It was bad enough before. Now I don't even feel I'm here. It's not that I feel I'm somewhere else, just not where I am. It's as though I'm no place in the world. I'm afraid, David."

"But you are here," David insisted. "We both are. We're both alive and we'll see this business through. We'll go back to Holland some day, and find Ruth and Father and Rachel. We'll eat good food together, as we did in the old days."

"I wish that were true," Saul replied. Without glasses, his eyes were slow to focus.

"It is; believe it. You know how things are going. The Allies are in Holland. I heard that yesterday in the latrine. Maastricht has been liberated. Rachel must be free already. And the British are in Arnhem. They say soon we'll be hearing the Russian guns." But all this was talk of the outside world, which Saul could scarcely imagine. Suddenly, with his glasses gone, his gaze had turned inward.

"Time for supper," David reminded him.

"I don't think I'm hungry," Saul replied.

"Come on. We both eat or neither one eats, and I'm starving." David hauled his brother to his feet.

This was the evening of October 4, 1944. The following morning, their detail was called for inspection but not sent out to work. There was nothing to do but rest and thrash over rumors. Perhaps the Russians were too close and the equipment was being withdrawn. Heavy explosions suggested they were under air attack. They heard rifle fire. A battle in progress? By nightfall all was quiet, and the diverse rumors had collected themselves into a single theme. The 12th Sonderkommando, facing extinction, had revolted, armed with explosives smuggled in the false bottoms of soup kettles. They had destroyed at least one crematorium and killed seventy SS soldiers before they themselves had been shot down to a man.

"One day a monument will be built to them," David said.

But Saul seemed less impressed. "What on earth for? All they did was die."

"Like heroes, Saul."

This was by no means all there was to the story. A prologue was perhaps more important than the main event. With the coming of autumn, the harvest of Hungarian Jews had stopped. To feed the furnaces, more and more inmates were being selected from the camp, and it was alleged that one of them, a young Dutch woman, had inspired the revolt. She'd been a dancer, one of the prisoners in the women's section, Frauen Konzentrations Lager, and she had not been selected because she was useless but because her courage was a threat to the blue-eyed, whip-snapping terror of the women's camp, Irma Grese. They were nearly look-alikes, both small and blond, and tough in their own way. No one seemed to know the Dutchwoman's name, but she was a wonder. As the tale was pieced together, David could picture the white cement building in the birchwood all aglow with autumn colors. The gray-faced victims, bodies wasted, heads shaved, naked, without a trace of dignity permitted them, waited outside the doors they knew led to death. They accepted death not so much because they had no choice as because it seemed the only way out, the only rest. Then the Dutch girl, standing straight in the coppery sunshine, moving with grace, became an automatic focus for all eyes, especially those of the SS officer in charge. It required a certain tact to encourage people to strip and go voluntarily to their death, though for him they had become less than mice or beetles in their thousands, incapable of stirring even a cheap sensation. Now here was this rare exception.

He smiled at the Dutch girl as he might smile at a domestic pet. He'd heard of this one. He lifted his hand, waiting patiently until all were silent. Without occasional diversion, how could anyone endure such a business? What could he tell his family after the war about the gap in his life if there were no human incidents? He must have bowed to her in mock politeness, but surely he did not go so far as to kiss her hand, a Jewish hand. "Madam, would you be so good as to dance for us?" And what would she have replied? "You wish a swan song, kind sir?" No, she would have been silent. If it was Ruth, as David felt sure it was, she would simply have stared, hard-eyed, her gaze a weapon in itself, and then slowly she would have begun to sway as though following a very personal ideal. She must have become her old self again as she danced, no longer an automaton doomed to die, but the old and fearless fighter, her nakedness, the very incongruity of the moment, giving her a balance and style she had lacked in the old days. She must have pirouetted there, eyes shining, her whole face glowing, the cold autumn sun seeming to shine through her as she danced for her executioner, so fine in this last refrain that he glanced at the ground, pinching his cigarette between slim fingers, spitting out a bit of leaf as she whirled closer, arms extended, seeming to float on the air. Then her strong hands had darted out as sure as eagles' talons to seize his pistol, and, in an instant of unbelief, they had pumped nine bullets into his astonished body, so fast they made a single roar.

And then they had killed her. Well, not quite. David heard at the factory an extended version. Before they cut her down, she ran. Of course, they wanted an example, a public execution, but she had run toward the wire, through the beech trees, an uncertain target in the pale light and shadow. They had fired first at her legs, not wanting to permit an instant death, and she had fallen. Perhaps she had felt no pain, only a shattering of attention, but as they ran to pin her down, she had crawled the last few yards to grasp the electrified fence. This might be called a death in the tradition of Kiddush Hashem, a martyr's death in the name of God. She had taken her life in her own hands at the end. She had shown others how to die, this marvelous Dutch girl whom they could not defeat, let alone destroy.

Even her death did not quite end the story that had been talked about for days until the revolt of the Sonderkommando overshadowed it. The SS officer, despite the number of bullets in his body, had not died immediately. He had lain on the ground directing the execution of the other prisoners. Only when the chamber doors had been sealed behind them had he uttered his expiring words: "My God, what have I done to suffer such agony?" Another version saw him alive all the way to the hospital, taken there in the Red Cross truck that had delivered the pellets of Cyclon B gas to the chamber. There, in a state of delirium, he had died, reciting from Rilke's *Madness:* "It's only a queen who dares to dance, yes, dance in a city street." Farfetched? Nothing seemed farfetched at Auschwitz, much less the possibility that this story involved Ruth. Ruth! She passed lightly, dancing across David's memory as he had seen her on a North Sea beach, a feather on the wind.

Saul would not speculate upon such things. Ruth had long ago ceased to exist for him. She had less substance than his dreams, in which he wore a black uniform. "I was one of them, all black with silver piping."

"How horrible," David replied. But not as horrible as his own dreams, which seemed always to involve people in flames.

"I'll tell you the most horrible part," Saul admitted. He closed his eyes wearily, as if the light burned them. He appeared for a minute to be dead. "In the dream, I didn't mind being one of them. I was overjoyed. I knew I wouldn't be hungry or cold any more. I knew I would never die."

The leaves had already fallen in that autumn of 1944 when, because of the rapid Russian advance, the munitions factory was dismantled and withdrawn. Those workers who survived selection were given other jobs, and David and Saul were assigned to one of the thirty-five vast warehouses called Canada. Here the private possessions of the dead were sorted, salvaged, repaired if need be, and packed for shipment. Every day a train left for Germany full of clothes, false teeth, artificial limbs, gold, shoes, and bags of hair packed in potato sacks to be used for U-boat calking and felt footwear. It was their job to sort out the pins and combs from tresses, bangs, and braids hastily shorn on the way to the gas chamber. Apart from what food they could "organize" in the warehouse, a fatal offense if caught, they were fed less than ever, so they worked slowly and fretfully, overcome with fatigue. Only when a guard appeared, or Camp Commandant Hoess with his gold bracelets and smart uniform, did they work with a will, slackening off again as soon as he passed by.

"We'll never pack it all," Saul lamented. "We'll drown in

this hair," and it seemed to rise above them like the billows in a stormy sea. "Look at my arms, David. Are they thinner today?"

"No. More muscular," David assured him, knowing all along that Saul was in trouble. For no special reason, he now seemed to tire quicker, cry more easily. "Nothing really matters," he would say, as much to himself as to David. He seemed to accept the justice of his lot as God's punishment for the age-old sins of the race. He paid little heed to David any more, but squandered his strength on useless SS orders such as washing his shoes inside and out, which only hastened their deterioration. He put shoe cleaning before eating, looked on idly as the grease hardened in his bowl, while David clung to the old rules. If a fellow prisoner died in the night, he was fair game for a search, and if under his body was a bit of bread, you fought for it. If you saw a frog in a ditch, you ate it alive if need be, in your soup if possible. What he found, he shared with Saul, forcing him to get it down.

"If you don't eat, you'll die," he warned.

"Then let me do it in peace."

"Saul, if you die in peace, then I can't live in peace."

What kept them going was a friendly kapo at the warehouse who slipped them tins of food when he dared and called them "Jew pigs" when the Nazis were around. One day he warned David that Dr. Mengele was searching the camp again for twins, a search that always ended in a fatal phenol injection to the heart, followed by dissection.

David panicked. His false papers would not protect them forever. He even considered hiding Saul under bales of hair. If they tried to escape, they'd be strung up with a sign around their necks, "Hurrah, I'm back home again." Ten barracks mates would be starved to death in reprisal. He was desperate until some Greek prisoners arrived in camp suffering from scabies, and this provided a new bent for the doctor's researches. By this time David had other problems. At last the warehouse kapo made him admit what he for so long had been denying to himself.

"Brothers like you two aren't found every day," the kapo began, "but, David, you can't keep this up. Saul's dragging you down, too. Look at him. He's sleepwalking in broad daylight. I mean, you can touch him, but he's not there. He's one of them. Death would be a judgment of mercy."

David denied it. "Saul's fine! He gets discouraged sometimes, but he's not one of them."

But Saul was, or would be soon, a Musselman. There were the infallible signs of withdrawal, the failure to wash, the withered, ancient look where everything seemed to melt away except the eyes, which rode wide open on his cheekbones. Saul's were nearly blind, and they seemed to overflow his face.

Left to himself, as the kapo advised, Saul would certainly vanish in the next selection, a proceeding that occurred more relentlessly as the eastern front collapsed. But David redoubled his efforts. He stole food for his brother, hand-fed him, stuffing his clothing with scraps of paper for a robust effect when the selections took place, even bodily kept Saul on his feet as Dr. Hauschild passed. "Are you shivering?" the physician asked David, who had no newspaper to insulate himself from the cold. "We can warm you up very quickly." But it was only a threat. Once again death passed over, but now David was beginning to wonder if it was worth such effort to go on enduring lice and cold and gnawing hunger. An hour of dull terror for those who were marched away, and then he found himself envying their repose. What else did any of them have to lose, really, except pain? Death itself had long ago lost the element of revulsion. So many were dead now it seemed indecent to go on breathing. But still something in him clung to life. If he died, then he would lose that last satisfaction of seeing the downfall of the Nazis.

Every hour it drew nearer. Rumors arrived daily, which ran the gamut. All prisoners would immediately be released because the guards were needed at the front. All prisoners were to be killed for the same reason. But they could not kill everyone in a single night. They would not have enough bullets left to fight the Russians, whose guns some prisoners swore they heard when the wind was from the east. If nothing else, the Germans seemed intent on destroying all evidence of their crimes, and the burning of bodies had long ago overflowed from the crematoriums into pits and from pits into smoldering heaps. Then, one day in early November, David awoke and knew without opening his eyes that something had changed. His eyes did not burn with the usual irritation. On the way to work, he realized that the great chimneys no longer belched forth smoke. That night a noncommissioned SS officer, who had been block leader for a short time, lurched into the barracks with a bottle in his hand. "We're all of us in the same sinking boat now, Comrades!" And he passed the bottle around. It made no difference that the next morning he was replaced. The fires at Auschwitz were out, the selections over. The Germans had quite literally run out of gas. David laughed out loud, a thing until now inconceivable in this house of death. He seemed to see the walls stripped away and all those disbelieving skeletons in their triple-decker bunks beginning to prance with the news.

"We've made it, Saul!" he shouted, throwing his arms

around his unresponsive brother. "I told you we'd make it if we stuck together!"

Saul just stared. David left him sitting on his bunk and went outside to look at the smokeless chimneys stark against the sky. It was a clear autumn evening. Forty miles away he could see the mountains, already crowned by winter snow. The camp was in shadow but the sky blazed, a biblical sunset free of man's contamination, red and gold. Other prisoners, clutching their soup bowls, came out to stand in wonder. Puddles of watery filth echoed back the glory until David had to exclaim, "How beautiful it all is!" He remembered his grandfather speaking these words as he stood on a high dune above the sea for which he yearned.

From beyond the horizon came faint thunder. Thunder in autumn? Bombs, then; a factory or a town being destroyed; but before morning he knew it was more than that. It was the opening barrage of the Russian offensive.

TEN

WINTER, 1945
Death March

As the autumn of 1944 became winter, fear of final extermination hung over the camp. Those who could walk, it was reported, would be evacuated back to factories in Germany. The SS needed them, counted on them as a gentleman counts on a cuspidor, for without prisoners the guards would be out of a job and would be sent to the front. This and the dwindling supervision were all that guaranteed that some Jews would live. The loosening discipline made it possible to "organize" more food through the warehouse, and though corpses continued to pile up, stiff as logs, outside the barracks, David and Saul were eating well. The newspapers David had organized to stuff their trousers were good insulation against the cold. He made vests out of empty cement bags with a supplement of warehouse hair to pad them. So they were better prepared to face the winter than most of the 64,000 survivors in Auschwitz when news came that the eastern front had collapsed before the Russian forces, and evacuation of all those fit to walk began. They left under SS guard. In the column, adding a note of bizarre unreality, were one hundred Hungarian dwarfs, saved by an SS sense of humor from the gas chambers. They were not built for walking, and most would perish along the roadside.

Left behind were the fences, the watch towers, the chimneys. There were still the guards and their dogs flanking the

204.

slow column, and there was the bitter Carpathian wind, a polar wind sweeping ceaselessly over the Auschwitz plain as though to tear the soul from the body. The prisoners walked hunched over, heads bent, to protect themselves. A few tried to escape into the bleak fields or patches of forest, but most of these were run down by the dogs. A man concealed himself and his wife in a shed beside the road, and a whole pack was unleashed upon them.

In a rolling leaden sky, there was no sun. Faces were gray, mouths hung open. Tendons protruded with the effort of movement as the captives dragged themselves westward. All track of time was lost. January became February and still they staggered on like an invasion of great gray worms.

Forcing them occasionally from the road were soldiers moving toward the front. They shouted at the SS guards, "You filthy swine! *Judenhelden!* Cowards!" The soldiers' only hope of returning home to Germany alive would be a severe wound.

Behind the cold wind came snow, and the ragged figures with purple hands and faces stumbled through thickening flakes. Gradually the tidy column was falling apart, with the old and the sick shifting to the rear. They did not cry out when they fell behind, for there was a wagon there to pick them up, a wagon that every so often turned aside. There would be a volley of shots, and then the wagon would catch up again until it finally threw a wheel. Subsequently, prisoners were shot where they fell and left to the crows that shrieked above the line of retreat. Many sought a quick death, calling on the guards to end it all and obligingly bending their heads for the *coup de grâce*. The alternative was to be stripped alive of clothing and left for the cold to do its work. Among the starving survivors there was macabre talk at night about how to nourish their failing bodies by any means whatever. Could human brains be digested if eaten raw?

Saul's overwashed shoes were in ruins. His legs dragged along the frozen road like sandbags. David kept an arm around him, though his own feet felt as if they were shod with lead. "One more step," he told Saul, "just one more step." There was no pain. He had passed beyond suffering, and now with detached curiosity he contemplated how much his anesthetized muscles would endure. In this state he was not even aware of losing touch with Saul until he heard his brother's cry.

"I can't walk any more, David. Help me!"

"Where are you?"

"I can't see you!"

It was dusk, and again the snow was falling.

"Here I am, Saul. Come on, now. On your feet!"

"David, I can't go any farther."

"Of course you can. There's nothing wrong with you," David lied. He had to lie. Saul was sick. Probably typhus. It was necessary to lie. To Saul's former self, he would not have considered doing so. "Now, left, right, left, right. That's it, we're marching. Left . . ." Together they stumbled forward. Saul's cough had a cathedral boom. "We're doing fine. Left, right . . ."

"I'm cold," Saul repeated, his eyes dull as stone. "I'm so cold."

Yet winter had dulled its sharpest teeth. The snow that fell was heavy and wet, telling of spring to come. At a bombed-out factory near a gutted town beside the railroad line they stopped. Though the factory was a dreary shell, having choked up its insides, it was a shelter from the wind. David dragged Saul to a corner, where he shivered like a wet kitten. The roar of the wind surrounded them, muffling human noise with an odd effect of deep silence.

Saul had reached the end of his strength. David slapped his cheeks to keep him warm and awake, and Saul turned blind eyes upon him. "You aren't cold, are you?" David said, astonished. His hand on his brother's brow told him that a torch flickered inside. Saul was on fire, with very little fuel for burning. Was it typhus, then? David couldn't be sure. Suddenly Saul began to shake. "Hold me! Hold me!" he gasped, and David closed his arms around his brother. Nothing but newspaper and bone. "Where am I? What am I doing here? Who are you?" He struggled to rise and then in his delirium began to shout, *"Sieg Heil!"* He moved on to a chorus of the "Horst Wessel Song" in shameless imitation of the SS squads who had shouted it out around camp. David could not keep him quiet, and the result was an SS guard standing over them. He pushed David aside and hauled Saul's trembling body to its feet. They sang together.

"So," said the German, "you want to join the SS?"

"Jawohl," agreed the dreamer's voice.

"You think you are suitable material?" The guard was having fun.

"Jawohl."

To David this arrogant figure was all Nazis: the one who had buried his father and sent him to the left, not the right; the one who had thrown a grenade into a Dutch canal; the one who had ordered a naked girl to dance. "I ought to kill him," he told himself, "I ought to bring the edge of my hand down on the back of his neck," but it was all he could do to remain erect.

Then the guard shoved Saul to the ground. "Come to your

senses, Jew!" and he slapped Saul's head forward and back. "No food for this one!" he called. "He's finished." The guard stalked off.

"Saul, listen to me. I'll get you food." And Saul, from deep inside his dream, murmured, "*Jawohl*" with every breath. He was smiling. He had joined the master race.

When a kettle of potato soup appeared, David lined up with both their bowls. There was plenty to go around. Many of the prisoners were beyond eating; others, with dysentery, cried only for water. David drank his own portion beside the warm kettle. It was an unsatisfying brew, so thin it would pass down a drain without so much as a gurgle. He started back with Saul's bowl full. Fearing that it might spill, he skimmed off some around the rim. Too much would undoubtedly make Saul ill. He drank a little more, then, driven on by unabated hunger, he finished it to the dregs. Guilt-ridden, he ran back only to find the kettle had been taken away.

All that he had left to offer his brother was melted snow, which he held to Saul's lips. It ran uselessly down his chin. So David pulled a thin, filthy blanket which smelled of pus and excrement over them both. Saul's skin had a dull pewter sheen and his enormous eyes seemed to fill his entire face. David remembered that the light of a star shines long after the star is dead. There was almost nothing left of his brother, though in his ruined chest the heartbeats were visible. Under the blanket, David found Saul's skeletal hand and wondered how it could be so hot.

Presently David slept, and the torments of the day, hunger, cold, exhaustion, the harassment by SS guards, turned into a formless nightmare of fierce violence. Tremendous guards howled orders at him in a language he could not understand, and in his sleep he flayed back at them. It was only a dream, but when he woke in the first watery light of dawn, both arms ached. He was confused at first about where he lay, then focused on the high, shattered ceiling through which occasional flakes of snow still fell. "Saul," he said aloud, finding that he had dragged the entire blanket about himself. Saul lay there, a shred of blanket around his ankles, as though torn from a winding sheet. The pale cage of his ribs showed through his ragged clothes like old ivory. "Saul?" The eyelids were not quite shut, and through narrow slits Saul seemed to peer accusingly.

In despair, David tried to chant the Kaddish, but the words eluded him. He wanted to scream until blood came from his lungs, but he had no strength. A monster seemed to take hold of him: guilt, rage, helplessness, all together. How dare Saul die and desert him after all he'd done? Then he remembered he'd stolen his brother's food and warmth. "Forgive me, Saul." There was a kind of envy, too, for in Saul all pain and fear had ceased, but David clung to life and to life's last freedom, the ability to choose one's attitude even when conditions are beyond alteration. There was relief in the thought that he had only himself to consider now. He could even elect to die without feeling he was letting another down, but for the moment he wanted only to cling to his blanket. Let the SS finish him with a shot behind the ear if they felt like it. Another kettle of food was brought. Again David drank for two, and by morning a desire to live had rekindled itself. Before the call came to fall in, he had stripped the shirt and trousers from Saul's wasted body and wore them over his own clothes.

"Fall in! Fall in! *Schnell! Schnell!*" Slowly the survivors gathered themselves. Those who could not rise were left behind, and this time no bullets were wasted upon them. A freight train was waiting at the siding. It was not the usual transport, but a conglomerate of box-, tank, and open coal cars. The coal cars were occupied first, then the boxcars. David was among the last to board. Without delay the train headed west under clearing skies. Through a hole that looked as though it had been punched by a partisan's bullet, David could see blue sky and thin, bruised clouds that let down blades of blinding light. For three days and nights the train proceeded haltingly. Once it was strafed in a siding. No food was provided, but under guard the prisoners were allowed to collect snow, which still lay in patches under the trees. David struggled down to quench his thirst, but few descended from the coal cars; they were freezing to death there in the open. On the third day the coal-car survivors were shoved into the covered cars. Many were frostbitten and beyond help. One of these, thrown down beside David, confided, "I no longer want to be alive. My friends are all dead," and by dusk he had expired with an uneaten crust of bread in his pocket. This David consumed, and it lay like broken razor blades in his contracted stomach. Certainly they would all die presently, except perhaps for a remnant of the sort who always defy probability, the sort, thought David, who sometimes emerge from the flaming ruins of a crashed airplane.

The train sat motionless in a siding for the better part of a morning. SS guards patrolled outside, and David watched them through the hole in the blotched and blood-stained wall with unfocused eyes. He knew that he had long since lost the strength to escape. Then something odd caught his attention. Beneath his gray greatcoat, one guard wore civilian trousers. Did he mean to desert? Take "independent action," as it was sometimes called? Late afternoon found the train in the same place, the guards still patrolling, but on the road beyond, men in field-gray uniforms were passing. Many lacked weapons or packs. They were accompanied by a nondescript parade of battered vehicles—horse-drawn carts, motorcycles, a fire truck, even a hearse, all packed with German soldiers, faces gray, beards stubbled, eyes red from weariness and gunpowder. It was the German army in retreat. Not until the sun lowered and David saw that the shadows advanced ahead of the stumbling, marching men did he realize they were coming from the west. Not from the east, from Auschwitz and the Russian advance, but from the west.

Daybreak brought the whistling of a shell overhead. He could hear it rip the air and then explode not far away. Schrapnel hissed in the air and clattered on the roof of the tank car. A rumor spread that the train's engine had been destroyed; it was a lump of torn iron and muttering steam. Their journey would end here. Outside, a German panzer had pulled up under the trees beside the road. The tank's turret slowly rotated until it seemed about to fire on the railroad car. Then the muzzle lifted for a farther target. Other tanks appeared among the trees. Fire was returned. The first tank shuddered, smoke poured from its vents, and the crew suddenly emerged from the turret, hurling themselves out with fantastic gestures and attitudes like clowns performing from a high-diving board. Their clothes were aflame. Machine-gun fire broke out, and the dancing men assumed absurd new postures on the ground. One crawled toward the shelter of the tank car. Features frozen, lips pouting like a blowfish, he vanished in the very star of an explosion. David felt the heat of it as long, jagged tentacles of smoke were flung out. Another, closer explosion rocked the car. Soon the woods were exploding. Fire glowed from the heart of one tank after another and their human contents writhed away, leaving red

smears in the slush. With the scream of an airplane passing
low overhead, the far end of the railroad car caved in.
Splinters filled the air and David, caught by the blast, was
hurled against the side of the car.

How long he was unconscious, David never knew. He
awoke to broad daylight, silence, and a head that felt as if it
were packed with cracked ice. A few figures slumped in the
shadows. One prisoner actually had the strength to leave the
car. He did not return, and there was no message from the
outside world until David became aware of a distant clank
and rumble that could only be more tanks. From the hole in
the car he finally saw them, like prehistoric lizards browsing
through the forest. They came lumbering toward him. On
the top of each sat a soldier with binoculars, like a statue on a
wedding cake. On the turrets were big white stars. Confused, he looked for the letters JUDE, thinking that because of
the stars, somehow they must be Jewish.

The tanks passed on. There was silence again. David could
almost hear the faint pulse beating in his wrist. Outside,
through the confined horizon of his bullet hole, he saw that
the flow of soldiers and refugees had stopped. There were
only the discards of war, the dead, the demolished. It was a
world of phantoms. The last trace of civilization had vanished. Degradation begun by a triumphant Germany seemed
now concluded by a Germany brought down. David dozed
fitfully. What might have been hours later, he was aroused by
the approach of a Red Cross truck. "*Sonderwagen!*" someone
muttered, recalling the death trucks at Auschwitz. They
dared not hail it.

Again he was gripped by a drugged euphoria, only to be
awakened by inhuman shouts and screams, men howling like
dogs and cats. Not until later would he learn how near they

were to a prisoner-of-war camp. The prisoners, released un-supervised, had come out to scavenge the train. They had no use for the dead and dying, but, in their search for food, they had discovered a tank car full of alcohol. When the valve would not turn, one of the prisoners had attacked the shell with a fire ax. Hats, shoes, mess tins were filled to overflow-ing. In the excitement, the warning voices of a few who could read German went unheard. It was wood alcohol, poison, but no one had listened. A horde of emaciated clowns in striped rags performed a dance of agony, then squirmed blindly on the ground.

Dusk brought to David a final awakening. He regarded it at first as only an unwelcome intrusion on the solitude of his dying. There were strangers in the car, big men in clumsy clothes who looked immune to disease and death. They probed with distaste through the piles of what they only remotely recognized as human beings. One, with a boxer's nose and a heavy stubbled chin, glanced at David.

"War stinks," his voice drawled in English.

"They won't bite you, man. They're all dead in here. Let's go."

David tried to call out, but his tongue was no longer moist and flat. It was dry and round. His lips seemed fixed by glue, and the sound he made had the harsh inhuman tenor of a par-rot learning to talk. "I'm alive . . . I'm alive." Not that he regarded himself within reach of human help. He awaited only the expunging of that final spark to share the fate of his comrades. Apparently he wasn't to be allowed to perish quietly among them. Rolled onto a stretcher, he was carried over the red slush where men had fought, through a camp gate ringed around with barbed wire, but the bunk they gave him belonged to no one else, and the blankets smelled of disinfectant and soap. Still, he would die. The walls of the room moved in and out, seeming to breathe, and he felt death coming toward him, no vengeful skeleton with a scythe but a starved rat to gnaw away the last threads.

Big, well-fed men with full faces came and stared and went away. Another, in white, attached a needle to his arm and he watched the drip-drip-drip from a bottle hung beyond his reach. He drowsed and woke and watched the bottle and drowsed again. The walls had stopped their breathing before they tried him on weak tea and soft bread and margarine. It flowed through his frame like fine oil, lubricating his joints and forcing him down into sound sleep.

After that he was like a small child, thinking only of nourishment. Had he been allowed, he would have eaten until he was sick. Nothing had ever tasted better than the contents of those khaki-colored waxy cartons full of veal loaf, Spam, and concentrated chocolate.

David still expected to die, though he could not really grasp what it meant. He would wake in the morning and imagine himself already dead. He would examine his own corpse, but what he could not understand was seeing it with his own eyes. His stomach said eat, live. His mind made no judgment whether this was a new day or simply the wreckage of yesterday. His conscience said, "Poor Saul. May God forgive the evil I have done him." He had been chosen his brother's keeper and he had been found wanting.

The barracks' ward contained other patients, a few of them former prisoners of war; typhus victims for the most part. The majority were survivors from Auschwitz, but there was no one within range of David's bunk who spoke Dutch or English. His only communication was with the Americans, and that was uncertain, for they lacked the British accent to which he was accustomed. One day an officer came in to address them all: "I'm from Tennessee." He made the place sound as if it were made of tin. They listened respectfully. America was talking with the help of an interpreter who stood with a pen behind his ear and appraised them up and down with a parade-ground stare.

The American officer spoke in slow, measured tones, his hands clasped behind his back. Disrupted by pauses, translations, and throat noises, the gist of his speech seemed to be that he did not mean to talk long, "ha ha," but that they ought to be acquainted with the situation. For the moment the camp was in American hands. It might at any time fall under Russian jurisdiction. Meanwhile, the Americans meant to use the German personnel who'd been left behind for menial tasks such as latrine and grave digging. There had been threats against these new prisoners and it had to stop. "The war's over, boys. It's up to us now to mete out justice." He chewed slowly on a stick of gum, rolled it with his tongue. "Justice, that's what we all fought for. Like somebody said, this isn't a day of triumph. It's a day of dedication." Once the translations were done, the patients applauded.

That afternoon brought a rumor that one of the SS guards had been trapped in a shower room. Those who were ambulatory responded. Among them was David, who, with a rest midway, was the last to arrive. The German was a fat reservist. They'd caught him in the shower, all lobstery pink, singing, *"Ach, du lieber Augustine."* Now, like a clumsy tortoise, he was trying to pull on his clothes, but the prisoners wouldn't allow it. They turned on the hot water full blast. Nothing but pure steam.

David was shaking. The mood was contagious. Murder ran in his veins; he felt his whole wasted body unsheathed like a talon.

The former guard was pleading for mercy, for his family's sake, for God's sake. "Forgive, forgive!" though no one could have understood him had his words been spun out above his head like a comic-strip balloon.

He was a great pink trembler of a man, slippery with soap. His appendectomy scar blushed rose red.

"Take my watch! Anything!"

They had cornered him, circled their prey without haste. For an instant David felt shame as he looked at the red, tear-stained face, but he could not feel the slightest stirring of compassion. Upon this naked stranger he was willing to heap the vengeance of his whole race, from Adam down.

The patients circled closer, jaws sagging, crooked bodies hunched, eyes glowing while their victim shook with terror. "I am a grandfather," he implored. From his pockets he pulled family pictures, a watch, his wallet, and held them out. The scalding steam billowed at his back.

"For the love of God!" he howled.

"Yes, yes!" Those who understood screamed back, in thin sea-gull voices. "For the love of God!"

None of the patients was in good condition. Not one could have done the thing alone, but combined they had a tiger's fury. As one they crowded around, forcing him back with lengths of stove wood until he stood under the shower's full blast, screaming from lips and cheeks puffed out round as a wind cherub's. The last shriek rose pure and irrevocable as the steam beat him down, no longer a human noise but like that of some engine which has jammed its gears. Then he was lost in steam and the cry that came from him was like a sailor's cry, "Ahoy, ahoy." Finally even that stopped and there was only the sound of the steam turning him into a lump of scalded flesh.

David felt nausea overcome him, and he sat down heavily against the wall. The German's watch lay on the floor beside his hand. Absently he picked it up. There was also a steam-shrouded fragment of a mirror, which he cleaned on his shirt. For the first time in months David saw his own face. Hollow cheeks, black holes for eyes, cracked lips. He looked like a corpse gazing back from beyond the grave. "Oh, my God," he said. If he hadn't been so tired, he would have gone to the latrine and put his finger down his throat, but it was all he could do to return to his bunk on legs so unsteady it seemed a wonder they clung to his body.

Outside, a gusty wet wind was stirring, heavy with the odor of thawing soil. After the long silence of winter snow came the music of water falling.

There was no reprisal for the murder of the SS guard. Of course the Americans knew, but the report read "accidental death." Nor was there ultimately any satisfaction in it for David. He could strangle a thousand Nazis and not bring back one member of his family. Roosevelt was dead. Hitler was dead. The wild cherry trees bloomed outside the camp. Where German mines were still planted, buttercups turned the fields into gold. Spring glowed about him. It was life and renewal, but David felt no part of it.

Every day his body revived. The flesh showed signs of filling out, scabs and sores began to dry and flake away. But why get well when inside he was still dying? What a waste of good health. Stretched on his bunk, his arms behind his head, David did not smoke or complain or chew gum. He lay there, alone, looking at the ceiling. The first spring flies gathered. He tried to recall a summer place by the sea, but the stains and smears on the ceiling took on shape and meaning, and he would begin to sweat with terror at the force of his imagination.

Sleep was the next best thing to death. He slept much of the time, and his dreams were haunted with the voices of the dead. Repeatedly he dreamed he was sleeping on top of other human beings laid out in tidy rows. Not a single row, but one row piled upon another until those below were flattened, pressed cardboard thin, and this was as bad as losing himself in the patterns on the ceiling.

Of course, he could not say for sure which of his family were dead, which alive. Perhaps even Saul had only been asleep. Then David would lapse into the void of being dead. Nothing mattered. Saul had said it first. Nothing mattered at all. This strange, quiet acceptance of death was new to him.

Abruptly one day there came a change in the camp. David had often heard of the Russian Bolsheviks who had machine-gunned the royal family in their nightclothes. Now the arrival of the Russians was for him like a hurricane at sea, glimpsed from many fathoms down. He was aware but almost untouched as the Americans withdrew to the official lines of occupation. Their jeeps and trucks pulled out. Then the Russian tanks and wagons rolled in, with their soldiers roaring out some deep and serious song as they came.

The Russians brought none of the bland processed food the convalescents were accustomed to. With them came great steaming vats of fat boiled ham. Not a voice among the Jewish survivors was raised in religious protest. They were beyond that. All gorged upon the rich fare and many were ill. In the excitement a woman inmate, Polish and afraid of Russians, gave birth. David had seen her before, so wasted that the child had hung before her like a gourd. Now she was carried to a cot, only two removed from him, where she screamed openly and rolled wild terrified eyes. After a last shriek there was silence, and then David glimpsed the new-born, dark of face and howling. Did children never come laughing into the world? A boy child, it glistened like a skinned rabbit. He could not crowd around with the others and grin at the mother, who lay like a dry and empty husk, and yet she smiled. She had only given birth to inevitable death, and still she smiled as though life were the winner.

As long as his life had been in hazard, David had clung to it. Now that his body was saved, there seemed no point to his being alive while all the others were dead. The meaning of life and the belief in God had died for him at Auschwitz and in the snows of Prussia. If God were not dead, He had turned into a vulture or become disgusted with his creations and moved away to some other galaxy where life was a darting flame.

With the first real warmth of summer, David was drawn outside. He paced the wire, read the multilingual signs warning of the mine field beyond. They were now all classified as DP's, displaced persons, but they were virtually prisoners until the Russians could move forward the slow machinery of exchange. David's only comfort was lying in the sun. It was the one thing that warmed him, and he had come to loathe the barracks. He would roll up his trousers and sleeves so that his thin limbs could absorb the heat. He would watch the clouds change. The cracks in the soles of his feet were beginning to close. Despite his overwhelming disillusion, his body said yes to life and health; but the more his body took hold, the more his heart seemed to wither inside him, communing with the dead. His hands now were his father's hands, white, long-fingered, and delicate, hanging from his sleeves: a surgeon's hands. If he had only somehow pulled his father to the right, but he had abandoned Abraham, as he had deserted Saul. To be alive was a continuing betrayal; never could he bury them deep enough to forget. While he lived, he was death's deserter, and now it seemed too late even to die decently. He was not alive enough to kill himself, but the past continued to beckon while the future seemed an empty cul-de-sac.

As the days passed, David knew only one thing: whether he was to live or to die, he would not do it here among strangers. His legs had begun to stir in his sleep like a dreaming dog's. They were growing stronger. He yearned for solitude. To live or to die? Whatever the answer, it must be made alone. There was a way of resolving everything. Let the decision be providential or pure chance, he must soon discover whether he was to go as a messenger to the living or to the dead. And as May passed into June this resolve grew and became fixed until there came a morning with dawn not yet in the sky. He awoke in darkness and knew the time had arrived. Silently he brought his feet down on the floor. Waves of tingling ran up and down his calves. No one stirred as he crossed the floor and went out. The stars were fading. He was not worried about the guards, who relied upon regular doles of food, the wire, and the mine field beyond to contain the DP's. David knew a place where the wire was rusted through. No light beamed his way as he followed the wire around. He caught his sleeve as he passed through the opening. Then he was over the ditch with its blackish water, and running through the wide field of posted mines. Behind him someone was shouting. A shot echoed away. He ran hard, knowing full well that every footfall might be the last. His lungs sobbed for breath, but he would not fling himself down for fear he could not rise. Traces of dawn showed him the burned-out skeletons of tanks, like petrified relics of the paleolithic age. His joints burned as though filled with hot sand. The remains of his shoes, stiff as wood, opened old wounds. He threw them aside and followed a path through woods down to a marshy patch of tall sharp grass. He inhaled the smell of the cool grass and he could taste it, along with a strange metallic flavor. Perhaps he had been hit! No, it was only from the unaccustomed running.

The sun was up. David found himself now in a cultivated field. His eyes had misted over from the effort, and the flowers of the field seemed to fly around him. I'm going to faint, he thought. I can't go any farther. As he sank to his knees, he realized the flowers were yellow butterflies. He was alive in a field full of butterflies. Life had chosen him. Death had refused. He began to cry. As he lay at full length, breathing hard, he heard old familiar sounds that reminded him of home. The trilling voice of a skylark, many skylarks, spinning over the fields. Far off, cows were lowing. Somewhere a dog barked. He smelled the rich dark earth and it was good. Then he lost consciousness.

ELEVEN

SUMMER, 1945
The Trek to Holland

David swam through warm and empty darkness into bright light. He moved his arms and groaned, then opened his eyes upon billowing summer clouds. He did not know how long he had been there. On his wrist was the dead German's watch. It had stopped, but the sun seemed to have moved toward the west. He was rested and at last he was alone, in a field on a summer day. He felt a lifting of his spirits. He stood up, pale and ragged, not a young man so much as a scarecrow shingled in rags. All around him were green trees, glowing yellow fields. "The world is still good," he thought, and yet somehow it seemed beyond his reach. He wanted to touch and savor it, but inside he felt as though the wires connecting sensation and will had been severed. None of it, nothing outside the barbed wire, was real. He would not have been surprised to see elves dancing in the grass or a lion emerge from the trees, so it was without the slightest alarm that he observed the approach of a figure through the tall grass. Nearly as threadbare as himself, she came like a banner flying from a beleaguered fortress, battered but still holding out and somehow joyous, with the wind whipping her tatters. As she drew near, he noticed the triangular patch of a political prisoner on her jacket. Her head hadn't been shaved, but she'd known starvation. She was a tall, spare girl with narrow ascetic features, neither beautiful nor entirely plain. He thought of medieval paintings of minstrels.

222.

"Who are you?" he asked in Dutch.

At this, tears welled from her eyes and she threw her arms around him. Normally David avoided touching strangers. Never had he held a girl in his arms before, but now he was embracing a total stranger. Though he felt no surge of electricity, it perplexed him all the same. She drew back and gazed at him. He could see streaks of gold in her irises, like pebbles he had once picked up on a beach. Her mouth smiled a little, but without changing the eyes at all.

"I come from Holland, too," she said. "What's your name?"

He told her. "And yours, miss? Your name, I mean."

"Hannah," she told him, "Hannah Cronk. I'm from Amsterdam."

The bones beneath her cheeks must be as delicate as those of sea gulls.

"Did you run away from camp, too?" he asked.

"What camp? No, I've been trying to get home for ages. I was near Vienna when the war ended. I'm not really sure where this place is. What day is it?"

"Day? July, I think. I've lived so long away from weeks and months. You're all alone?"

"I had a friend. He was killed back there." She pointed beyond the trees.

"By Germans?"

"No."

"Russians?"

"No, no. By accident. Come on, I'll show you." There was no reason for him to view another corpse, but he had no reason to refuse, so he followed her as she ran, a pale butterfly fluttering ahead of him. She moved well. She must have been athletic once. Now she was as thin as a reed. She led him through the woods to an abandoned dairy. All the cheese was gone, but there was a row of shining vats with ladders to ascend to the rims. Beneath one stood an overloaded baby carriage stuffed with odd bits of clothing and food: sausage, bread, jam, a pound can of lard, and all of it surmounted by a homemade Dutch flag.

"He's in there," she said sadly.

"In the carriage?"

"No. He drowned in the vat. It's full of buttermilk."

David measured the ladder, closed his eyes to see where the strength was to come from, and then ascended, rung over rung. Looking down, he saw a round white moonlike surface of pale liquid in which a figure floated face down.

Life must be nourished, and he picked up a bucket, but she told him, "No, not from that one. I can't drink from that one." So he had to climb three more vats, all empty, and finally the fifth and last, before finding any milk. By this time his head was swimming and he had only enough strength to fill the containers half full. It was more than enough. He offered her the prize and she drank deeply. The milk left a white mustache on her upper lip.

"Now you need a shave, like me," he said.

"You don't look so bad," she said. "When your hair grows out, I think you'll look very nice."

They took turns sipping from the bucket.

"Any more and I'll be sick," David admitted finally.

"I wonder," she asked, "would you know which way I ought to walk from here?"

"Which way? Well, I suppose it depends on where you want to go."

"Home, to Amsterdam, of course. I thought you would be going there, too."

"Honestly," David admitted, "I hadn't thought." He explained about the mine field.

"You were going to kill yourself? That's horrible."

"Yes. No. I mean, it didn't really matter."

"All right." She looked at him a bit foxily from beneath a crown of soft hair. "Pretend you're dead and come with me."

"Amsterdam's my home," he said, "but no one's there. I was at Auschwitz. I'm the only one of us left." He could scarcely attribute his survival to a guardian angel; no angel would take an entire family, leaving only one. "Of course I'll go, if I can keep up."

"Oh, you're undoubtedly faster . . ."

"Than I look?"

"I wasn't going to say that," Hannah said. "For all I know, I may have no one there, either. When they took me away—you see, I was with the underground, in a small way—I had my father and my brother there." She talked rapidly now, letting it all flow as the last barrier dissolved between them.

"Your mother was killed?"

"Not exactly. We call her the dear departed."

"She died naturally?"

"No. Just departed. Before the war. Ran off to God knows where."

He couldn't help but laugh for the first time he could remember. "You're funny," he said. "Let's go to Amsterdam."

The first thing to do, of course, was to find and cross into either the American or the British occupation zone. That meant heading west. David could be no more definite than that, and by now the sun was setting. "That way," he pointed. "In the morning. It's too late to start now."

Dawn blazed like a forest fire in the east as David and Hannah prepared to start out. For a moment they lingered. The dairy took on shape and color. The last stars vanished in the west.

"One gets so callous," she said. "I hate it."

David knew she was thinking of the body in the buttermilk vat; just leaving it there. "Was he a good friend?"

"He was Dutch," she said. "I didn't know him that well, really. He must have risked his life a dozen times in the war, and now this . . . We ought to put up a plaque or something. 'Here floats . . .' " She was trying to joke. It was her way of warding off pain, but he saw the tears in her eyes. "It just doesn't make sense."

"None of it does." He put an arm around her. He was thinking of the millions of gassed and cremated Jews. "Thank God it doesn't."

A paved road passed the dairy, and they took it. David pushed the baby carriage at first. There were trees along both sides of the road, a meandering stream, and fields of grain. The road descended, then rose toward a hill crowned by a castle. Farm workers were already out, gray-haired women and children for the most part.

The road itself was not empty. Civilians pushed baby carriages or wheelbarrows full of firewood, rarely more than twigs, taken from the forest. There were former prisoners of war, forced laborers, the riffraff of chaos moving in what they hoped was a homeward direction. Most bore meager loads and foraged for food by day; others, particularly a large group of French soldiers still in faded uniforms, staggered under bundles of organized loot. They had broken into a wine cellar and were singing, tilting up slender green bottles to their lips. The Russians paid no attention. They guarded the important bridges but intercepted only those who tried to escape from their zone of occupation, an obstacle that David and Hannah would have to face sooner or later.

By midday they arrived at a small town, where the baby carriage passed with difficulty over the cobbled streets. They stopped to rest and eat in the square dominated by a statue of Bismarck, the Iron Chancellor who had been the first to propose solving Germany's problems with blood and iron. The pigeons seemed to lack respect for the old warlord, for his shoulders were white with spectacular dandruff. Around the square itself, shops were shuttered for fear of looters. White flags still hung from the windows, as well as red ones in honor of the Russians—red, but still showing the circle where swastikas had been removed. The Gothic-style town hall had been broken into, and David and Hannah entered to see what might be organized. The place had been thoroughly rifled; broken pencils, strewn papers, a trampled portrait of Hitler in armor. The only thing of value was a map of Germany, too small in scale to show where they were, but they found Erfurt. They had seen signs pointing south to that city and east to Weimar. The barrier, then, that they would have to surmount lay perhaps fifty kilometers farther on, the Weser River west of Mühlhausen, where the northeast corner of the American zone touched the area of Russian occupation.

On the way out of town they were driven into a ditch by a flock of liberated bicycles inadequately controlled by Russian POW's. They seemed to believe that inanimate machinery had a will of its own and might be intimidated with shouts, like a nervous horse.

No liberated prisoners hesitated to forage, no defeated Germans dared refuse them. They might lock their doors, hide in their cellars, but, once confronted, they were obliging lest they be reported as former Nazis. David and Hannah's first stop was at a small farm back from the road where a woman of about fifty with gray strands in her dark-brown hair worked the shrieking wheel of a well. She looked at them with brooding eyes. Her mouth was sullen and sad. David, who had learned some German in camp, had no confidence in his ability to communicate. Hannah, who knew no German at all, believed she could, and did, essentially by pronouncing Dutch with a German accent. The result was a barn for the night. Dry litter squeaked in alarm as they tiptoed in. Later the farmer appeared. They were startled by what looked like a gun in his hand. It was only a hammer, and he grinned at them from a smooth, wind-carved face. His front teeth had rotted away.

"Willkommen," he said, gracious as a Bethlehem innkeeper with only a stable to let. They would be hungry, yes? Apples? He pulled a handful of withered apples from a barrel. They still tasted good. David had forgotten that apples existed. There was also cheese and salty bacon, which the farmer evidently supposed they would eat raw, and in the end they did.

"A month ago I couldn't have kept half of that down," David said.

Hannah looked at him with heavy, drugged eyes. "I'm not sure I can now," and he had to help her outside, where she retched miserably. They were both exhausted. After long drafts of cool, metallic-flavored water from a mossy stone well, they crept back into the barn, where David fell asleep as though he had taken a potion. He didn't stir until nearly noon, when Hannah shook him gently.

Their hosts were out in the fields. They waved goodbye, and that was that. David would never know whether they were simple people with compassion for derelicts or former Nazis trying to appease a guilty conscience.

Fifteen kilometers was all they were able to cover that afternoon. The foothills of the Thüringer Wald lay to the west and south, and the slopes were steep. Downhill the baby carriage tried to run ahead. The weather was sultry. Beneath a hazy sky the countryside rolled away. Woods, meads, hamlets, and, far in the distance, the thread of a river with lush green banks, snaking to the horizon. The Weser?

The road led down toward the river, over which thunderheads built up so clear and brilliant they seemed unrelated to the earth. The early-evening sun touched them with gold. It made David think of the sunset at Auschwitz and he shuddered involuntarily. As though plugged into his mind, Hannah said, "It reminds me of Dresden when the raid came. Those great clouds of smoke. You, too? Or something worse?"

How could he explain? Words would only leave her understanding less after he had tried. "You don't need to look at me like that," he said.

"How was I looking at you?"

"You were pitying me."

"I don't pity you, Mijnheer Ullman."

"You're a liar. I can see it in your face."

Neither wanted to quarrel. Perhaps it was only the tension of the approaching storm, which rose as though heaven were preparing for an assumption. Flies buzzed in swarming, biting galaxies and a bulge of thunder formed along the western horizon. The darkness swallowed the sun and yellow tongues of lightning licked the hilltops. David thought he felt a raindrop, though it was only a bead of sweat sliding down his cheek. The smell of rain accentuated the odors of pine trees and turned earth.

In the Russian zone, evening meant curfew, and the on-coming storm, which had already brought darkness, was added incentive for quickly finding shelter. A gaunt pariah dog slipped through an imposing wrought-iron gateway; there must be a house beyond the stand of trees. They fol-lowed, passing on the left a cherub fountain so mossy green they could hardly distinguish it from the surrounding trees. Its right arm was raised and oozing water. Lightning tore through the air. Path, trees, fountain, flickered pale yellow, as did the flinty gray stone façade of a large house beyond. The light continued to glimmer and flash like an old movie film as they approached. In a zinc tub set out beside the front door reposed the body of a middle-aged man, clothed and drenched, not with water, but with honey. Had he been drowned in honey? The color of his eyes was lost in staring white, and his tongue lolled from his mouth as though fixed forever in licking the sweet adhesive from his face.

Hannah covered her eyes, though it was only a fatal sort of joke to David, who had seen worse, and yet behind the joke, what implication? "Let's leave here," Hannah begged. Al-ready a beaded curtain of rain had begun to fall. Like a lower-ing scale of piano notes, the rain beat down. Where else could they go and not be drowned?

The front door was open. David tiptoed in as though not to make footprints. Leaving the baby carriage in the marble-floored entry, Hannah followed. A light glimmered from under a doorway. Above the patter of the rain, they heard sounds of activity and laughter. Kneeling at the keyhole, David saw in the light of candles several square, Slavic faces and red-starred caps: Russian soldiers playing in a lavish nursery full of toys.

A finger to his lips, David drew Hannah away. They were upstairs before he explained. "I think they're drunk," he said, adding, "Lord, this place smells like a sewer." Around them, the damp deserted rooms reeked of contamination. Hannah hung back. They should have passed this place by, but it seemed too late to consider that now, and something else drew David on. If there were toys, what other treasures might a place like this hold? He tried a light switch, which produced nothing but a hollow click. Lightning, however, showed half-open double doors, and, with a perception more subtle than sight, he felt there was someone there. He entered the room slowly, with Hannah nearly stepping on his heels. A bed, a desk, chairs, the sweet odor of decomposition. David had matches, but the lightning was sufficient to show him that a woman lay on the bed: no sleeping beauty to raise with a kiss, but a suicide with one arm trailing down into a bucket of dark water.

There were candles here, grouped in a candelabrum. David lit them and the result was the discovery of three more corpses. A man slumped over the desk amid the smell of decay and peach blossoms. "Prussic acid," Hannah said. Shiny black boots jutted out from under the desk. Another figure lay on the floor, mouth open, staring surreptitiously from under half-lowered lids. A sofa leg had cocked his head forward so that he seemed to be assessing the bullet hole in his chest. He wore a black uniform. SS. What other course had such a one, but why shoot as well the dog that lay at his feet? The effect was strange, rather like the tomb effigy of a crusader.

Three years before, David would have fled from this tableau in trembling horror. Now he coolly considered the boots and wondered if they would come off. No use. Summer heat had made them part of their owner. Only a knife would separate them. Meanwhile, Hannah had opened a closet. She was trying on a coat and a floppy hat, which filled him with affection and pity for her poverty and hope. She turned once around, a model. There were men's clothes, too, silks, stout trousers, polished boots, and shoes with Italian labels.

They emerged from that room of death and disillusionment a fashionable couple, even though the fit left much to be desired.

"My dear!" He bowed her out into the corridor, holding the candelabrum high.

Turning a corner, the carpeted gallery enlarged into a baronial dining hall: long table, gilded velvet-cushioned chairs, huge fireplace, cupids and goddesses painted on the ceiling, and rows and rows of antlered heads. Scavenging further, they found a larder stocked with dried meats, hard cheese, beer, and wine.

"I'm hungry," Hannah said.

"Starved!"

There seemed no alternative. They sat down at the vast table for a banquet.

"Not exactly the coziest room I've ever dined in," she said. "It looks like a movie set for Belshazzar's feast."

"Once I ate twelve meringues," David told her. "I could do it again right here."

"Pig."

"I used to want to be a cook in a famous restaurant; you know, a real chef. What did you want to be?"

"A princess. No, a queen."

"What a nice world, with nothing but cooks and queens."

"All like you and me."

Their words echoed back and forth.

"More beer?"

"Why not?"

For a few moments, they were the whole world. The storm outside drowned the noise of approaching feet and they had no warning when the doors burst open. In leaped a wild figure, a Russian officer waving a pistol. He was handsome in a primitive way, with broad shoulders and a broad face upon which grew a ragged mustache trained to conceal a scar, like honeysuckle cultivated on a rough wall. His open shirt revealed the dark pelt of his hard and heavy chest. Crouched in suspicion, he looked like an ape. Seeing Hannah, he clearly wished to play the rooster, but in a gentlemanly way. Not wishing to antagonize David, he silently offered a bribe, a fine Leica camera, undoubtedly picked up on the floor below, in exchange for David's woman. David shook his head. The Russian, whose name appeared to be Slava, jutted his chin. He would take what he wanted; the spoils of war. Even if the Russian hadn't been brandishing a pistol, David was no match for him, but he had known absolute terror, so that nothing now could really frighten him. "You leave my sister alone," he said. This obviously did not register, so David began an elaborate charade that worked very well, since Russian is not a language of the lips alone but is spoken with the eyes, the hands, and the entire body. This was his poor sister. She had suffered very much in the hands of the Nazis. They had tortured her in ways that only a woman could be tortured. Though they had much respect for the Russian heroes, for him to press his desires would, under the circumstances, be unspeakable cruelty. By this time three other Russians had shouldered their way into the dining room. They brought bottles. The first Russian conferred. Suddenly they were all comrades in suffering, a group with arms linked. They would eat together. One Russian produced a raw potato, chewed it powerfully, handed out others. They drank vodka like thirsty horses. Their leader, Slava, his feet planted, his head thrown back, poured it down. David showed his concentration-camp tattoo. They all looked very serious, shook their heads. He must drink, too, and the vodka shot through him like molten silver. Then one of the Russians ran off to return up the corridor amid the green whiteness of the lightning flashes. He dragged the honeyed corpse with him, proudly unveiling on the corpse's arm the tattoo of that despised legion the SS. With thunder rumbling and tricks of wind guttering the candles, he set the dead man up in the high-backed chair at the head of the table. Their host was dead, and good riddance. Germany was dead. Not only was he SS, he had profaned the Russians' laundry. From the charade, David could only conclude that the Russians, unfamiliar with modern plumbing, had mistakenly used a flush toilet as a laundry basin and then, finding their reluctant host using it in the prescribed manner, had killed him for the insult.

All that was over. Killing was over. Twenty million Russians were dead. They would fight no more. A toast to the millions of Jews who had died. Another toast to their lolling host. No more wars. No more boundaries. To the good, simple people of the world. A toast to Hannah. May she recover and bear many strong, peace-loving sons. Warmed by food and drink, David sensed the beaming of an inner sun. He was thrilled by a vision of the brotherhood of man.

Toasting led to Russian singing, and the plaintive, off-key

melodies gave meaning to the words. They sang of mothers and sweethearts far away, of defeats and terrible victories. Tears gushed down their faces. Then it was time for David to reciprocate. Two Russians swung him up onto the table. Hannah was assisted up as though she were a queen entering a carriage. They conferred, trying to recall a song they both knew. The vodka muddling his memory, the only ones David could recall were those roared out by squads of Germans marching home after an execution. In the end he settled for a mindless kind of "Jaba-jaba-jaba" song, letting himself go in Chinese, a language he did not know, and to his surprise Hannah joined in with her own version of Chinese. The Russians loved it. Slava leaped from chair to table and began to dance in a squatting posture, flinging out his booted feet until the bread and glasses began to fly. Plates smashed on the floor. Outside, thunder bellowed. The shadows leaped while their silent host looked on, goggling with frozen astonishment.

The next morning David and Hannah were not permitted to slip away quietly. Their baby carriage had to be crammed full of edibles, even half a bottle of vodka. Slava was again offering the camera in trade, this time for David's wristwatch. The Russian displayed an armful of wristwatches, none of them working. "You have to wind them, like this." David showed him. Delighted, Slava pressed one, then another, to his ear and seemed even more eager to trade. Remembering his uncle's camera, David took off his watch, and so it was done.

Slava stood massively smiling. All comrades, they embraced solemnly and Slava sang once more, an old song of the East with no hint of Western melody, which made the world seem vast and strange.

The morning's hiking brought Hannah and David to the bank of a river somewhere near the juncture of the Weser and the Werra rivers. Here was the first DP camp set up for people trying to cross into the American zone. Any stray boats had long ago been appropriated, and the river was wide and swift. Neither wanted to be put at the mercy of Soviet officialdom, for without papers it might be months before they were exchanged.

Perhaps they could build a raft. In any event, there were thick forests where they could retire and think it over. Hannah led the way, walking so erect and effortlessly that David longed to run after her soundlessly, catch her by her thin shoulders, and whisper something foolish into her ear. But the baby carriage snagged on a stump and nearly upset. He could barely keep up, lost sight of her for a moment, then heard her singing a hiking song, *"O Taler wiet, O hoen."* She had stopped at the edge of a stream, one of the Weser's many tributaries.

In this small area, nature was triumphant. Rabbits pelted through the thickets. Birds sang in the trees.

Hannah had already established herself in a sunny spot. "If I were St. Francis, I'd say to all the living things today—grow—grow—and replenish the earth."

"The place is undoubtedly alive with snakes," David observed.

"So was Eden. Let's eat. You sit down and I'll do the work. After all, you're my banner, sword, and shield, as they used to say. I want you to just sit back and enjoy the beauty of nature."

It was there, of course, spread out before him as it had been in the butterfly-filled meadow after his escape, but

David felt numb to it still. So far, this girl alone had aroused in him any response. He didn't want to lose her.

"There, doesn't that look good?" she asked him.

"It looks fine," he said.

She put her hands against his face, spreading his lips. "Then smile. That's right," and she shone back at him. He took her hands and for a moment didn't let go.

"Now," he said, "suppose the earth turned upside down. We'd go sailing away, but I wouldn't lose you."

"Where would we go?"

"The island of my dreams. Where else? Just us two." He was weary of other faces. They were only masks hiding savages. "As long as we're together, it wouldn't be lonely."

She laughed at him. She understood and still she laughed. He wondered why.

"I just like you. No price tag; for free. Do you like me?" he asked.

"Yes."

"But you wouldn't say no, would you, if you didn't."

"No, but I really like you a lot," she said.

"I like the way you walk," he said, "and the way you eat. I even like the way you look. You're beautiful, Hannah."

"What?" She sounded surprised.

"I said you're beautiful."

Now she laughed out loud. "Lord, I'm a skinny wreck. Once upon a time I was sort of pretty."

"You still are."

"David, you've been in prison too long. My brother used to say I had an interesting, off-beat face. My father's nose. The only trouble was it had gotten stuck on upside down."

If she wasn't beautiful in a classic sense, her sum was certainly more than her parts.

"I bet you've had plenty of sweethearts," he said.

"Don't be silly."

"And don't you lie."

They tried to look at each other, but their eyes wouldn't hold.

"How's the food?" she asked.

"When we get to our island," he said, "I'll raise cattle and vegetables and you'll make bread." This was his secret dream, his grandfather's dream. He knew, of course, it was no more than that, but this did not diminish the sincerity with which he spoke. "My grandfather really did go off to wonderful places," he said. "East Africa. He saw the elephants come down to the beach at night. Once he sailed on an Arab dhow all the way to India. I don't know why he ever came back to Amsterdam."

"Can you swim?" she asked.

"Yes, but not very well."

"Like me," she said. "Let's swim."

Where they were, the stream widened, becoming a pool into which the sun flung its rays to the very bottom, reflecting off every flat stone and pebble until the water was as golden-brown as sherry wine.

"That's how holy water should feel," Hannah said, sticking in her toes.

In the camps they had been robbed of modesty. Now they both rediscovered it. David retired to a thicket to remove his clothes, then slid into the stream like an otter with only his eyes and nose above the surface. The water was a shock against his sun-heated skin, but it seemed to carry with it a blessing and a rebirth.

Hannah paddled from the other end of the pool. They met in the middle, gazing back and forth with sparkling eyes. Then she clasped his hand and laughed with such effortless candor that he decided he loved her, as he suddenly loved this day. The two of them out of so many millions were triumphant.

The water was too cold to linger long, but Hannah's lips were blue before she turned and swam away. She swam like a child who has watched dogs in the water. David, used to rough surf, thrashed his way to the bank.

Dry and clothed once more, they followed the bank of their stream as though it might indeed lead them to that retreat where men brown as fresh-baked bread basked under palms waiting for the coconuts to fall. Instead they came upon a figure in the gray uniform of the German army. He sat with his back against a tree, his head tilted to catch a patch of sun. His eyes were closed. Beside him was a double-barreled shotgun.

David was caught short. There was no such thing as a decent German, and he seized the gun as the stranger opened his eyes. Never again would David be helpless in the presence of an enemy.

The German looked at him, his face empty of expression. It would have been easy to jam both muzzles against his chest, pull both triggers. There would be very little noise.

"*Sprechen sie Deutsch?*" the soldier asked calmly, and then, noting the Dutch flag on the baby carriage, he said in that language, "If you wish to shoot me, you will need shells." He produced a couple from his uniform pocket. "Here. I don't seem to have the courage. I've been sitting here looking down the empty barrel. The trigger is hard to reach. Go ahead. I'll be grateful." Again he closed his eyes and leaned back as though awaiting oblivion, and David felt his resolution drain quickly away.

"I'm sorry," he said. "I'm not an accomplice to suicide."

"I'm sorry, too," the man replied. "I take it you're looking for Holland, if Holland still exists." The soldier could not be called jolly, but there was sardonic laughter in his eyes that David liked.

"We're both from Amsterdam. This is Hannah, I'm David."

"Amsterdam? I was an art student there once," the soldier said. "It seems a long time ago. My name's von Weichs, Erich von Weichs. I had dreams of being another Rembrandt, but then the war came and saved me from the disillusionment of finding out I have no more talent than Adolf. Sit down. Yes, please sit. Tell me sad stories of the death of kings."

Hannah looked at David, shrugged, and sat down. They unpacked their lunch, and talked. The indescribable years were filled out in a series of stark headlines. Erich von Weichs had missed the Polish campaign, but had ridden into France with Guderian's supply column. Later he'd been sent to Russia, where he'd met an officer named von Stauffenberg. There had been a conspiracy against Hitler, which had almost succeeded. "Well, they're all dead now. I would be, too, if I hadn't stepped on one of our own land mines. Strange, to think of one's foot and shinbone meatless and bleaching somewhere in Russia."

David had never before held a real conversation with a German. Now he and this stranger talked well into the afternoon. When David broached the subject of passing over into the American zone, von Weichs said, "On that score, I may have a helpful idea." He looked first at the sky where the sun had slid far off center, then at his watch, adding, "It's late. Come along home. My widow's expecting me. Who knows what we'll come up with by tomorrow?" Never questioning that they would follow, he rose, giving his artificial leg the help of both hands. It cracked and snapped as he half-walked, half-hurled himself along. David and Hannah followed. Both pushed the baby carriage as if they could not shake off the spell of the afternoon and could not bear to be separated.

Erich pointed ahead as they left the woods. "There," he said. "Built by my grandfather, the knockwurst king, for his knockwurst queen." Frowning down on them from above the river was a giant's castle conceived in a fairy tale.

As they drew nearer, David saw a light burning in a high, narrow window. A light in daytime; it gave him a lonely feeling. The baby carriage rumbled on the drawbridge and, as they arrived in the courtyard, an old woman in a long coat hobbled past them, holding a chamber pot before her like a crucible. She fixed the visitors with a gloomy stare, set the pot down, and made the sign of the cross.

"We still have a few servants," Erich observed. "One of Castle von Weichs's many afflictions." Another figure appeared. "Ah, here's Mother."

Under an enormous hat structured of feathers, an elderly woman had appeared. She awaited them in a doorway. Her lacy dress was black and she carried an umbrella with a carved ivory handle. Long, yellowish teeth gave her the appearance of laughing when she wasn't amused at all.

"The Baroness von Weichs," Erich introduced her. "My two friends, Hansel and Gretel, who were lost in the forest. I'm sorry, you call yourself Hannah now. Yes, Hannah and David—my mother."

The baroness lowered her eyes and actually smiled. Then she ushered them inside, and said something in German to her son, which he translated.

"Would you care for champagne?" he said. "Or would you prefer to see the castle before refreshment?"

They chose the latter.

He showed them first an old guest book going back to the days of the Kaiser. A recent page had been torn out, which their host explained had been soiled by a single signature: A. Hitler. The last entry seemed to be that of a drunken American soldier who had written: "Winston Churchill, 10 Downing Street. Ooh, la la, this place needs a plumber."

They proceeded through a dusky corridor aglow with polished wood where armor stood at attention. The last thing David expected to see was another playroom, but they now entered one full of delicately fashioned toys, small musical instruments, tiny animals, and particularly human figures, all carved in wood. "There are almost all the characters out of the tales of the brothers Grimm and of Hoffmann," Erich said. "They are quite old. In those days, ogres were content to put on their slippers and enjoy a tankard of beer beside a fire. I love the past, though not as much as my mother does. It was so charmingly fond and foolish. There has been too much sanity in Germany of late. It has driven us mad."

From a high turret he showed them the countryside, the river below, the old bridge broken by bombs, and the new one made of pontoons, beyond which lay the American zone of occupation.

Presently a bell sounded in the castle, a call to dinner.

"Come," Erich said. "You will meet my wife. She is a bit strange, like myself and my mother, but she has good reason."

The dining room at Castle von Weichs was even larger and more depressing than the one they had occupied the day before, though it did have electric lights to supplement the candles. It was full of grim portraits that scowled down from behind layers of yellow varnish. The baroness sat at one end, wielding a powder puff with an elegance befitting the flowery days of Marie Antoinette. There was a place set beside her in honor of the baron, dead since before the war.

At the other end Erich sat beside his wife, a small, thin woman with a graceful figure, which a low-cut gown showed was beginning to run to bone. Her face was long and narrow, the features fine. Hannah and David sat on one side where there were empty chairs for ten others. No one sat across from them, though three places had been carefully set.

Erich's mother conducted the meal with the pomp of a dethroned empress. "In this heat, Mother insists champagne is much more refreshing than tea or coffee." The old chambermaid they had observed in the courtyard entered with an enormous bottle, which she wiped with a towel. "Mother prefers champagne from magnums. It tastes better."

The old servant poured solemnly and returned the bottle to a silver cooler in which the ice appeared to have entirely melted away. Then she vanished briefly, only to reappear with a heavily laden silver platter. "Fresh venison. I believe that's what Mother ordered." The baroness served and the plates went around. They ate silently in the ghost-ridden room with only an occasional comment from Erich. Then the old baroness began to ask about *"der Kinder"* and David realized she was speaking about children. For a moment she was ignored. Then Erich's wife put down her fork. Her eyes flashed around as though she'd been accused of a crime. She rose, looking very young herself, a careworn child with tears just about to form in her eyes. "I must go and find the children," she apologized in English to her guests. "You will excuse me."

Erich said nothing, though his skin seemed to tighten over his face so that he resembled a revivified Egyptian pharaoh.

Presently the baroness found fault with the food. The servant was called and admonished. What had they done with this venison? Servant and mistress departed together, leaving only three at the table, drinking spring water that flowed from an old champagne bottle and eating a kind of meatless hash made from long-stored kale.

"Have you children?" David finally broke the terrible silence.

Erich looked up. "Yes," he said. "That is, perhaps. They are missing. You will excuse the ladies. I have known physical pain myself, but there is worse. You see, while I was in the hospital, with this"—and he motioned to his leg—"members of my family became involved in a plot to kill Hitler. As you know, the plot failed. Many were punished, with torture and death. In our case, our three children were seized. If they're still alive, they have probably been given different names; they were young enough to forget their own. It's a hard thing to bear. And now the Russians are threatening to take over the castle as quarters for their officers. What are we to do? My wife and mother are accustomed to comfort. Do we live in the stables? The horses won't mind. They were eaten long ago. Or do we go to relatives in the American zone?"

With such decisions David could give no help, but it presently became evident, as they were shown to their rooms, that their host could help them and meant to do so.

"Now, tomorrow," he said, "I shall be going into the American zone. The conspiracy against Hitler has at least left us in good standing with the Allies, and there may be some information regarding the children. I'll take you two with me if you like. The car will not be searched."

David slept hard that night, but he awoke early when a bird outside uttered so strange and human a cry that he could not sleep again. Breakfast was another banquet of kale and spring water. The ladies did not attend. A staff car, spattered with bullet holes and looking as though it were a casualty from the Western Desert campaign, waited outside. The baby carriage was left behind. With odd reluctance David saw it standing in the courtyard as the car swung over the drawbridge and down through fields where a woman looked for her lost children and did not wave. The Russian DP camp occupied the river's eastern bank. A line of inmates were being hustled through a cattle dip to rid them of lice as the car passed. It slowed at the bridge, where a sentry in hob-nailed boots paced five strides forward, five more back. He waved the staff car ahead and, with no questions asked, they clattered over to the American side. Again they were summarily passed through. A hundred meters up the road Erich von Weichs pulled over.

"Down there," he directed. "You'll do better to stop at the American DP center than to wander about on your own." Then the hated-loved foreigner stuck out his hand, and David took it.

"Keep your shotgun empty," he said. "This country will need you one day."

"Don't worry," von Weichs replied. "I have three children I hope to find. May we all have good luck in our quests."

As the old staff car stuttered away, David and Hannah were undecided whether to proceed on their own or to submit to the mercies of the Americans. As they stood debating, a jeep stopped nearby and a tall black man in khaki emerged to pound a "SLOW" sign into the ground. He was sweating profusely and paused to fan himself with a helmet liner. "Man, it sure is hot," he said to himself, to them, perhaps to the sultry weather itself. "I'm heading down thataway to the center." He motioned toward his jeep in case they didn't understand him. "Pile in if you have a mind." And so they went, not so much from resolve but almost as though they were hypnotized. There was no guard outside the DP center, only a machine for dispensing soft drinks and candy. Both stared at it, not from a craving for sweets, but in a kind of wonder that such things still existed.

A nurse behind a desk took down their names and sent them on for a delousing with DDT powder, and from there they went to the showers. David, shown to the men's section, was given a green sponge bag and a strong-smelling bar of red soap. Despite his recent swim, the dirt of ages seemed ground in. He felt as moldy and green as a long-buried corpse when he stepped under the scalding spray that shot at him at high speed from an assortment of nozzles. It did not bring him the picture of a Nazi guard melting in steam, but of times long forgotten, of his mother laughing, squeezing water from a sponge down his back. Then, gleaming like a fish, he rubbed himself down with a rough towel until his very bones were warm.

When he saw Hannah again, she, too, looked clean and scrubbed all through. Her hair had taken on a curl and he stopped and stared while she, like a self-assured model before the camera, absorbed his admiration. Then she gave a big, in-

voluntary yawn that blossomed into a laugh when she tried to quell it. They laughed together.

For dinner they had fried Spam, a delicacy to David that the Americans seemed to despise, along with cloudy piles of mashed potatoes puddled in thick brown gravy.

"I'm so full," Hannah finally said. "I'm so full and so sleepy I think I'll be sick."

"Not again," implored David. He watched her with a smile in his mind if not on his lips. There was only one thing to mar a day when everything was going right. Though they were not obliged to stay at the DP center, which had been designed to process people into the Russian zone, they could not get into Holland, either. For the first time they heard what Holland had suffered at the end of the war. There had been starvation and flooding in the northeastern portion, which the Germans had held until that spring, and destitute refugees were being kept from entering the country until the situation improved.

The DP center was overflowing with eastern-bound refugees. The dormitories were full and all that remained in the way of accommodations were beds in the main corridor, but they were real beds with springs and mattresses, softer than anything David had slept on since leaving Amsterdam. In fact they were so soft he could not sleep, but in chagrin finally rolled up in a blanket on the floor. It was there that Hannah found him. She couldn't sleep either, but it was her own merciless imagination as much as the bed that kept her awake. What if Amsterdam had been flooded? For the first time she was facing the possibility that David had long accepted about himself: total abandonment. An impression that she was about to cry made him catch her by the shoulders. They embraced with a sort of anguish, not kissing but simply trying to satisfy a terrible need for closeness. "Rest against me," he said, "and don't worry, Hannah. I'll take care of you."

"Yes," she said, "why not? I'll take care of you, too, when I feel better." Together, they no longer feared the darkness.

"Maybe you'd feel better if you said a prayer," he whispered.

"What sort of prayer?"

"Whatever you used to say when you were little."

"Now I lay me down to sleep? That's just something to say at bedtime. It's all right if you believe God's watching over you. For years, nobody's watched over me, not until now." For a moment it was as though they had fallen in love from sheer dependency, as though no one else existed in the world. "I shouldn't be afraid if only all the people who ever cared for me could be here around me like a wall." She was growing quieter in his arms, and he more alarmed. She needed him now, but he wanted to be all that she needed. Where would she be if he had not come along? Never mind, he was here, and he would look after her. But what if she had a family still? He seemed to see Amsterdam sunk in the sea like a modern Atlantis. Let it be, as long as he did not lose this girl, his only living link with a world that had died.

TWELVE

SUMMER, 1945
Back to Amsterdam

They remained at the DP center for a month or more. David kept no count of the days. He even had to think twice to name the year. While Czechs, Poles, Bulgarians, and thousands of Balkan people flowed east through the center, Dutch, French, and Belgians plodded west. But David was in no hurry to move on. He was gaining weight, though he did not look forward to Spam and powdered eggs as much as he had at first. He was content. He had Hannah.

All the while there came from Holland reports and rumors upon which their imaginations fed. Amsterdam, or whatever part of it had survived high water, the rats, and the Nazis, had not been liberated until the eighth of May. The Nazis, in retaliation for a Dutch railroad strike, had withheld food from the civilian population for almost a year, and starvation had been widespread until the German surrender. Coastal fisheries had been depleted by the occupiers' practice of fishing with hand grenades. Those dogs and cats which had not already been seized as food for concentration camps disappeared from the streets. Sugar beets and nonpoisonous varieties of tulip bulbs were about all the nourishment that remained at hand, unless one had a diamond ring that might become the price of powdered milk for a baby. Children turned to crime, as did adults. People would not leave their homes for fear of looters, and doctors gave up house calls because their cars would vanish while they were inside a patient's home.

"That can't be Holland. It can't be," Hannah said with tears in her eyes. And it was beyond the reckoning of either of them to determine what bombs and flooding had done. They knew the Walcheren dikes had been opened by the British, a necessary strategy of war, and that toward the end the Germans had blown up the Wieringermeer dikes for no reason other than spite. But there was no imagining what more they had done, and Hannah could not stop speculating. She wept at night and murmured in her sleep. Then David did what he could to comfort and reassure her. Sometimes he caught himself bringing grim bits of news to her attention; then he despised himself for his selfishness. He knew her well enough now to realize there were two Hannahs, and he thought of them as the nighttime and the daytime Hannah. The first he could say anything to, such as "Did I ever tell you I care for you so much, well, it's damned upsetting?" He nearly blushed for the silliness of his words, but he was in good hands. "You make me very proud of myself," she said. Then they clung together, needing one another, seeming, apart, to be no more than dead leaves blown by the wind. At night in early August they counted the Perseids hurtling down the black sky. He talked of far-off places where they could bask on palm-lined beaches and bathe in turquoise water hot as blood, and she agreed: "Take me anywhere; just keep me warm." So David talked and talked, spinning out dreams. Beyond the cloud shadows of the unknown they would find their place.

"If I kissed you, you wouldn't hit me, would you?" And she, without answering, touched her lips to his. Then he covered her cheeks, her eyes with kisses, and their future seemed so impossibly fine that his eyes filled with foolish tears.

The daytime Hannah was crisp and self-contained, an entirely different person who spoke of proceeding on foot to Holland if no transportation was made available. She was a contradiction, saying, "It seems to me a person should live where he was born. I mean, people who want to live in another country, speak a different language, are sort of odd. Well, maybe not odd, but sad, as though their clothes never quite fit."

So David faced the inevitable return. He ought to go, just in case someone who had been dear to him was still alive. There was Rachel, whom he had especially loved.

"When we get home to Amsterdam, I may try courting you. I mean, if such things are done any more," he said.

"I don't know how I'd get along with anyone else. We've been through things other people couldn't understand."

In August they heard of a food truck heading north to Holland. They could ride with the driver. Hannah was overjoyed. David pretended to be.

"What's wrong with you?" she questioned. "You ought to be dancing and singing."

"It's the bomb, I suppose. That atomic thing the Americans dropped on Japan."

"Japan's a long way off."

"I know. It's stupid of me"; but the news had come as an eerie portent of what another war might be like.

Their driver turned out to be an old friend, the black man who had first brought them to the center. He stood a good two meters tall, had a wide, face-splitting grin full of white teeth, and a booming laugh. He must have made a recent trip into France, for he smelled overpoweringly of perfume: Chanel Number 5, according to Hannah.

"Name's Raddie," he said. "I'm from Georgia. You-all from Amsterdam?"

He drove fast, taking the autobahns that Hitler had built for military traffic. Occasional Red Cross stations provided coffee and doughnuts. The retreating German army had blown up all the bridges and overpasses, which made for slow going and traffic jams. The morning carried them as far as Giessen.

"How'd you folks get so far from home?" Raddie asked.

"Pardon?" said David.

"You don't hardly talk good English, do you?"

"Excuse, please?"

"I said, your English ain't so sharp."

"Sharp?"

"Where'd you pick it up? Learn to talk?"

"In the Gymnasium."

"Gymnasium? You learned English in the gym?"

"How do you say it—high school?"

"Never did get to high school myself. Listen here. You Jewish? How come you want to go back to that place?"

"It's our home," said Hannah, who, not being Jewish, had none of David's complications in answering.

"If I was you-all, I'd go to the U.S."

"But I always heard you people had problems there yourselves."

"Us coloreds? Well, we had trouble, but no more. No, siree. We learned us how to fight, and that's a fact." He shifted gears, and the truck shot ahead of the traffic pile-up.

From Giessen, they headed north through the Westerwald Rothhaar, slow going on a bad road, with trucks ahead and behind. It began to rain, and the metronome sound of the windshield wipers put David to sleep. He woke to find they were at Siegen, lined up to cross the Sieg River for clearance into the British zone. While they waited, Red Cross volunteers passed out tea and toast, a welcome change from coffee and doughnuts. Evening was coming on before they headed into the setting sun. They were now in the industrial Ruhr Valley. It was bomb-cratered and looked to David like the face of the moon.

"Wait'll you see little ole Cologne. Now that place is really somethin'." David was beginning to understand the driver's speech, which was accented differently from any English he had heard.

Cologne occupied the Rhine's western bank. It was dark before they arrived at what had once been a great industrial city. Hannah had seen Dresden in the throes of destruction, but David was unprepared for this by his hazy memory of Rotterdam's bombing. It was now months since the war had ended, but Cologne was a gray and jagged memorial to the inhumanity of man. All that remained were roads, which had been bulldozed through the rubble, and the specter of the great cathedral, a black skeleton reaching for the moon.

It wasn't until Raddie burst out laughing that David realized they were lost. They pulled over beside a standing wall pierced by a window that looked both ways on rubble. Whitewashed on the brick were words in English, six feet high: GOOD NEWS! GOD IS LOVE!

Raddie climbed out of the truck. "Don't go 'way, now, you hear? I'll be right back."

Few people were abroad. Perhaps there was still a curfew, and those that passed the waiting truck had a gray, caged look that David hadn't observed in the countryside. They appeared to be half-starved. If they guessed what the truck's cargo space contained, he was sure they would attack. It was a relief when the driver returned, though he himself sounded discouraged. "Ain't a livin' soul 'round here can tell his ass from a hole in the ground, far as directions go. Reckon we'll have to spend the night right here, cozy as peas in a pod."

Raddie was soon asleep, his head flung back so that it seemed he would fracture his spine with snoring. Hannah, who was increasingly nervous as they drew near to Holland, and David, who was again used to beds, slept hardly at all.

At dawn they took discreet turns behind the cover of the wall and then they were off, taking the longer route via Aachen because of traffic problems and the heavy bomb damage along the Rhine route. Charlemagne's old citadel of the Holy Roman Empire had suffered little from air raids but, toward the end, when all was inevitably lost, the city had been defended against an Allied ground attack. The result was ruin. Aachen was a corpse of a city. Roads had been cleared through heaps of plaster, brick, and wood that breezes stirred into clouds of reddish dust.

"You-all hungry?" Raddie wanted to know. The only new and intact structure in sight was a Red Cross shelter. Tea and toast again, with K rations from the back of the truck to supplement them.

From Aachen they crossed over into the southeastern tip of Holland, then turned north along the river Maas with its fleets of barges. Here there was little evidence of war beyond an occasional wrecked and rusting vehicle. The land was high enough to be beyond the reach of flood waters.

"It's all right, isn't it?" Hannah began insisting. David knew her apprehension was growing with every mile, as was his own, for different reasons. Yet even he was aware of a mounting compulsion to return and see his birthplace, if only to be quit of it forever.

One more night intervened before they reached Amsterdam, with Raddie at an army post, themselves sheltered at a hostel. Soon after breakfast they reached the outskirts of Amsterdam. First came the "people's gardens," where city folk tried to be small-scale farmers. They passed over the first canal. It was unbelievable.

"Lord, look at this here town! Hot damn!" proclaimed the driver. Not a brick looked out of place. Not a window was broken. They swung round the Weeper's Tower and observed that the harbor had indeed been damaged. Hannah was giving directions now. David felt his heart accelerate its beat.

"Stop. This is good," Hannah said at last.

"You live here?" Raddie sounded surprised.

"No, but it's a dead end. Besides, I'd like to walk the last little bit."

"Sure 'nough." Raddie climbed down, helped Hannah and David with their few bundles. A wide grin slashed across his dark face. "Well, folks, so long. You send for me if you have trouble, hear? 'Cause nobody calls this here nigger 'nigger,' and nobody calls my friends kikes. You ever come to the U.S. and my mama'll feed you up. You could do with some good eatin'."

"We'll do that," David assured him. He would miss the truck and its cheerful driver. He and Hannah watched silently as it drove away. Next to them, children played in the canal on a makeshift raft made of food tins roped together.

"I wasn't much older than those kids when I left here," David said. He stooped and picked up their belongings. "Well, where do we go?"

"This way."

They almost tiptoed, cautious as housebreakers. A child ran by, his face covered by a German gas mask. Nothing was left of the war but toys for children to play with.

"There." Hannah was pointing. It was half a block to the house.

"So here we are," David said.

"Yes, here we both are."

He sensed that something was ending.

David followed her to the front door. Knocking drew no response, but the door was open. They entered a small foyer, which smelled as if a lot of smoking and drinking had taken place with the windows closed.

"Doesn't it smell awful?" she said, but she sounded delighted.

Abruptly an inner door was flung open and a man squinted suspiciously at them. His mouth folded down at the corners, and his cheeks were loosely hung, but above the mouth his face was hard, suggesting that age crept up from below.

"Papa!" she cried out, near tears.

"Hannah? Oh, my God!" Father and daughter were in each other's arms. "Gerard! Gerard! Come down here! Your sister's home!" Gerard, a younger, plumper version of his father, came bounding down the stairs. At first he did not seem to believe his father.

"Come here, Gerard. I'm not a stranger. Come here," Hannah insisted.

David still stood just inside the door, feeling himself an intruder. It seemed as though he did not exist.

Finally Hannah's father stood back, his arm still around his daughter. "It's been so long, Hannah, but let us pretend you have been away only a day."

At last it was David's turn. Hannah performed the introductions, adding, "If it weren't for David, Papa, I wouldn't be here now."

"Then we're deeply grateful to you, David," said Zes Cronk, clasping David's hands in both his own. "If you've no place to stay, please stay with us for as long as you wish." He turned to his daughter. "And tonight we must celebrate. Tonight rationing doesn't exist."

Hannah took charge in the kitchen. She said dinner would be a surprise, "if I can still remember how to cook," and by virtue of certain black-market purchases, it was.

"Rice table," she announced proudly. "David, you're always talking about it." There was beer to wash it down, and even half a bottle of Genever, that Dutch gin to which Zes Cronk admitted addiction. At first they ate silently. There was much chewing and swallowing, much tinkling of forks and glasses. Hannah's father belched discreetly behind his napkin. "Delightful, my dear. We haven't eaten like this since you left."

"I'm eating too fast, but I won't forget a bite," David said. "My grandfather always said my brother and I had an unimaginable ability to absorb rice table."

With this he had to disinter Saul, bury him again.

"Will it bother you to answer some questions?" Zes Cronk said.

Hannah turned on him a bright, quick smile. He felt it rather than saw it.

"No, no," he said hastily. "I guess I wouldn't be here in Amsterdam at all if there weren't questions to be answered." He felt the muscles of his throat contract in swallowing. "Really, I feel that I'm eating for my whole family. Rice table was sort of 'our' dish."

"You know, David, it's good to talk," Zes Cronk assured him. "Sometimes you can talk the sadness out right through your mouth. I was able to do that in the case of my wife."

But David had more than a vagrant spouse to lament. He felt his head spinning around from the gin, the beer, the hotly spiced food. He must presently laugh or cry. Laughter came first, with a rush of blood to his cheeks, then for no apparent reason tears rose from the depths, a hemorrhage of tears at last.

"That's all right. We understand." Zes Cronk patted him on the shoulder as though trying to quiet an emotional horse. "Get it out of your system, lad. Tonight misery is a punishable crime."

But it wasn't that easy to put loneliness and loss aside. Hannah finally took David by the hand and led him to a small, quiet bedroom. He felt full of gratitude toward this independent girl with her observant eyes. "You're only twenty, David. Life isn't over. This is just the beginning. You have years and years ahead of you."

"I know," he managed. "What could be more frightening?" His voice trailed off like a timid ghost.

"Now go to sleep," she said. "You're welcome in this house. You're home."

But it wasn't this house or those who lived in it that bothered him. It was memories of another house and those who had lived in it that gnawed at his sleep. For the first time he faced the fact that he was not one of the dead. He had left them all behind, and still this could not take death out of him entirely. He had never felt more lonely. "I must never forget them." Once he had tried keeping a diary, but that was no good. Now he could not truly say if Hannah's version of rice table had tasted like his grandmother's. Pretty soon people would be telling him about the past and he would say, "Yes, I suppose that's how it was." But just because they were dead was no excuse for letting them down, and he didn't mean only his family. For thousands of burned corpses he should be a voice and a witness, but what had he seen, and what could he say about it? In ancient times, Jews often chose a martyr's death, believing they did so to glorify God's name. But Auschwitz had no glory, no divine inspiration. It was totally without purpose.

The next morning David was urged by Hannah's father to stay on, though he qualified this carte blanche with "for a while." Clearly, Hannah was home for good. She had taken over the house, thrown open the windows, and scrubbed them down. She was becoming indispensable to her father and brother. The island, the far journey was, as David had always known, only a dream. Her reality was here. And his? He could not be sure, but there were things that had to be done before the past could be laid entirely to rest.

First he must visit his old home. He made his intention clear at breakfast.

"You may have a shock," Zes Cronk warned him. "During the fuel shortage last winter, much of the old Jewish quarter was stripped of wood. You can hardly blame people who were freezing."

It didn't matter; David had to see for himself. Hannah showed him to a padlocked shed where a bicycle was kept. Most bicycles had been confiscated by the Germans, and this one remained because the tires were gone. Riding on the bare metal rims of the wheels was a bit like ice skating, but faster than walking if one had a good sense of balance and a tough backside.

"You'll be home for supper?" she asked.

"Of course."

"We'll always be friends, David, won't we?" and her searching, always candid eyes forced him to agree.

"Forever and ever," he said, though he knew that life was not like that. It was meetings and partings, and she knew it, too.

"I hate to think of you being gone even for a little while," she said.

He took her face between his hands. To be deprived of Hannah was his one regret, and he felt a sad emptiness for what he knew in time would come to pass.

It was over two miles to the old Jewish quarter. There were signs of revival along the way: a barrel organ attracting children, a market with pigeons being sold from willow baskets, fishmongers with their stalls announcing "Hollandse Nieuwe." The silvery herring were coming back. He heard no church bells, and supposed they had been taken for their metal content, but it was not until he entered the old quarter that he saw real signs of war. This artificial ghetto had been emptied of all its inhabitants by 1943, two years before, and into the vacuum had come looters. At first they were criminals who tampered with locks and windows in search of valuables. Then had come squatters, vagrants, and finally anyone who was cold, to strip away doors, banisters, panelling, even the supporting timbers, so that the result was almost as thorough as a heavy air raid.

David was appalled. At least his own home was standing, though the windows gaped or were boarded up. His shoes crackled in the debris of broken glass on the front steps, and a boy stared at him from the doorway. He was a thin child of perhaps ten years, with eyes as hostile as those of one species of predator turned upon another.

"I've come back," David said. "This is my home."

This was too much for the boy, and he ran into the house as David climbed the steps. He would see this through no matter how distasteful. Almost invisibly a shutter flickered like a winking eye, and then a large blond woman with a dark mole beside her lower lip looked at him around the corner of the door.

"This is my home," he repeated. "My name is Ullman. I used to live here. I want to see the place."

The woman turned back inside to tell someone else, "It's a Jew," as though that explained everything.

Next, a man appeared. Thin, in threadbare clothes, he emitted an odor of sweat, grease, and abject poverty.

"We live here now," he said. Then he coughed, a rending cough of advanced tuberculosis.

"I've only come to look," David told them. "Please open the door." The pair, the boy behind them, stood firm, until David unlimbered the cased camera from his shoulder, threatening to swing it like a ball and chain. Then they gave way, and he stepped into the flood of memories that the house evoked around him. Even among these hostile strangers he felt the old sense of well-being. At least the squatters had kept the interior from being plundered. There was his grandfather's study with most of its books, the great eternal desk.

"I told you that when the war was over the Jews would crawl out of their holes! There'll be more Jews than before the war. Remember what I said?" The woman spoke loudly, tossing her head about. "You can see who's got the good cameras and the bicycles."

David paid no attention to her or to the man, who added, "All the decent Jews are dead. It's the bad ones that turn up."

David walked upstairs to his old room. The plants were

gone from the window ledge, but he seemed to see Saul and Rachel there, leaning out, listening for a make-believe war. Downstairs again, a committee was waiting, the man and woman side by side. The woman was armed with a pair of long shears, their blades erect.

"Don't worry, I'll be going soon," David said, "but if you come any closer, I'll beat out your brains." The camera strap was wrapped around his wrist, and he held it out from his side as the David of old had held his sling.

They stepped aside. The sound of the man's cough was like strange bitter laughter, and the woman, who must have noticed David's wrist, said, "Why don't you join the circus? You can be the tattooed man!"

David wasted no banter. Except for the kitchen, he was finished here forever. Surprisingly, the blue Delft tiles were all in place. He counted up and to the left. With a meat cleaver, he stabbed around the edge of the tile, pried it loose. There was the small leather bag and a notebook. He had all but forgotten his diary. With both in his pocket, he advanced again on the trio.

"I'm leaving," he said. The cleaver was still in his hand, and they let him through. He was down in the street before the woman dared hurl after him, "If God were just, he'd have given Hitler one more year! You Christ crucifier!" Then the door slammed.

David had considered leaving a message outside the house with a forwarding address, but it would do no good. The squatters would surely efface it. As he mounted the bicycle, a cat ran around the corner of the house to stop on stiff legs, back hunched, moving sideways. "Here, kitty, kitty, kitty!" he called. Clearly it was a survivor, a canny veteran who'd outlived the war. Rachel's kitten? He couldn't be sure, and the cat made off, padding softly into a derelict building.

"Good luck!" he called after it, adding, "And scratch out their eyes!" There was no sign of Rachel's canary, though he scanned the trees that lined the canal. How could it be there? It was in the Canary Islands.

David stopped only once on his return journey, to check the lists at the Jewish Center: lists of the known dead, of the missing, of survivors. The list of survivors was shortest of all, giving their new addresses. To this he added ULLMAN, DAVID, CARE OF CRONK, without any hope that this year or next or ten years from now anyone would find it there and try to follow him.

The Cronks were all out when he returned, and the house was locked, but Hannah had left a penciled message: "Back soon. Shopping."

That gave him some time to sit on the steps in the sun and examine the contents of the little leather bag. There were his grandmother's gold rings, a small hoard of pearls. He was wealthy by refugee standards, but that was no source of joy. He would trade them all for five minutes with his grandfather, who was not so much dead as simply gone from the physical world to live on in David and nourish his soul. He thumbed idly through the diary, seeing a sentence here or there on which he could not bear to reflect. There were a few blank pages at the end, but before that there was some other handwriting, which began with a date, "November, 1942." It was a message from his grandfather. "Dear David. If anyone reads this, I feel somehow it will be you. You and the rest of my family have just left, and you will forgive an old man his sentimentality. I am alone, David, and I will not be here long, but I want you to know that even now I do not despair of life. Life is a wonderful gift. Like the tropic sun, it can strike you blind, but it is magnificent. Never despair of it. If you could hear the dead, they would all tell you, 'live.' That is the whole answer. Live, and if you can, love. At the bottom of all human renunciations, buried under so many 'no's,' there is that last indestructible 'yes,' and it is sufficient to rebuild everything. When you read this, it will be your turn. I have nothing more to leave you except the contents of the small leather bag. But even now I do believe that life is good, and that men can be good, or, at least, a bit better than their circumstances.

"If I had it all to do over, I would not conduct myself in any other way. I have known the worst that the world can do to me, and yet it has my praise. Do not linger with the dead. They must be left in peace. Carry forward their living, and be careful of yourself. Do not forget what has happened, but do not live in bitterness. The past is the past; do not dig it up. Look for the pot of gold at the rainbow's end, and even if you do not believe it is there, go on looking." And then the signature: "Your loving grandfather, Moses Ullman."

David slipped the notebook into his pocket. Walking down toward the canal, he caught his foot on a loose cobblestone and nearly fell. At the edge of the canal he leaned against a tree. The water below was dark and sluggish. A breeze from the harbor made him shiver. Another autumn was coming. A crowd of unseen people seemed to sweep around him on that wind, aimless, unable to stop. They would always haunt him here. This was not his place any more. Turning back toward the Cronk house, he felt the stirring of new conviction and a relaxation of his will. His heart was sad, but his mind was made up. Europe, with its ingrown hatreds, was not for him.

Not even with Hannah could he share more than a fragment of the past, and his future had to be elsewhere.

He told her his decision that afternoon. "Before I can live with other people, I've got to find myself."

She knew. "When will you leave?"

"Tomorrow. I have to see if my sister is alive."

They parted after breakfast with an embrace, tearful, passionless, very private.

"I don't know how to say goodbye," he admitted. "We've known sad times together, and without you . . . I don't know."

"Take the bicycle," she said. "You'll need it."

"But I may not be back this way. I may have to keep on going."

"Take it, David."

"Then you must have this," he said, and placed in her hand one of his grandmother's pearl necklaces.

"Oh, David, I can't." She was near tears.

"Keep it, in memory of a wandering Jew." Then he turned and mounted the bicycle. She had filled its basket with food wrapped in a heavy sweater. He did not look back. If he did, he would see her standing there and he might not be able to go on. The corner was turned. His future seemed to close about him as he went.

David's first objective was the summer house. He arrived before dusk to find the place in ruins. A charred book, a broken fragment of china, raised inside his head the voices of childhood. He remembered walking here with his grandfather. He could almost hear the crunch of Moses' cane on the gravel. He remembered Rachel singing and his mother admonishing them all to wash before dinner. But there was nothing to salvage, and the wind from the sea was cold.

It began to rain as he pedaled down to the mill. It looked entirely unchanged, as well as he could see it in the dim, watery light. Empty, empty, empty, and silent as the grave. Bats had reclaimed the secret room, but in it he spent the night, curled on the bare floor.

Nothing remained there, either; no message. In the morning he dug up the buried pistols, all three rusted beyond use. A last stop was the Catholic church. A little priest with feathery gray hair opened the door for him. David told his story briefly.

"My poor boy," the priest said, clearing his throat and making a gesture into the air as if scattering holy water. He spoke consoling words in Latin. Perhaps, David thought, he expects to achieve a miraculous conversion.

"What's become of Father Lebbink?" he asked the priest.

"He has gone to his rest."

"Dead?" Another blind alley.

"Oh, no, retired." There were no wrinkles or marks on the priest's face to suggest spiritual struggle, nothing to indicate that the passing of two world wars in his lifetime had left any mark. "Actually, he's gone to a rest home for elderly clergymen."

"Where is that? I'd like to see him."

"I'm afraid it would do no good," the priest sighed. "You see, poor Father Lebbink is disturbed. He began to have one-sided chats with the Devil down in the church's crypt. That was in '43. Since then, you might say, he's taken a vow of silence. He does his beads continuously, regular as clockwork, but he will not speak, poor man. He suffers. No good Christian can be completely free of our Lord's suffering. Christ did not endure pain to save us from pain, you know, but to teach us how to endure it ourselves."

"Have you any word of Daniel Ullman?" David asked. The priest looked blank. "He would be about forty—a dark, fierce-looking man. He was in the underground."

"I wouldn't know about that," the priest said. "I could look in the records." Not in the burial records nor in any others did David's uncle's name appear. He was more likely to be dead than alive, but, without evidence, David chose to believe that Daniel lived.

One place remained, the caves near Maastricht. He would have to traverse the better part of Holland, and for what? Part of him yearned to return to Amsterdam. If he did, Hannah's face would be the only good thing he could be sure of—but then what? Was he to become a ghost haunting his old neighborhood? He made no decision that day, but pedaled back down to the beach, where the salt waves broke and the voices of the drowned whispered on the wind. He skimmed flat stones into the foam and wondered what had become of a message in a bottle and whether horses still cantered here. The gulls hovered on the wind, waiting for him to leave.

David turned and strode up the bank, kicked at a pile of leaves with the lightness and energy of what remained of his childhood. There was only one way to go, and after another night at the mill, he took it, pedaling south. He would pass inland of Rotterdam. There were not so many flowers as there had been in 1940. Many of the mills had vanished. As natural observation posts in the flat land, they had been flattened by the retreating Germans. An occasional concrete bunker marked the route, and after a day's clattering on the bicycle, David spent the night in one of them near Arnhem. Outside were fields of white crosses: British, Canadian, Polish. The great bridge across the Rijn was down, but he crossed over on a span supported by pontoons. The bicycle was becoming a torment, but he persisted along the last of the flat canal roads. There was a haziness in the air as if here morning yawned perpetually. The barges moved slowly as though in their sleep. As Holland narrowed between Belgium and Germany, the landscape became more wooded and hilly. There were deer crossings and pheasants in the thickets.

A long slope took him down toward the ancient city of Maastricht. There the canal widened to accommodate barges moored like log jams against the bank. Children in the street were drawing chalk pictures for a prize, their efforts streaked by the passing of bicycles. David nearly fell off his own thinking one of the young artists was Rachel, only to realize he was seeing Rachel as she would have been over two years before. That night he indulged himself at a French-style sidewalk café, eating sausages.

The next day he went to the tunneled mound of St. Pietersberg, not far from the city. Cavemen had been the first to tunnel in the chalky soil, and now there were over two hundred miles of tunnels and galleries. Famous men, including Voltaire and Napoleon, had left their signatures, and some twenty thousand hiders—resistance workers, downed airmen, and Jews—had taken refuge there toward the end of the war, along with such national treasures as Rembrandt's *Night Watch*. Now very few of the cave's inhabitants remained, but there were lists of those who had been there and gone. The names were often illegible, blotted, pencil-smudged. Some were crossed out or written over, usually with addresses not given. Many of the Jewish names were followed simply by "Palestine." It was in the third such ledger, with his eyes aching from strain, that David made his discovery. "Rachel Ullman." Moisture had blurred the writing and had smudged the name below it into an indecipherable blot. Yet in both cases the address was the same, "Palestine," and seemingly, it had been inscribed by the same hand. Rachel and Daniel gone together? There was no guarantee in either case, but somehow he felt sure that, if he followed, he would find them.

At the end of the ledger he placed his own name in large bold letters on the unlikely chance that Ruth or Abraham or even Saul might somehow, like Lazarus, rise and follow. After his name he wrote, "I have gone after Rachel and Daniel to Palestine."

So it was written. The doing was another matter, for many wished to go. If all who desired were aided and abetted, an Arab land would be overrun. David felt his best chance was from Rotterdam, if his grandfather's friend, Van Walsum, still lived there.

Once more he took to the abominable bicycle and headed northwest to Rotterdam, hopeful that, in that seaport where the war had become a reality for him, he would finally lay those dark years to rest. Rebuilding was beginning to get under way, and supreme in the middle of it all still stood the great mill "de Noord," with the legend that had given heart to the Dutch resistance: "Through all tempests, undisturbed, the sails of the mill have kept turning. God always has the last word."

David made his way to the docks, where, despite the war's devastation, Rotterdam's reputation as Europe's greatest port was being reborn. Stevedores swarmed among bags and crates of cargo, loading, unloading, cursing in a babel of tongues. Ships' horns droned in the harbor. A radio blared out the latest jazz hit from America.

His first few inquiries yielded no results, and then David

saw, amid a forest of rigging, masts, cranes and smokestacks, a name that jolted him. On the bow of a down-at-heel steamer were letters in peeling gold: *Texel Queen II.* From there it was easy. A stevedore pointed out a small waterfront office, the windows all sooted over, a dark desk inside, and a man behind it hunched over piles of papers. Gray of mustache and hair, Van Walsum had large eyes shadowed with weariness, and his brow was deeply lined.

"I'm David Ullman," he said. "You must be Van Walsum."

"What if I am?" came the reply. "I'm a busy man. Who is David Ullman to me?"

"Moses Ullman's grandson."

"My Lord," said the old man, standing up. "You're supposed to be in England. No, by God, you're supposed to be dead."

David told what had happened.

"So my old friend is the one who is dead. Lord. At least he is at peace. Well, you're not here to pass the time of day. What can I do for you?"

"I want to follow my sister to Palestine," David replied. "I was hoping . . ."

Van Walsum sat down again. He began to write. "Here," he said finally, "take this. I only wish my old friend were going with you."

"And this is all I need?" David stared at the paper in disbelief.

"Go down to the dock."

"Now? I can go now?"

Van Walsum fixed him with a steady stare and asked, "Why are you still here?"

The note was to the captain of the *Texel Queen II*, which

was to sail the following day for the Mediterranean with an undisclosed cargo, a portion of which, labeled "flowers," was bound for Palestine. Fearing that he might again be left behind, David went out in the first available launch, through great floating walls of black and rusty iron.

Compared to the adjacent aircraft carrier, vast and complex as a gothic cathedral, the *Texel Queen II* was tiny, shabby, and low in the water. Her solitary stack looked like a tall red candle. Her engines thumped erratically as a damaged heart, and the green-black portholes chattered in the wind.

That night the wind swung around to the sea and a thin cold rain began. David lay awake listening for the last time to Holland. A freight train shuttled to the dock, a tram clattered, there was the agonized creak of ships at anchor. He was finished with the past. From anxiety he had passed to fear, and from fear to sorrow. Fear was a terrible wandering that destroyed the spirit, but sorrow was an arriving, a new beginning. He was not running away from something, but going toward it. This was no longer flight, but pursuit. In Palestine, he felt confident, he would reestablish what remained of the family, and those who were dead would have a place. He would not weep for them. Like pearls in an oyster, they had painfully worn a place, and now they were safely lodged in his heart. Yes, the night had been long and full of terrible dreams. Many were left behind in it, but he was emerging. He would be part of a new dawn and a brand-new tradition. In Palestine, men would live as brothers. They had known the desolate cities and the house of bondage. There would be no more war. Surely his grandfather was right, and his mother, too, for though man had come from the ameba, the killer reptile, the raging ape, and had become Adolf Hitler, he had become Gandhi and Einstein as well. What Hitler and the Nazis had all along proclaimed had finally been proved: the fittest, in the end, survived. The fittest were the good men of the earth, not the bad.

Of course, one must be on one's guard. Evil was not dead. It might break out again and again, and that was why he must not forget; why he must always remain a messenger from the dead.

Perhaps there was no God, which only meant it was up to man to fend for himself. David seemed to have outgrown that child's God whom he had promised to believe in forever. Perhaps in time he would reconcile himself to a man's God, or perhaps he would fill that void with man alone. Only time would tell, but if any covenant had come out of the fires of the European holocaust, as it had come to Moses from the fires of Mount Sinai, it would be found in Palestine.

The rising sun gilded the dirty glass of the porthole. The *Texel Queen II* shuddered as the anchor chains lugged free of the river's mud. A whistle sent a shrill challenge to the gulls as the current swung her bow around toward the sea. They were pulling away, cutting a brown furrow through the dark water. Let the ship carry him. Tomorrow? The future remained a question mark. What mattered was that it no longer frightened him.

Temple Israel

Minneapolis, Minnesota

In Honor of the Bar Mitzvah of

KENNETH LANDSMAN
by
His Parents
Dr. and Mrs. Gordon Landsman
September 2, 1978